Nick Valentino

Thomas Riley

A Steampunk Novel

Shakin' up
Young Readers

quakeme.com

THOMAS RILEY

A Quake Book

Shakin' Up Young Readers!

First Quake paperback printing / February 2010

Cover © Nathalie Moore

Artwork © W. Routon

QUAKE

is a division of

Echelon Press, LLC

9055 G Thamesmeade Road

Laurel, MD 20723

www.quakeme.com

13-Digit ISBN: 978-1-59080-700-2

10-Digit ISBN: 1-59080-700-6

eBook: 1-59080-701-4

PRINTED IN THE UNITED STATES OF AMERICA

10 9 8 7 6 5 4 3 2 1

*To Stacey Valentino,
without whom, I could not go on these adventures.*

PROLOGUE

The industrial revolution sparked an inventive firestorm that inspired people across the earth to delve head first into the seemingly endless endeavor of science, alchemy, mathematics, and metallurgy with a fervor the world had never seen. Rivaling any surge in human knowledge in history, this new industrial way of life was fueled on harnessing the power of steam, gases and the limitless imagination of the human mind.

1
LIFEBLOOD

Thomas Riley's eye peered through his brass microscope at a gelatinous mass smashed between two thin glass slides. He watched with great interest as it writhed and wiggled of its own accord like a liquid octopus. Thomas reached up, clicking the gear-shaped adjuster on the lens to get a closer look. He smiled as the blob became twice as big in his eyepiece, revealing hundreds of tiny black spots on the inside of the mass.

Thomas wore a white buttoned-up shirt with a high collar and a grey suit vest. He wore a blue neckerchief tied in a fancy knot and his pinstripe black slacks were held up by a thick brown leather utility belt. Hardly an inch of space was left from the endless pouches and copper colored tools hanging from it. A thin man of twenty nine years, Thomas was clean-shaven, with long thin sideburns and close cropped but messy black hair. While many of the women of West Canvia frequently called on him, he never indulged due to work-related obligations.

"This is it, Cynthia," Thomas exclaimed, backing away from the microscope. "This is how the soldiers are getting sick. I've found it."

Cynthia put the blowtorch she held on the nearest table and lifted the copper face shield of her welding mask.

"What?" she asked. "Is that the sample from the prisoner?"

She twisted a rubber tube on the side of her welding mask making a *phush* sound and almost dropped the mask as she ran to Thomas' side.

Cynthia Basset, Thomas' twenty-five year old assistant, wore short curly platinum blonde hair that dangled in curls down to her chin. She always appeared overdressed for the hands-on scientific and alchemic work she performed at Thomas' company, Mercury Craft Industries. Today, Cynthia wore a wide-bottom black and white striped dress with a grey corset that limited her flexibility. Her black boots came up to her knees and she wore arm stockings that served as protection as well as a strange utilitarian fashion statement. Her black and gold goggles hung around her long pale neck and while she'd applied makeup earlier that morning, most of it had come off from the heat of the welding mask.

She pushed Thomas aside and eagerly jammed her face against the microscope lens, quickly readjusting the knob Thomas had just focused.

"How do you know for sure?" she asked, with her eye still pressed against the microscope lens.

"Can you see the black dots inside the sample?" Thomas asked.

"Yes," Cynthia replied.

"That's the difference. That's the actual bacteria. I wonder if they are infecting their own soldiers so that our men get sick. That would be strange indeed," he said.

Thomas rubbed his chin as if he was stroking his nonexistent beard and paced around the laboratory. Mercury Craft Industries was sponsored solely by Duke William Beaufort, the primary ruler of their fair country of West Canvia. The laboratory, a large one room building filled with all manner of machinery and scientific equipment, featured huge windows lining the sides like a church but with clear rather than stained glass. At one point the lab had been a clothing warehouse, but once cleared out it had provided ample space for almost every type of experiment Thomas and Cynthia could dream up. Great brass and copper tanks and inventions filled every corner of the laboratory. Every type of tube, beaker, wheel, box, scrap, and myriad tools lay strewn in an unorganized fashion all around the giant room. Dozens of copper colored gas lamps hung on the walls–currently extinguished until evening. Thomas and Cynthia primarily made their money designing and constructing new weaponry for the West Canvian forces, which were at constant war with the neighboring province of Lemuria. Thomas and Cynthia had constructed dozens of weapons and weapon systems for the duke, which included an array of steam-powered tanks, steam-powered clearing vehicles, and a multitude of light firearms and handheld cannons. Their inventions had turned the ongoing border war in the duke's favor, giving them popularity about town along with a virtually limitless budget from the duke.

"Well, what does this mean, Thom?"

"We have isolated the bacteria. That is the most important part," Thomas answered. "Now we need to make antibodies from it. We will have to be careful. I don't know how much can infect someone, so we will need to test it on mice first."

"I hate doing that."

"I know," Thomas said. "It is better than more people dying from this. I don't even know what the death toll is just from the bacteria."

"I heard it was close to ten thousand," Cynthia said solemnly.

Thomas sighed. "The war is bad enough; we don't need our men getting sick. If enough succumb to it, we simply won't have the power to keep the Lemurians at bay."

"What about making more Mercury Clearing Machines?" Cynthia asked.

"We could, and I'm sure the Duke will want more soon. We would need thousands of them to do any real damage."

The 'Mercury Clearing Machines'–or MCMs, as the military liked to call them–were small brass tanks the size of an outdoor trashcan on treads. They held a heating device, a tank of water, a flamethrower and a compartment of explosives. These machines were simply put on the front lines and when the heating device was turned on steam would build, propelling the small tank forward. The soldier would also ignite the flamethrower and the machine would roll forward for a set distance. The more water that was put in, the further the machine would go. When the steam propellant ran out, the flamethrower would die down until it ignited the explosives, thereby making a clear path for any number of yards the soldiers desired. When these devices were applied in mass, it could clear a path through forests, towns, or anything in their way. This provided a particularly frightening and emotionless opponent for the enemy as there was no practical way to stop them. Fences, walls, ditches, and gunfire were pretty much useless. If the MCM ran into a blockade, it would just sit there until it ran out of steam and exploded, shattering the obstacle.

Thomas continued to pace around the laboratory, now fiddling with the green tinted brass goggles he'd pushed up on his head.

"We will worry about the machines later," he said. "I need as many mice and rats as you can get me."

"Should I use the spiders?" Cynthia asked.

"Yes, and set the traps."

Cynthia rushed over to a wooden chest where she opened the heavy lid and extracted two metal spiders, each the size of her palm. They were complex in appearance, full of tiny gears and joints. Their brushed chrome bodies were bulbous but gave them the weight needed for pinning a mouse or rat. She placed them on a nearby desk and proceeded to insert small glass cylinders in the head of each spider.

"Should I use the Delirium or the Sleep Serum?" she asked.

"Use the Sleep Serum. I don't want them damaging any more of the spiders. Last time three went missing. They take too long to build to just disappear."

Cynthia repeated her action until the desktop was covered in menacing metal spiders, each with sharp, finely forged legs and small pointy fangs to inject their prey. When she was done, she pulled a small key from her pocket and placed it in the first spider's back. When she made a half turn, the spider came to life, legs clicking loudly on the wooden desk. She repeated the

10

process on the rest of the spiders. Fearlessly, they hopped off of the desk and clumsily ran across the floor until they found the front door, which was cracked open. The army of mechanical spiders sprawled out, scouring the city streets for their prey.

"They were supposed to be a better mouse trap," Thomas said.

"They are a better mouse trap," Cynthia rebutted. "Their habit for biting dogs and house pets makes them a bit of a liability."

Cynthia walked over to another trunk where she pulled out small metal boxes with trap doors on the front. "Same serum for the traps?"

Thomas nodded without looking at her, still pacing the laboratory. "I will need a cadaver," he said. "That way, if it works with the rodents, I can use human blood to synthesize it."

Cynthia made a disgusted face and groaned at the thought of her macabre assignment. "Fine, I'll go to the morgue. I'm sure there is a soldier without a family there."

"You're a good woman," Thomas said. "We can really make a difference if we can make vaccinations for the disease."

Cynthia ran her fingers through her wavy hair, puffing it out as she did. She fastened her goggles on top of her head and picked one of the weapons off the wall. She chose a short pistol with a fat cylinder and an oversized snub nose barrel. The gun was pearl white with ornate gold filigree decorating the entire weapon. Opening the cylinder, she checked the cylindrical bullets and snapped it back in place.

"Be careful out there," Thomas said.

"Nothing will happen," Cynthia replied. "However, you are aware that the price on our heads went up last month?"

"Yeah, I know. Don't dilly-dally. If they have one, just have someone deliver the body here."

"They'll have one," Cynthia mumbled.

An hour passed before Cynthia returned. Thomas spent the time scrutinizing his sample of the bacteria under the microscope. He pulled several other samples of the same material and began applying different elements to the samples, hoping to dilute or kill the bacteria without doing damage to any human elements. Nothing seemed to work.

The door to the lab swung open and Cynthia came dashing in covered with sweat, her wind-blown hair springing up in wild angles. Thomas swung around from his microscope lens, alarmed by the quick footsteps on the laboratory's hard wood floors.

He blinked rapidly trying to focus on her as she approached. "Are you all right?" he asked with concern in his voice.

"Yes," Cynthia panted. "There was a skirmish at the Duke's residence."

She bent over, holding her knees to catch her breath.

"There were at least five men shooting at the house. A fragmentation bullet hit a wall right next to me, so I fired a couple shots back and ran."

"Did you hit anyone?" Thomas asked.

"I don't think so. I was hardly looking at them as I ran and fired."

"How did the bullets do?" Thomas asked. "Did the phosphorus burn like it was supposed to?"

Cynthia wore an angry expression as she stood upright. "So gentlemanly of you," she snapped. "I'm fine, thank you very much. I didn't see the bullets impact. I was too busy running away."

Thomas waved his gloved hands in the air. "I am sorry Cynthia. Please accept my apology. Sometimes I just get carried away with our work."

"Sometimes?"

"All right, most of the time," Thomas said. "I'm sorry. Please sit down. Is there anything I can get you?"

"Thank you, but no," she replied, "I will take a short breather."

Thomas hurried over to a silver tank and lifted a brass lever so water flowed from a spigot, pouring Cynthia a glass of water despite her wishes. "Do you know if they recognized you?"

"I am not sure they even saw me," she replied. "I think the fragmentation bullet might have gone astray. It doesn't matter, there were only about five of them and there were at least fifty men stationed around the Duke's house. The attackers have to all be dead or captured by now.

"Besides," Cynthia continued, "if they did recognize me, I'm sure I would have been in a lot more trouble. Anyone would abandon their mission for the amount of gold they are offering for us."

Thomas approached her with the glass of water. "You are probably right," he said with an uneasy smile. "Please forgive my heartlessness."

Cynthia smiled and took the glass from him. "You are forgiven, you obsessed fool."

Thomas' face relaxed.

"I think the phosphorus bullets did well. I didn't see them, but they popped and cracked after I fired," Cynthia said with a devious smile.

Thomas pointed at her. "See, you wanted to know if they would work too! Me obsessed? You share my insanity, young lady."

"Did any of the spiders come back?" Cynthia asked between gulps of water.

"Not yet. I've been trying different things to the bacteria ever since you left, but I have gotten no positive results."

"This could take forever," Cynthia said.

"Oh, don't be so–"

Someone banged on the laboratory door as if they were going to knock it down. Thomas ducked and ran to the far wall, from where he quickly lifted a large wood and copper rifle from a rack. It had a large tank mounted on top and metal tubing flowing into the stock. He pulled a lever on the side and aimed the horn shaped barrel at the door. Cynthia had drawn her fat pearl and gold pistol and instantly dropped to the floor, also aiming at the door.

"Did anyone follow you?" Thomas asked in a harsh whisper.

"I don't know, Thomas," she hissed.

The rapping on the door came again. They could see the door vibrate in its frame as if it was being hit with a battering ram. Thomas pressed his back against the wall.

"Who is there?" he shouted.

"By authority of Duke William, open this door now," A huge voice boomed from outside.

Thomas took a few steps forward. "Stay there," he whispered to Cynthia.

"Who's calling?" Thomas yelled at the door.

"Chief Marine Karlis Volmer! Open the door now, Riley, or we will break it down," his burly voice yelled back.

Thomas knew the Chief Marine. He was a huge man, one of the tallest Thomas had ever seen, with a thick black beard. He was in charge of an elite group of Marines who personally guarded Duke William and his family.

He raced to the door, unlatched the bolt and flung the heavy door open. Karlis Volmer towered in front of him, his body almost completely blocking out the sunlight. The man was so tall his head was just a few inches from the top of the laboratory door frame. Dressed in a combat uniform, a black vest with multiple utility pockets, heavy grey trousers, he had black tank goggles on his forehead and a soft grey safari hat with the brim curled up on both sides. He had three of Thomas's top of the line revolvers strapped to his thick black belt and a Mercury Craft T-7 rifle looped around his enormous shoulder. Thomas and Cynthia had only made a hundred of those rifles as they were very complex, but boasted devastating firepower. Only the top officials had one of these rifles.

"Make way," Volmer said, putting his huge palm on Thomas' chest and pushing him aside. "Clear off a table, Riley!"

Lowering her hand gun, Cynthia popped up from her position on the floor. The movement startled Volmer, but he just shot her a dirty look with his deep weathered eyes.

"I told you to clear off a table," Volmer ordered.

Thomas scurried around trying to find a table to clear. He chose a table with the least amount of materials on it and began relocating items to the floor.

"Are you deaf, Riley?" Volmer roared.

The man took two thundering steps to the closest table which was covered with beakers, dozens of test tubes and scientific instruments. With one swipe of his club-like arm, Volmer sent every piece of equipment crashing to the floor.

Cynthia winced, squinting her eyes, not to avoid shrapnel, but from all the work that was in those test tubes. Thomas' hands balled into fists and he bit his lip to keep from attacking the ignorant Marine. "What is the meaning of this intrusion?" Thomas yelled. "You have no right to–"

"Shut up Riley," Volmer yelled.

The huge man turned his head to the open door. "Bring her in!"

Thomas put the items in his hands gently back on the table and squinted into the doorway. A large group of West Canvian soldiers congregated outside and four of them gingerly entered the lab, each holding a corner of a stretcher. They went to the cleared table and set the stretcher on its top as if they were lowering live dynamite.

On the stretcher a young woman with dark hair, about Cynthia's age lay bleeding and unconscious.

"What are you doing?" Thomas yelled. "I'm no doctor."

"All the other doctors are on the front line hospitals. The Duke's personal doctor was just killed. You are the only one with this kind of experience," Volmer growled.

Thomas gave a frustrated sigh and walked over to the woman on his table. Upon getting close to her, his eyes grew wide and he sucked in a desperate breath of air. Lying on his laboratory table was none other than Lillian Beaufort, Duke William's oldest daughter.

Her face was porcelain white, her long brown hair strewn across the stretcher, and the shiny black ribbon that once held her hair up was now tangled around one ear. She wore a tight black dress with black and white striped sleeves. Around her shoulders she wore a red sleeveless high collared top, a mark of nobility in West Canvia. But it wasn't the red fabric that caught Thomas' eye. Lillian Beaufort's blood was pooling on the stretcher and she had a hole in her torso the size of Volmer's fist.

"What am I supposed to do with her?" Thomas yelled. "Is she even still alive? I'm not a doctor. Sure I can patch a small flesh wound, but this…this needs a real surgeon!"

Cynthia ran to Thomas' side. Seeing the girl, she gasped and put both hands to her mouth.

"She's not going to live," Volmer said.

"So why did you bring her here?" Thomas asked. "I can't do anything with her."

"Yes you can," Volmer said.

"Are you crazy? I can't work magic," Thomas yelled up at the looming Marine.

"I was sent here by Duke William's personal assistant with specific instructions that you can help her," Volmer barked.

"How many times do I have to tell you? I am neither a doctor nor a surgeon," Thomas rebutted.

Volmer raised his thick hand in the air. "Out," he yelled at his subordinates. "And shut the door!"

The four men who had carried the stretcher darted out of the room, slamming the heavy lab door behind them. Volmer noisily inhaled, bracing his tree trunk arms on the table with the dying woman on it. He leaned in toward Thomas, smelling like sweat and gunpowder. Thomas stood still, determined to not appear intimidated.

"I was told you can save her, Riley." Volmer said in a very serious but calm voice. "You know what I am talking about."

"Oh no, no, no," Thomas protested. "That is dangerous on many more levels than you know."

"I don't care how dangerous it is," Volmer said. "You will at least attempt it."

"What's he talking about Thomas?" Cynthia asked.

Thomas cleared his throat. "He wants me to use the Lifeblood and remove her soul."

"Lifeblood isn't even real. That sort of alchemy is a myth," Cynthia said.

"It's real, but it is very dangerous. Its results are different in

16

every occurrence. Karlis, please, don't make me do this. It could do anything. We could level an entire town block, or it might dry the wells up, it could poison the earth beneath us for hundreds of years, it can do anything."

"But it will remove her soul, correct?" Volmer slyly asked.

"Yes, but it will do no good if we don't survive to contain it."

Cynthia gave Thomas a look with which he was quite familiar. It was the oddly disappointed look Cynthia aimed at him when she knew something wasn't right, or when she knew something that he didn't.

"Wait a minute, Thomas," Cynthia said with a raised voice. "Everything I have ever been taught says that Lifeblood is not real. Why have you never told me about it?"

Thomas sighed. "Cynthia, Lifeblood is so incredibly dangerous, I wouldn't even want you to know about it. I am not sure how Mr. Volmer here knows about it."

"If any harm came to the Duke's family I was given this letter to open," Volmer said, reaching in his pocket and holding up a tattered brown envelope.

Thomas snatched it out of the man's huge hand. He read it carefully. The note, handwritten in calligraphy with the royal wax seal broken, was signed by the Duke himself, accompanied by another official stamp in deep purple ink. Just as Volmer said, it contained instructions that if any of the royal family was gravely injured or killed that he was to immediately find Thomas Riley or a comparable Alchemist to administer Lifeblood.

Cynthia looked put out. She crossed her arms and stepped back, angry Thomas had never taught her about Lifeblood's reality.

"Well, Riley?" Volmer asked. "I need not inform you that if you do not do it, this will be considered an act of treason."

Thomas wiped his brow and put the letter on a box of beakers near him. "I will do it," he said with disappointment in his voice.

"I thought you said it could do immeasurable damage, Thomas?" Cynthia said.

"Cynthia…" Thomas searched for a way to explain.

"Miss Basset, please do not interfere or waste time. Treason can be applied to interfering with official royal business as well," Volmer said.

She couldn't hide the ugly look that appeared on her face. While she wanted to scream at both of the men who seemed so ignorant, she held her tongue. A small part of her wanted to see how this forbidden act of administering Lifeblood worked. She'd only read about it as legend. She knew it could do bad things, but the fairy tales from the old books mainly focused on how wonderful it was to get loved ones back. After the soul was extracted, they simply had to find a suitable body to place it.

"Time is wasting Riley," Volmer said.

Thomas sighed again and turned to his ingredient shelves to do the unthinkable.

2
LILLIAN'S STATE OF MIND

Thomas rushed to a large, dark wood cabinet with two dusty glass doors on the front. He opened the doors and quickly snatched up vials and small bottles filled with an array of different colored liquids.

"Hurry, Riley," Volmer said impatiently. "We need to do this before she dies."

"Not necessarily," Thomas said. "But it would probably work better. I'm going as fast as I can."

He ran back to the dying woman and gently put the bottles on the table next to her. He snatched up a black granite mortar and pestle and a silver Verso-Sator, a crude hand cranked centrifuge.

"Step away," Thomas ordered as he put his instruments on the table.

Cynthia and Volmer took a few steps backward.

He opened a long test tube and poured almost all of the contents into the mortar. The silver flowed out like a thick, shiny molasses. Hurriedly, he opened a brown bottle and tapped a rusty powder into the silver mix until it was almost thick as gelatin. Next he added a handful of rock salt, a pinch of powdered sulfur and finally he produced a small vial no larger than a ring finger. He looked up at Cynthia and Volmer to make sure they were standing at a safe distance.

"What is that?" Cynthia interrupted.

"I'll explain later," Thomas said.

"I've never even seen that vial."

"Please Cynthia. I will tell you later," Thomas said, not looking at her.

"Thomas I need to know what you are doing. I am you

apprentice for a reason."

"Ok. It comes from the Far East. It's called Angel Blood. No one really knows the source, but its purity can be tested with fire. If you put the liquid over fire it will glow a bright green. It's sold by merchants in the mountains of China. Happy?"

Cynthia nodded with an unsatisfied look.

Thomas carefully poured a thin stream of the brownish-red liquid from the vial into the bowl, watching it as if he was measuring it with his eyes. The gooey contents of the bowl seemed to react immediately with the liquid. It fizzed like water on a hot skillet. Thomas slipped his goggles off his forehead and over his eyes. He grabbed the pestle and jammed it in the bowl kneading and twisting it as if he was making dough. Volmer had taken another precautionary step backward, but Cynthia took one forward. After putting her own goggles on she stood on her tip toes to get a better look. She took a few more brave steps forward, watching the goo writhe under the pestle in amazement. It looked like it was alive, moving like a jellyfish in water. Thomas wore a determined but uncomfortable expression as he ground away at the mess. A light steam began to rise off the goo, indicating it was producing heat.

"Gloves, Cynthia. I need heavy work gloves. This is getting hot," Thomas said.

Cynthia dashed over to her welding station and grabbed the gloves she'd used earlier. Thomas paused only long enough to put them on and then continued kneading. After two short minutes, Thomas was perspiring profusely and the goo had changed into a liquid, releasing a steady stream of steam from the heat it generated. Without warning the pestle cracked and split violently in Thomas' hand. He yelped and stepped away from the mortar instinctively.

Quickly regaining his courage, Thomas stepped close to the bowl and peered inside. "This is it."

"That's Lifeblood?" Cynthia asked.

"Yes, Cyn."

The Lifeblood gave off more steam at the verbalization of its name.

"It was that easy?" Cynthia asked.

"Yes it is that easy. The problem is obtaining the last ingredient. It is very rare and very expensive."

"Riley," Volmer interjected. "This isn't a biology class. Get to work!"

Thomas bit his lip and picked up the steaming bowl with his heavily gloved hands. He approached Lillian and held the bowl over her wound.

"Thomas, please wait. This seems–"

"Just step away, Cynthia," Thomas said, looming over Lillian's motionless body.

He tipped the black mortar over her wound and let the steaming liquid run into the woman's body. It violently steamed, briefly obscuring his vision as the elixir touched flesh and blood.

He put the bowl down next to her and leaned over to examine what might be happening. Besides the smell of burning flesh and the steam that rose from Lillian, the process seemed to be doing little.

"Riley. If you didn't do this right…" Volmer threatened.

"Just wait," Thomas interrupted. "Give it a minute."

Two minutes went by as the three of them stared at the dying girl. Lillian's breathing became shallower by the second. It was a matter of minutes before she would expire.

"Riley," Volmer barked. "For such a brilliant machinist, you are a terrible Alchemist. You know if she dies and this little experiment doesn't work, you could be looking at jail time!"

"Karlis," Thomas yelled back. "I told you to be–"

Lillian's large open wound made a brief crackle, quickly followed by a deafening explosion. The air seemed to compress, then expand within three meters of the dying woman. When the explosion released itself, it roared outward like an air bomb, the shock wave instantly rendering Thomas, Cynthia and Karlis Volmer unconscious.

The wave of mysterious power lifted all three of them off their feet, sending them flying like rag dolls in different directions. Thomas was twisted around, landing under a table, Volmer's head snapped violently sending him hard into the floor of the lab, and Cynthia was tossed through air onto a table of microscopes. Every glass instrument in the immediate vicinity shattered, and the mechanical prototypes on a nearby shelf were thrown from their resting places.

Thomas' eyes blinked open. With his face pressed uncomfortably against a table leg, his eyes rolled around in his head as he tried to gain some sense of what had happened. After a few seconds, he noticed the air stank of blood and chemicals. He sat up and his back roared with pain. He did a quick examination, patting his arms and legs to make sure they were still attached. There were no visible wounds, just the terrible ache in his back from the rough landing.

His next thought was of Cynthia. Jumping to his feet as fast as he could manage, he ignored the pain to search for her. The room was a mess. Not a single object or tool in the area had gone undisturbed. The table holding Lillian had collapsed and split in half, her lifeless body crumpled in the middle. Karlis Volmer was still unconscious, lying by the front door of the lab, a bloody halo circling his head on the hard wood floor.

Thomas found Cynthia lying on a table amidst bent and broken microscopes, boom-orises, and rota vehos pneumatic tubes. Her legs were hanging off one side and her arms were splayed above her head, hanging off the other side.

Thomas' heart sank. He'd killed a high ranking soldier and failed to capture the soul of the Duke's daughter. There was surely going to be a price to pay, but he would face that later. Rushing to Cynthia, he prayed to any entity that would listen that she was not dead. Glass crunched beneath his boots and his awkward gait kicked pieces of shattered objects across the floor with each step. When he reached her, he almost cried out in glee when he saw the slow rise and fall of her chest. Aside from a thin abrasion on her cheek, she didn't seem to be visibly wounded. He touched her slim arm and squeezed, grateful when he found a pulse.

"Cynthia," Thomas said desperately. "Can you hear me? Wake up. Come on, Cyn."

She didn't move. With his forearm, Thomas cleared the remaining debris off the table. He picked up her legs and laid them gently on the table. She eerily reminded him of how Lillian looked when Volmer brought her in. When she looked comfortable enough, Thomas shuffled over to the Marine, who appeared in the worst shape of the three. More bits of smashed scientific tools crunched beneath his feet, but the thought of the hours of work that was destroyed paled to the panic he felt for the injured soldier.

Surprisingly, Volmer was still breathing, though his massive chest hardly moved. Thomas heard gun fire in the distance, probably another skirmish or ambush within the city walls. It was an abrupt reminder there were soldiers outside. Thomas checked Volmer's pulse–which was faint–and maneuvered over debris to the heavy front door of the lab. With great pain, Thomas bent and grasped Volmer's arms which were splayed wildly. As gently as he could, Thomas dragged the man aside so he could open the lab doors. He pushed them open, hoping to find some of Volmer's soldiers, but they were gone. No one was outside. The sound of the guns increased as Thomas poked his head out the door.

He deduced from rapid gunfire in the distance that there must have been trouble and the men probably left to assist their comrades. Something big must have happened for all of Volmer's men to leave. With no help available, Thomas turned his attention back to the victims in the lab. He was glad he'd been able to wake up from the blast, but his heart ached for Cynthia, and despite wanting to tend to her first, Volmer was in worse condition. Kneeling close to the giant man, Thomas inspected his head. There was a sizeable gash on one side, just over his ear. It was a gruesome wound, but fortunately it had already begun to clot. Thomas went to his first aid cabinet and pulled out a metal flask full of alcohol, some gauze and bandages. Carefully, without moving Volmer's neck too much, Thomas poured the alcohol on the gash and dressed the wound as best he could. Worried he would cause more damage by moving Volmer if the man had a neck injury; Thomas left him on the floor until he could find more suitable medical assistance.

Back in the first aid cabinet, Thomas retrieved some smelling salts for Cynthia. As he hobbled through the lab, he was forced to push toppled lab tables out of the way and his back protested every step. He gently wiped the trickle of blood from the cut on her cheek. The bitter stench of ammonia always made his eyes water. Not wanting it to appear he was crying he rubbed his eyes. Then with a quick crack, he snapped the smelling salts capsule under Cynthia's small nose. Only a few seconds went by before she responded. The heavy chemical scent set her eyelids fluttering and she grumbled something unintelligible.

"Cyn, wake up," Thomas said quietly. "That's right. Wake up."

Cynthia's glassy blue eyes flipped open and she looked at him with a peculiar and angry expression.

"What is this?" she asked groggily.

Confused, Thomas didn't answer. He just waved the smelling salts around to aid her waking.

"Stop waving that disgusting thing in my face." Cynthia said with an uppity tone.

Something was wrong. Cynthia was a spunky young woman, but she rarely took such a tone with anyone, especially Thomas. He tossed the smelling salts on the debris-covered floor behind him.

"Who are you?" Cynthia asked with the same ill temper. "Wait. Are you the Gunmaker?"

"Um, Cynthia. Just take a moment. You will feel better soon."

"What did you call me?" Cynthia asked arrogantly.

Thomas didn't know what to say. "Cynthia," he replied sheepishly.

"Don't you know who I am?" Cynthia asked. "Wait, you are not working for the Lemurians now are you? That is treason, sir. If you have taken me hostage, there will be hell to pay!"

"Relax Cynthia," Thomas said. "Please just take a moment and you will feel better soon."

"Stop calling me that," Cynthia snapped. "I don't know who you think I am, but I demand to be returned to the West Canvian palace immediately!"

Thomas paused in fright. "Excuse me? Who are you?"

"I am Lillian Beaufort, daughter of Duke William Beaufort and Duchess Marian Beaufort. And what is your name?" she demanded.

"I…I'm Thomas Riley."

"Why am I in this dreadful place? I demand to be taken home right away."

"Um, my Lady," Thomas said nervously. He instantly felt strange calling Cynthia 'my lady'. "I think there's a small problem."

"And what is that mister…what was your name again?"

"You were gravely injured in an attack on the palace, and–" Thomas tried to explain.

"Was I?" Lillian snapped back. "I feel perfectly fine, besides a slight headache. If I was so gravely injured, why is there nothing wrong with me?"

Lillian looked down at her body and began to pat herself down when she noticed the clothes she was wearing. "What is this?" she yelped sitting up on the table. "What are these dreadful clothes? What have you done to me, Gunmaker?"

"Please remain calm, my lady," Thomas said. "I can explain."

"Explain?" Lillian yelled. Her voice was getting higher in pitch with every sentence.

"Why am I wearing working clothes? Ah! What is this? Why are my nails filthy like an animal?" she questioned, holding her hands in front of her face. "Look at me! What have you done to me? I don't care what you've done in the past for this country. I'll have you hung for this, Gunmaker!"

"Please calm yourself, my Lady," Thomas said as calmly as he could. "Let me explain."

"Is that Captain Volmer on the floor?" she yelped, finally noticing the bloody soldier a few feet away. "You have kidnapped me and killed a Marine officer?"

"No. Please. My lady, give me a moment," Thomas pleaded.

"I will not give you a moment. Summon my guards now, or I will do it myself. And trust me Gunmaker; you don't want me to do that."

Thomas couldn't get a word in, so he walked to a table where he retrieved the hand mirror he used to reflect light in sunlight heat experiments. It was cracked, but he handed it to her anyway.

"And what am I supposed to do with this?" she asked defiantly.

"Please, just look at yourself," Thomas answered.

Lillian sighed as if it was a burden to lift the small mirror and held it in front of her face. She didn't say anything for a full ten seconds. Then, slamming the mirror down, she jumped off the table, her legs wobbling under her. Thomas prepared to catch her if she fell, but she shot him a look of such pure hatred he remained still.

"Gunmaker," she said, her voice filled with royal wrath, "you will be publically hanged for whatever it is you have done to me. Some kind of black magic or alchemy I assume."

"No, not at all. Well, there was some alchemy involved. Please let me explain, my Lady."

Before she could get another word out, Thomas dashed to where Lillian's crumpled body was resting on the fallen table.

"This is going to be a shock."

"I have had enough *shocks* for one day," Lillian shouted.

Thomas scooted one half of the broken table out of the way so Lillian's body was in full view of the woman.

"What? What is this witchery?" Lillian shrieked.

"It isn't witchery," Thomas explained quickly. "You were wounded. You were moments away from death. Captain Volmer and his men brought you to me to extract your soul before your body died, and I did, but somehow you ended up in my apprentice's body."

Lillian turned ghostly white. Trying to hide her uneasy legs, she stumbled closer to her former body. She stared at her former face, which was obviously dead. Without another word, her legs gave out from under her and she fainted on the spot.

Thomas rushed to her but wasn't close enough to keep her from hitting the ground. She crashed to the floor with a heavy series of thuds as she went down. "I told you it was going to be a shock," Thomas muttered to himself.

He thought maybe it was best to leave her unconscious for the moment. A thousand worries rushed through his mind. Had he actually killed Cynthia? Was she trapped inside of herself? Never hearing of this condition before, he knew no way of reversing such an occurrence. He grew angry at Karlis Volmer for making him perform such risky alchemy. Thomas would forever place the blame on Volmer if his best friend and protégé was dead and this arrogant woman now possessed her body.

A light clicking sound came from the front door, pricking Thomas' attention. It sounded like tiny typewriters gathering outside. Thomas cracked the door, but saw no one. As he opened the door further, three of his metal spiders dutifully came clicking into the room, each with a small rat asleep in their undercarriage.

"Well, at least you work like you are supposed to," Thomas said to them.

They clicked across the floor and deposited the rats in a gilded cage in the corner of the lab. For a moment, Thomas wished he was one of those brainless spiders. They had nothing to worry about. No cares, no fears to consume them.

He shook his head at his self pity and stomped over to the Narro Phone–a large wood and tarnished silver box on the wall–and picked up the receiver, holding it to his mouth. The Narro Phone's large horn-shaped receiver tapered into a thick tube that connected into the box. Small round, typewriter-styled buttons with symbols printed on each one adorned the front of the box. He punched a few buttons and a distorted voice blared from the other end of the receiver.

"Yes, this is Thomas Riley at The Mercury Craft Industry building. I need a doctor right away," he said loudly into the open end of the horn.

The voice garbled something back to him.

"I know there's a battle going on, but I need a doctor right away. And I need Duke William's guards to assist me."

The voice on the other end mumbled something Thomas didn't like.

"I don't care if there is a skirmish going on," he yelled. "The Duke's daughter is here at my laboratory and she is in need of help. Send someone right away!"

The voice on the other end changed its tone.

"Thank you," Thomas said, exasperated.

Not ten minutes went by before a platoon of soldiers arrived at Thomas's door. Karlis Volmer and Cynthia were still unconscious. Thomas had taken the time to inspect Volmer's wound again and to straighten out Cynthia's leg which looked rather uncomfortable.

The men who arrived looked like a hardened group as they burst through the doors and three of the eight subordinates dashed through the half-smashed laboratory to secure the room. All of them were decked out in the most sophisticated armor with reinforced brass chest plates and razor knee guards. Two of the men had Mercury steam jetpacks strapped to their backs, and all of them carried Mercury T-7 rifles at the ready. They were led by a tall man with a short cropped beard, who looked like he worked out ten times a day. The patch on his arm indicated his rank of sergeant.

"Where is the Duke's daughter?" the bearded sergeant asked sternly.

"Well, that is going to be a bit hard to explain," Thomas replied.

"And why is that?" the sergeant asked suspiciously.

Thomas took a deep breath, but before he could get a word out, two men discovered Lillian's body in the midst of the broken table.

"Sir," the soldier yelled. "We found her."

The sergeant's face creased with anger. "Hold this man," he ordered.

Two men rushed Thomas, pulling his arms behind his back and binding him with heavy metal handcuffs.

"No, wait," Thomas tried to explain.

"She's dead sir," the soldier said, hovering over Lillian's body.

The sergeant got so close to Thomas' face that he could smell the potatoes the man had eaten for lunch.

"Who did this?" the sergeant asked angrily.

"Karlis Volmer brought her in. She was wounded in the palace skirmish and he ordered me to help her."

"Really?" the sergeant asked. "So why is this place destroyed and I have a dead duchess on my hands? It seems Captain Volmer is in no position to vouch for your story either. Did you do that to him as well?"

"No," Thomas protested. "He asked me to do some risky alchemy to extract her soul before she died. The results are questionable at best. He brought a letter ordering me to perform the procedure from Duke William."

"And where is this supposed letter?" the sergeant asked.

Thomas looked around the room. A fourth of his laboratory was in shambles and he had no idea where the letter was in the debris. He glanced around desperately looking for any sign of it, but everything around them was broken and in pieces.

"I don't know where it is. You have to understand. I extracted her soul. It worked! Her soul somehow ended up in my apprentice over there," Thomas said quickly.

The sergeant looked at Thomas with a doubtful eye. "Wake her up," he said, nodding at the two soldiers holding Thomas.

"Do you mind?" Thomas asked, lifting his cuffed hands behind his back.

The sergeant sneered and nodded at the soldier again. Once unlocked, Thomas went for the bottle of smelling salts again. He noticed the soldiers who'd just freed him now had their rifles trained on his head.

He tried to remain calm, but his nervousness showed through. His hands shook as he picked up the bottle and unscrewed it. He knelt beside Cynthia's body and cracked another smelling salt under her nose. Just as before, her eyes flickered open.

"Thomas? What happened?" she asked groggily.

"Lillian?" Thomas asked. "Are you all right?"

"Lillian? What are you talking about Thomas?" Cynthia asked with a curious look.

"Cynthia?"

"Well, it is very nice to see you too," Cynthia said sarcastically.

"Good story, Mr. Riley," the sergeant interrupted. "Men, arrest him!"

Two soldiers rushed Thomas again, screaming, "Get on the ground! Hands behind your back!"

As Thomas crouched to follow their orders one of the soldiers kicked him in the back, sending him hard to the floor where they attached the handcuffs.

"What are you doing?" Cynthia yelled. "He didn't do anything wrong! We were just following orders!"

"Arrest her too," the sergeant ordered.

Two of the soldiers quickly clamored over the debris in the lab and with no hesitation they twisted her arms behind her back and slapped the heavy handcuffs on Cynthia.

"Get your hands off her," Thomas shouted. "This is my company and my building. There is no reason to arrest her."

The Sergeant sauntered closer to Thomas. "Mr. Riley, your weapons have saved many of my men's lives, and because of that contribution, I will treat you with respect. Don't push it. Until I know exactly what happened here, I am placing you both under arrest."

"Get a stretcher for Captain Volmer," The sergeant barked. Two more soldiers darted off into the street.

"You are in big trouble, Mr. Riley," the Sergeant said. "You better pray Captain Volmer recovers and has a good alibi for you both."

"Take these two to the brig right away. I will need an additional stretcher for the Duke's daughter," The sergeant barked his orders again without looking at any of his men.

The soldiers hauled Thomas and Cynthia to their feet. Cynthia wobbled on her unsteady legs, but the soldiers held her up firmly by her shoulders. With guns planted hard in their backs, the sergeant's men marched Thomas and Cynthia into the bright sunlit street in front of the Mercury Craft building for all to see. Sporadic gunfire still clacked in the distance, but that was the least of Thomas' worries. How was he going to explain this to anyone? If Volmer did not recover, then he could easily be tried for killing the Duke's daughter.

3
SYMBIOSIS

Thomas sat alone in his jail cell for two full days without any explanation or consultation from a legal representative. The only human contact he had was the cell guard who brought his meals three times a day. He had not seen or heard from Cynthia and was ignored when he questioned the guard.

The cell itself was covered in thick brown pipes that completely hid the concrete walls behind them. The pipes contained ultra-hot steam, so that if any of them were broken, the super heated steam would fill the cell, killing or severely wounding the prisoner. Even the cell's front bars were hollow and full of the same steam, making them unbearable to touch. The heat radiating from the pipes was designed to make the room uncomfortable and break the will of the prisoner. These safety measures insured no one could escape by force.

Thomas knew the cell well, as he'd consulted on its design. With no way out, he would just have to wait until word came from Volmer or some representative of Duke William.

All of his belongings had been confiscated; even his pocket watch and his jacket had been taken. He sat on his thin mattress with no shoes, just his undershirt and trousers. He felt sticky and filthy. There was no shower in his cell and the constant heat accomplished its goal of making him feel less than human.

Late on the second day, he heard the cell block door at the far end of the hall open just after his lunch, so he knew that it wasn't another meal. Heavy booted footsteps clacked against the concrete floor, echoing off the cell walls. He stood up and approached the front bars, but refrained from grabbing them.

Just within his sight, an armed military man and woman

marched down the cell block flanking none other than Duke William himself. The soldiers were dressed in suit-like black and grey uniforms and were carrying his T-7 rifles. They wore black officer hats which were angled at the top like a high pitched roof and the woman was carrying a wooden chair.

"Back away from the bars," the woman ordered.

"At ease," the duke said. "Thom and I are old friends."

The soldiers shouldered their rifles and stepped behind the duke. The duke was in his mid fifties with short salt and pepper hair. His long mustache curled slightly upwards on the ends and his face bore the wrinkles of a leader. He was a man under constant stress and it showed. He wore a grey suit styled more for a formal engagement than a visit to the prison. Around his neck his royal seal hung as a medallion from a fire-gilded gold chain.

The female soldier with the chair sat it next to the Duke and stepped back into position behind him. The Duke sat down and stroked the right side of his graying mustache.

"I am sorry we had to keep you here... Thom," the duke said. "We had to be sure things were as you said they were."

"Is Captain Volmer all right?" Thomas asked.

"He woke up yesterday," Duke William said. "He has a concussion, but the doctors expect that he will make a full recovery."

"So he told you the story?"

"His memory is spotty at best," the duke replied. "He said he gave you my order to extract Lillian's soul in an emergency and that you performed some alchemy. He only remembers a noise and a quick explosion."

"That's correct sir."

"Here's the problem. When Lillian died, why did you say that her soul was in your apprentice?" the duke asked. "We buried Lillian this morning and, Thom, I am in no mood for games that my daughter is still alive inside Cynthia. You can tell me the truth."

"Sir, when I woke from the explosion Captain Volmer and Cynthia were unconscious. I dressed Captain Volmer's wound and I woke Cynthia with smelling salts. When she came to, she was not Cynthia at all. She spoke differently, she referred to herself as your daughter and she ordered me to call your security to take her back home. When she saw her former body, she fainted. When I woke her up again, she was Cynthia once more."

"Is this possible?" Duke William asked, his bushy eyebrows rising at the possibility.

"The results of using Lifeblood alchemy are completely random. It's rumored only the best Alchemists have actually been able to bottle a soul. Captain Volmer and your letter were quite specific when it came to having me try it, so I did as I was ordered."

"We have spoken with Cynthia already and she is slightly conflicted on what happened. She says the same thing you say, but she says she was completely aware when Lillian was speaking through her. If this is true, is there any way to get Lillian's soul out of Cynthia?"

The Duke looked worried. Thomas could tell he was trying to reject any false hope that his daughter was still alive in some form. The man had already started mourning and Thomas could mess things up by giving him hope that did not exist.

"Honestly, sir, I'm not sure what happened. It was not Cynthia that spoke to me when I woke her up the first time. Cynthia wouldn't speak to me like that, nor would she try to impersonate your daughter seconds after being revived. I can't say for certain until I can examine and speak to Cynthia more."

"How could this have happened, Thom?" the duke asked.

"With all due respect, sir, I didn't want to do the Lifeblood. No one really knows what it will do. Like I said, only the best of the best Alchemists can get a handle on it."

"You are the best of the best, Thom," the duke said, his voice rising with frustration.

"I do have a fair knowledge of alchemic processes,"

Thomas admitted, "but I am no master. There are just a handful of masters in the world. And most of them are continents apart."

"If this is true and Lillian is somewhere inside Cynthia, who do I contact? I will spare no expense and stop at no end to get my daughter back."

"I know that William Backhouse is in the island colonies, but I am not sure on which island he resides," Thomas suggested.

"He's a Temeculan," the duke said. "I don't know if he would help if I offered him the entire kingdom. Is there anyone closer?"

Thomas paused, considering. "The closest Alchemic master is Isaac Maier."

"Wouldn't that be the day?" The duke tugged on his mustache. "Our Lemurian nemesis freeing my daughter's soul from your apprentice. That's nonsense."

Isaac Maier was as important to the Lemurian war machine as Thomas and Cynthia were to the West Canvians. Maier and Thomas played a real life chess game with machines, soldiers and armament. Maier's job was to outperform, match and counter everything that Thomas did. While he was better in Alchemy than Thomas, he was not considered as good a weapons developer. This was largely why the Lemurians used more explosive elements in their weaponry rather than machinery like the West Canvians.

"What if we kidnapped him and made him do it by force?" Thomas suggested.

Duke William looked at the ground. "He would never willingly do it. He would love nothing more than to be able to kill Lillian and Cynthia–even under the penalty of death or torture."

"Could he be bribed?"

"His drive comes from his family and friends who have died in this war. You know as well as I do that the man isn't sane. I don't think any amount of money would change his mind. Again, I feel like he would take the money and kill them both. He would be happy to martyr himself to strike such a blow on us."

Thomas stood and paced around his cell, thinking. "What about using Sinope?" He asked,

"What's a Sinope?" The Duke asked.

"In Alchemy it is the closest we have come to a mind control drug. It is a mix of ethanol, sodium thipental, caffeine and alprazolam," Thomas explained.

"Thom," Duke Williams said. "I don't really know what most of those things are, nor do I care. Can it actually work?"

"It will render him like a zombie for eight to ten hours per dose," Thomas said. "He will be groggy, but he should be able to perform whatever duties we order him to do. From what I have read most subjects are completely obedient to suggestion."

"If this works so well, why has this never been used in combat?" the duke asked.

"The subjects are completely lethargic. It is only the high dose of caffeine that keeps them awake and viable. The only trick is actually capturing Maier. He is in the heart of Lemuria and I am sure he is well protected."

The duke looked away from Thomas, his mind obviously whirling with emotion and possibilities.

"Captain Moore, bring Miss Basset in please," the duke ordered.

The female officer behind the duke immediately walked back down the cellblock hall and exited. The heavy door crashed closed in her wake.

"Can you administer this Sinope, Thom?" Duke William asked.

"With a little research, I don't think it would be a problem."

"Be honest, can Maier extract my daughter's soul from Cynthia?"

"He's one of the few people in the world that can perform such alchemy. If it's possible, I believe he can do it."

"Such a risk," the duke said to himself. "If we kidnap Maier, there will be reprisals."

"If successful it could cripple the Lemurian war effort as well, sir," Thomas added.

A moment later, Captain Moore brought Cynthia into the cell block. She was not handcuffed and she looked in good spirits.

"Thom," she squeaked upon seeing him. "Are you okay?"

"I'm fine, Cynthia."

"You look awful," Cynthia said.

"Thanks," Thomas replied sarcastically.

"Tell Thomas what you told me, Cynthia," the duke said.

Cynthia paused for a second and glanced at the soldiers around them. "Well. She's inside of me, Thomas. Lillian is inside me. When she spoke to you I could hear everything she said. I could feel my body moving, but I couldn't speak or control what she was making me do. It was like I was listening to her on a Narro Phone."

"Miss Basset," the duke said. "Please be sure you're telling the truth. I would rather hear that my daughter is dead than go on some wild goose chase for her soul which no longer exists."

"No, sir," Cynthia said. "I swear it's the truth. I know she is here now. If I could hear her, then she can surely hear me right now. Besides, when I sleep she is there as well. She's in my dreams."

The duke sighed heavily. "Please understand this is hard for me to accept. There is so little proof. What if this is just a memory? What if she possessed you for only a short time and is gone now? What if this is some strange occurrence or stress induced side effect from the incident?"

"I can't prove it, sir," Cynthia said. "But something isn't right with me. It's like she is in my head at all times. She clouds my thoughts with her thoughts."

"I'm not sure what to do," the duke admitted. "Making an extraction of Maier could cost hundreds of lives with no guarantee of success. Even if we do get him, and successfully administer this Sinope, there is no proof that he can perform this feat."

"You want to kidnap Isaac Maier?" Cynthia asked doubtfully.

"He's the only one that might be able to free Lillian from you," Thomas said.

Cynthia paused and thought about the situation. No doubt she was wracking her brain for any other master Alchemists who could do it, but with her list as short as Thomas', she didn't say any more.

"Sir," Cynthia said. "When Lillian spoke to Thomas through me before, I was knocked unconscious by the Lifeblood. Maybe if we can put me under, you can speak to her again. Is that proof enough that I am the host for her soul?"

"It would make the decision about Maier much easier," Duke William said. "If you are willing to do that."

"Of course I will try it," Cynthia said with a brave enthusiasm in her voice.

"Captain Moore," the duke said. "Please release Mister Riley from his cell."

Captain Moore quickly went down the hall, opened a large rivet studded cabinet and pulled an oversized lever. The entire cell block seemed to rumble and steam hissed from the bars of Thomas' cell as they retracted into the ceiling. Without hesitating Cynthia ran in and threw her arms around him. "I'm so glad you are alright," she said. "But you're filthy!"

"Thanks again," Thomas said sarcastically.

Along with the duke, Thomas and Cynthia were escorted to the infirmary within the prison. Cynthia happily hopped on the medical table and rolled up her sleeve.

"I hope this works," Cynthia said.

A few moments later a nurse entered, carrying a syringe. It looked menacing with its long needle, copper colored base, and large round finger loops on the side. Cynthia's chipper expression vanished when she saw it. The nurse wore a stark white dress, plainly ornamented with thick black stripes

39

outlining the seams and hem. Her hat resembled those of the officers standing outside the door, but hers was white instead of black, with a black outlined red cross stitched on the front. Thomas stood next to her while Duke William sat on a chair in the corner of the room.

"Just tell me it isn't going to hurt," Cynthia said to the nurse.

The nurse paused for an uncomfortably long moment. "It won't hurt a bit," she said with a smile.

"Ack," Cynthia yelped, as the nurse jabbed her arm with the syringe. "That hurts, that hurts, that hurts!"

"All done," the nurse said, holding the needle in the air.

Cynthia rubbed her arm vigorously. "You said it wouldn't hurt a bit!"

"You asked me to say that," the nurse replied with a smirk on her face. Obviously, this was a well rehearsed line. "Now just lie down and let the sedative take effect."

Thirty minutes ticked by and Cynthia started showing signs of the drug's effect. Her eyes blinked slowly as if she was falling asleep and every now and then her body would give a small shudder as if she was shedding nervous energy. The nurse checked in every ten minutes to take Cynthia's pulse. When she fell asleep, the nurse re-entered with smelling salts in a cup.

"Would you like to do the honors, Mr. Riley?" she asked, holding the little cup out.

Thomas removed the tablet from the cup, put it under Cynthia's nose and cracked it in half. He wafted the fumes so she got a full dose of the stinging chemicals.

Even in a drug educed sleep, just as before, the smelling salts began to stir her. Her eyes flickered open against the foul stench.

"What…" Cynthia mumbled. "Leave alone."

"Cynthia?" Thomas asked, still waving the salt under her nose.

"What is that disgusting smell?" Cynthia muttered.

"Cynthia can you hear me?" Thomas asked.

Her eyes flipped all the way open. They were glossy and full of water.

"You, Gunmaker? Again? I thought I told you..."

"Lillian?" Thomas asked. "Is that you?"

Duke William stood up from his chair and hovered over Cynthia.

"Daddy?" She asked. "Am I..."

Her eyes were opening and closing involuntarily.

"She will have slurred words for as long as she is under the drug's effects," the nurse said.

"Honey? Lilli?" the duke asked. "Is it really you?"

Cynthia's mouth smiled. "Of course, Daddy," she said. "Where am I?"

"You're in a hospital dear," the duke said. "Can you answer a question for me?"

She smiled again as her eyes rolled. "Yes," she said with a slight giggle.

"When you were little, what was your favorite doll's name?"

Cynthia bit her lip and paused for a moment. "Victoria," she said in a child-like voice.

Duke William took a step back, clearly overwhelmed by what he was witnessing.

"We are going to help you," he promised. "Are you alright right now?"

"Yes, Daddy," Lillian said through Cynthia's mouth. "But I don't like this lady."

He hid his feelings well, but Thomas was sufficiently uncomfortable by the situation. Cynthia was truly possessed and there was nothing he could do about it.

"Sleep," Cynthia mumbled.

"No wait. I want to talk to her," Duke William said.

Thomas waved the smelling salt vigorously under her nose, but her eyes closed automatically.

"Can she be revived?" The Duke asked the nurse.

"I imagine she can be. Maybe a dose of caffeine."

"No, forget it," the duke said. "I don't want her even more drugged up. This is good enough for me."

Duke William glanced at Thomas. With tight lips beneath his mustache, his ice cold eyes narrowed in the brackets of deep crow's feet. It was almost as if his hair was standing on end, he looked different, like someone not to be contested.

"Captain Moore," he said loud enough for his voice to be heard through the door.

The Captain opened the door. "Yes sir!"

"Get the Jupiter ready for departure by tomorrow at nineteen hundred! Full crew and fully armed. Air to air and air to ground armament. No bombs."

"Yes, sir," Captain Moore barked back in a voice that belied her figure.

She turned quickly and exited the room.

"What are you going to do?" Thomas asked as he threw the used smelling salts in the trash.

"I am not going to do anything," Duke William said. "You and Miss Basset are going with my team to extract Isaac Maier."

4
THE H.M.S. JUPITER

Captain Moore led them up the oversized ramp and into the back of the Jupiter. The ship's innards were so vast that Thomas wondered if the entire Mercury Craft Building could fit inside the air ship. He felt like he was walking into a flying cathedral of metal and wood. Brass beams curved around the insides of the ship like the ribs of an unimaginably giant whale. Crew members scurried around checking the interior and battening down any loose objects with leather straps the width of a man's torso. After passing through the cargo area, they entered a room with a spiral staircase and ladders leading to other floors of the craft. Already sitting and buckled in were the Marines who would be escorting Thomas and Cynthia on their mission. They were the gruffest looking bunch either of them had ever seen. Five men and three women all decked out in full body armor with large rifles at their sides. Thomas recognized most of their weaponry had been made by him and Cynthia. The Marines carried modified T-7 rifles and H.H.E. Steam Grenade Launchers. Their eyes were blacked out with bands of dark makeup which made them look even more steely and cold. Even the women, with their short cropped hair and blackened military issued goggles looked as menacing as the overly muscular men.

"This is where I leave you," Captain Moore said. "Sergeant Michaels will guide you from here."

She quickly saluted a tall man with gold sergeant bars on his arms, then turned and raced up the metal staircase.

The only Marine not strapped in was a huge man standing at least six and a half feet tall. Wearing a grey and black combat uniform and chomping a fat cigar, his horse-like chest bulged beneath his uniform. No doubt he had some kind of chest plate on under the shirt, but the man was so big it threatened to burst through his uniform. His square jaw sported a beard of several days' growth, making him that much surlier looking.

"So much for formalities," he said sarcastically. In a deep voice, he introduced himself as Sergeant Michaels extending his hand to exchange shakes with Thomas and Cynthia.

Thomas couldn't help thinking the sergeant's hand was so large that it would have dwarfed Karlis Volmer's not insubstantial palm. Cynthia's hand completely disappeared within the Sergeant's iron-gripped paw.

"Duke William wants you to change into Lemurian garb for the mission," Sergeant Michaels said. "There's a changing room just beyond those doors. You'll find the proper clothing in the foot lockers. We will have you dressed as Lemurian Special Operations so if questioned about your weaponry, you will have a good alibi. Many of their special forces have black market weapons they have gotten from…less loyal West Canvian soldiers."

Cynthia remained quiet though she wanted to protest immediately. She disliked the idea of having to change clothes again, especially when she had dressed in her favorite and most mobile outfit.

"When we land, you are to follow my orders. If something happens to me, you are to follow any and all orders from my team. Do you understand?" Sergeant Michaels asked.

"Yes sir," Thomas and Cynthia answered almost in unison.

"Good," Sergeant Michaels said. "When we land we will escort you to Maier's Laboratory. We will have a backup team waiting on the outskirts of the property and you and four of my team will infiltrate and extract Maier. Easy enough, right?"

The two nodded their heads with an uneasy yes.

"Good. Do you have any questions?" Sergeant Michaels asked.

"Do you expect any confrontation?" Thomas obliged.

"We always hope for no confrontation, but I assume that Isaac Maier has a group of security personnel at his lab at all times. Our intelligence says that he has a platoon of soldiers stationed at his home and a backup platoon with artillery stationed a half mile south of the lab. To answer your question, we are expecting a confrontation, but we hope to do this as quietly as possible. We welcome your assistance if things do get hairy, but you are to only fire if there is an all out fire fight.

"Duke William specifically ordered Miss Basset as our number one priority of protection. If her safety is compromised, we are to abort the mission."

Cynthia felt a rush of mixed emotions. She didn't want to be the china doll of the operation, but she understood she was carrying the soul of the duke's daughter somewhere inside her.

Sergeant Michaels showed them to the room where their clothes were hung above the footlockers he mentioned and he waited outside the door while they changed.

"I can't believe we have to wear this," Cynthia said with a sour look on her face, holding the crimson uniform in the air. She folded the enemy jacket over her arm and looked at Thomas. "I'm not sure why we are even here."

"That was my first thought as well," Thomas said. "But it occurred to me that Maier probably has the necessary elements and equipment in his lab to perform the Lifeblood Alchemy safely. After how I performed it, I don't want him over here scrambling your brains because he doesn't have the right machine or vial to collect the soul. The Duke and I spoke on the subject while you were asleep. He feels it's a necessary risk as well as an opportunity to gain valuable intelligence from Maier's lab."

She opened her foot locker revealing a thick black belt, a pair of boots, black leather boot covers and a standard issue Lemurian side arm.

"It's for our own good," Thomas said.

"I know you're right," Cynthia said. "It just feels so wrong.

45

We make things to punch holes in these uniforms. Not to mention, they're ugly as hell." She snatched the boots out of the footlocker and looked around the small room angrily. "Where am I supposed to change?"

"Um, I have no idea," Thomas answered, already taking his vest off.

Cynthia grunted in annoyance. "Turn around and don't look."

Thomas turned, facing the wall. "Go on."

"Don't look," she said again.

"I am not looking! Just hurry okay?"

Cynthia didn't answer, nor did she hurry. While his patience wore thin, he remained a gentleman. Ten minutes later she gave Thomas the okay to finally turn around.

When he was allowed to see Cynthia, she was wearing the pristinely pressed and starched deep crimson Special Operations uniform of the Lemurian army. She had a short jacket, with a matching ruffled blouse and black pants that seemed to be cut a bit short for Cynthia's height. The crimson jacket had large shoulder pads, a high collar that nearly covered her entire neck, large black buttons, and two decorative black ropes that encircled the upper arms of the jacket.

Thomas' outfit was similar in style, with the high collar, black buttons and roped arms, but his jacket was longer and heavier with black trim on the bottom. His pants were black like Cynthia's skirt, but with two thin crimson stripes running down the sides.

"Hideous isn't it?" Cynthia asked.

"Well, not you, but the outfit? Yes," Thomas answered.

Once changed, Thomas and Cynthia were escorted to the cockpit by Sergeant Michaels, where Captain Moore was already in the Pilot seat checking the vast array of instruments and dials that covered every part of the dashboard and ceiling in front of her. Tubes, switches, meters, levers and pull strings all covered or decorated in brass casings lit the cockpit up with the sheen of a lost king's treasure room.

Like the flying machine itself, the cockpit was enormous, with four seats in the front, and two seats on each side for navigation, mission control, weapons management and flight integrity. In the back were a row of four plush brown leather seats.

"You two have a seat in the VIP section," Captain Moore said sarcastically. "If something bad were to happen, this cockpit is a detachable escape ship. Duke William doesn't want anything to happen to you two, so buckle up tight. I've rarely flown into Lemuria without getting in some kind of trouble."

She craned her neck around her seat showing Thomas and Cynthia a huge mischievous fire engine red lipstick smile.

"That's a nice thought," Cynthia said to Thomas as they slumped in the cushy seats.

"Also, above your seats are flight helmets and breathing masks," Captain Moore said. "If the Cabin pressure drops for some reason, put them on right away. Understand? Nice duds by the way. You look like Lemurian clowns."

Cynthia shot her a dirty look, and buckled herself into the seat next to Thomas. The cabin filled up quickly with a variety of officers manning their stations and doing the last pre-flight checks. Thomas and Cynthia watched in glee as everyone did their jobs. Being scientists, each job on the airship had its own technical niche that fascinated the two bystanders. They watched in wonder as each person marked their charts, dialed in coordinates, and tapped out codes on metal buttons and switches. After forty minutes of preparation, Captain Moore pulled down a flexible ribbed tube from above her head and spoke into the silver cone that hung off the end.

"Five minutes until take off," she said. "Make your final checks and hold onto your butts."

The five minutes felt like an hour. The anticipation of flying in one of the world's largest flying machines was exhilarating for Thomas and Cynthia. They squirmed in their soft seats like children waiting to take their first flight. When the time came, Captain Moore pulled a brass lever next to her seat and flipped three switches near her ornately molded steering handles to the on position. The ship shuddered and the sound of rushing steam hissed inside the cabin walls. It was so loud Thomas couldn't hear what anyone was saying. All of the crew members had strapped the flexible tubes with the metal cones to their faces to communicate with each other. After a few moments of building noise, the ship seemed to release steam from nearby portals causing a raucous squeal like a teapot boiling. But this teapot was the size of a house.

The ship shuddered again, and with a mighty lurch it jerked forward off the ground and out of the stadium-sized hangar. The noise of the ship was so loud, both Thomas and Cynthia had plugged their ears with their fingers.

Captain Moore turned around and pulled the speaking cone off her face. Her hair, nearly as red as her lipstick, poked out from under her leather flight hat. She yelled something at them and smiled again, before returning to the controls. Cynthia had no idea what she said, but Thomas was pretty sure it was something to the effect of *Having fun yet?*, with an expletive thrown in for salty measure.

The Jupiter shook and roared its way down the runway and quickly gained altitude. Everyone in the cockpit was completely focused on their specific jobs, monitoring the hundreds of blinking lights and pressure gauges. While they were deaf to what was going on, Thomas and Cynthia enjoyed watching the crew work. There were no windows where they were sitting, but they could see out the front windshield into the dark sky filled with clouds and tiny dots of starlight popping through. From where they were sitting, it looked like they were going to fly straight into space.

Twenty minutes passed as The Jupiter climbed at a sharp angle. Finally the ship began to level off and as it righted itself, Captain Moore pushed the large lever next to her back down.

The ship shook again and whistled as it did on takeoff. When the pressure was released the sound died almost completely and only the low, warm hum of the back turbines mumbled through the cabin.

Captain Moore snapped the cone off her mask so it hung off of one side of her face. "How'd you like it? Terrifying isn't it? She's like a rhinoceros in the sky!"

"Wonderful," Thomas said, with sarcasm in his voice.

"Would you like to take a look?" Captain Moore asked. "This is the best part."

It took little more than a second for Thomas and Cynthia to unbuckle their safety harnesses and stand up. They both wobbled as they attempted to walk toward the pilot and co-pilot seats.

"Take your time beaker geeks," Captain Moore said, laughing. "You'll need a moment to get your air legs."

They ignored her, fighting the slight rocking of the ship with every step.

"Suit yourselves," Captain Moore said, returning to her flight controls.

When they reached the forward seats, Thomas and Cynthia gripped the high backs for balance and peered out of the windshield of the cockpit. What greeted them was a most serene sight. The moon was almost full and as bright as a white sun. Below them a thick layer of clouds covered the world below like pillowed fields of unwoven cotton. Nothing marred the view of countless dots of stars above them and the moon lit up an entirely new world above the land.

It seemed so quiet and peaceful. There was no war here, no violence, and no need for people like Thomas or Cynthia to make weapons. It was just vast air with nothing to disrupt it except the gentle flow of wind. They stood in awe looking at everything and nothing all at the same time.

After an hour of standing in silence daydreaming at the scene in front of them, Captain Moore interrupted their trance. "Hate to be a buzz kill, but you guys need to sit down shortly.

We are approaching Lemurian airspace."

Thomas and Cynthia gazed at the balmy night sky for a few more moments before strapping themselves back in their seats.

"How long until we land?" Thomas asked.

"About two hours," Captain Moore answered.

An hour went by as The Jupiter started its gradual descent. The huge craft barreled through the clouds and popped out moments later with a view of the far-off ground beneath them.

Cynthia was still daydreaming at the sight. She wondered who was down there, walking on the earth thousands of feet below. What they were doing? Where they soldiers? Where they farmers? Who knew? She let her mind wander happily.

"Captain," the man next to Thomas called out. "We have bogies five point one miles to the East." The Foreign Object Tracking Officer's face glowed in the light of the round blue screen in front of him.

"Full Report," Captain Moore shouted back.

"Looks like ten fighters," he said. "There is a much larger vessel in the middle, but it is moving away from them."

"They don't know we're here?" Captain Moore asked.

"Not sure," the F.O.T.O officer said. "It looks like they are already engaged with the large vessel. If they don't see us, they will any second."

"Double time. Hard starboard," Captain Morris bellowed into the metal cone hanging from her face. "Maybe we can slip away without being seen."

The Jupiter lurched to the right. Despite its size, the flying machine seemed to turn pretty quickly.

"Too late," the man yelled. "Four have broken off and are headed our way. Intercept in one minute!"

Captain Moore started flipping switches above her head. "All weapons at the ready," she yelled in her speaker cone, slipping her large oblong goggles over her eyes.

Cynthia looked nervously at Thomas as The Jupiter groaned again with noisy build up of steam to gain speed. He gave her a confident look.

"Everything will be fine," he said. "This thing is a fortress."

The one minute seemed like five seconds as the large guns of The Jupiter roared to life from the starboard side of the ship. In between bursts, they could hear the *pitter- patter* of return fire tapping the sides of the great air ship.

"One down," the F.O.T.O officer next to Thomas said as he checked another blue screen. "The rest are breaking off and the large vessel should be in view any second!"

"Pirates," Captain Moore said. "They were attacking a pirate airship!"

Thomas and Cynthia could see the lights from the pirate ship in the distance. It too was a large vessel, shaped like an old sailing ship with a reinforced dirigible and sails on top. It had two massive propellers on each side and one was smoking from damage. It let off a salvo of shots at the Lemurian fighters as they sped away toward The Jupiter.

"We're being hailed," one of the communication officers said in the front row. "They want us to help."

"We have mission priority," Captain Moore said. "Tell them we can't help them."

The Jupiter flew quickly toward the pirate ship as the guns clattered away. Large cannon bursts thumped away from the warship's multiple guns.

"Two more fighters down," the F.O.T.O officer called out.

Cynthia dug her fingernails in the arm rest of the leather seat and looked at Thomas with crossed eyes. "I think I am going to be sick!"

Thomas couldn't hear her words well, but read her lips and put his hand on her knee in a paltry attempt to calm her. "Please, don't!"

Just then the pirate ship, complete with a glow in the dark Jolly Roger flag, let off all of its side cannons in a coordinated flash of destruction. Not a second later The Jupiter rocked as all cannon fire hit her.

"The pirate ship is shooting at us now," one of the officers in the front said.

"Hail them," Captain Moore yelled. "Tell them to stop or we will obliterate them!"

"Number five engine is down, Number three engine is damaged. Steam center number three is about to erupt!" The mission manager sitting next to Cynthia yelled in his speaker cone alerting the entire ship over the intercom.

"No response," the communication officer said.

The Jupiter made an odd clicking sound and an explosion that wasn't gun fire sounded from the rear of the ship. Out of nowhere, The Jupiter violently shook and dropped, losing several hundred feet of altitude. The screaming, yelling and the blur of the moment were surreal.

Thomas couldn't even lift his arms to reach the helmet the captain had told him to put on in an emergency. He turned his head to see if he could help Cynthia in any way, but she was unconscious from the drop in air pressure, her head dangling forward. Those five seconds of pure terror convinced Thomas they were all going to die. There was nothing he could do except live out the one minute or so of life he had left.

But death would be denied.

The Jupiter groaned with the thunderous sound of massive amounts of steam being released, then the flying fortress jerked and stabilized in the air. Warning lights and alarm buzzers were going off from every console in the cockpit, the din made Thomas think of a massive cuckoo clock gone insane.

Captain Moore and her crew were frantically pushing buttons and pulling levers, and all of them were shouting directions and orders at each other. When the ship seemed to have recovered, gun fire and cannon blasts erupted once again from the sides of The Jupiter.

"The Lemurian fighters are making another run, Captain," an officer said.

"Are we out of range from the pirate ship?" Captain Moore

asked. "I need a damage report now!"

Thomas got his first glimpse of one of the enemy fighter planes as it buzzed the cockpit window. It looked like a backward ice cream cone with a large propeller engine in the back. It had three stacked wings like a tri-plane and a half canopy where the pilot sat.

"The pirate ship is still in range," the F.O.T.O officer said. "They look silent. They're probably reloading."

"I am taking her down three thousand feet," Captain Moore said. "Concentrate all guns on those fighters!"

She pushed on her flight stick and the Jupiter angled downward so the black earth beneath them appeared like a void of nothingness. Only a few tiny ground lights shined up at them. The gunfire from both sides continued to rage on. Vibrating blasts bolted from The Jupiter's cannons and small machinegun taps from the Lemurian fighters continued to pepper the ship's hull.

"Two more fighters down! Wait! The pirate ship is turning toward us," the F.O.T.O officer said.

Even through the noise of the ailing Jupiter, and the gun fire from outside, the multiple grumbles of the pirate ship's cannons could be heard. There was no time to react. The sky lit up from the muzzle flares, illuminating the puffy clouds and dark smoke billowing from The Jupiter. Within a second, the Jupiter shook again as multiple cannon hits slammed into the side from the ship, causing it to list almost ninety degrees. Only the seatbelts were keeping everyone in their seats. Almost every light on the dashboard of the cockpit lit up in unison. Thomas glanced at Cynthia again. She was still unconscious. He was glad she didn't know what was going on. He felt scared enough for both of them.

"Rudder is gone! Ninety percent steam tank failure! Ejection module is inoperable," the maintenance manager yelled.

Captain Moore frantically hit every button that could possibly do any good. She yanked up on the control stick but nothing happened.

"All crew prepare for crash landing. Get strapped in," She yelled into the speaker cone.

The Jupiter lumbered downward. Captain Moore and her co-pilots all pulled back on their control sticks, hoping to get the best angle when they hit the earth. This time The Jupiter responded a little by raising its nose a few degrees.

"Get this thing level," Captain Moore ordered through gritted teeth.

The Jupiter continued to right itself, but there was no way the crew could avoid a crash landing. Even in the dim grey night Thomas could see trees through the window.

"Here it comes," Captain Moore yelled.

The bottom of the ship skimmed the tree line, snapping large trees in half and punching holes in the hull. The clamor threatened to rattle Thomas's skull off his neck. Upon impact, a rush of pain and intense fear rushed through Thomas. Enormous pressure from the safety harness weighed upon his chest and for a brief moment he saw the terrible sight of dirt and tree debris crashing through the cockpit window, then blackness.

5
SLEEP MOSCA'S & MECCA BEARS

Thomas awoke to the rotten taste of dirt in his mouth and the ring of small arms fire nearby. Still strapped in his seat in the cockpit of The Jupiter, he wiped the muck from his face to get a better view of what was left of the cabin. A single beam of moonlight gleamed through the broken cockpit window, shining soft light into an otherwise black scene.

Surprisingly, the cabin was primarily intact. A single large tree had collapsed over the left side of the windshield, which bent it inward. All of the glass was broken and the chill of the night air rushed over his sweaty face. Two of the four captains chairs were ripped from their bolts and the copilot and the navigator were lying lifeless on the cabin floor. All the other seats were empty, including Captain Moore's.

Cynthia! Thomas thought. How could he have forgotten? His head yanked to the side to see Cynthia still strapped to the seat next to him, her head still dangling forward.

"Cynthia," he cried out.

Panic stricken, Thomas struggled against his safety harness before he remembered he could just unbuckle it. Glancing at Cynthia, he could tell she was alive by a strand of hair gently waving under her nose. Her face was covered in dirt and she had a large welt under her eye, presumably where debris had hit her.

Thomas put his hand on her shoulder. "Cyn. Wake up."

She rocked limply under Thomas's pushing.

"Come on Cynthia," he said, shaking her a little harder.

He pulled the helmet with the oxygen mask closer and put the tube on her face. No air was coming out so he threw it on the cabin floor. Thomas saw the first aid kit open and hanging on the wall. He stood up and rummaged through the contents. Judging from the bloody hand prints, someone else had used it before he woke up. Fastened to the back of the kit were three syringes. He grabbed two and held them in the beam of moon light. One was labeled adrenaline and the other was an anti-airsickness drug. Popping the cap off the needle and stepping close to Cynthia, he quickly checked the fluid contents of the syringe and jabbed her in the arm through the thick sleeve of her Lemurian jacket.

Within a couple seconds, Cynthia's body shuddered and her legs jerked with spasms as the drug rushed through her body. She coughed loudly and her head snapped back against the seat.

"Thomas," she said hysterically. "Are we dead? We're dead aren't we? I knew it! This doesn't look like heaven!"

"No calm down, Cyn," Thomas said, unbuckling her safety harness. "We crashed and there's fighting outside. Are you alright? Are you hurt anywhere?"

Cynthia stretched her hands out, then her legs.

"I don't think…Ahh, what happened to my face?" she asked, patting the swollen lump under her eye. "I feel weird, I feel crazy, what is wrong with me?"

"I don't know. I passed out as well. I just gave you a shot of adrenaline, so it will be a bit before you calm down. I guess you were hit with something when we landed."

Cynthia unsnapped her harness and stood up quickly, still holding her face as if it would make the swelling go down.

"Thomas. Are they dead?" She asked, noticing the two bodies on the cabin floor.

"Yes."

More gunfire and muffled yelling blared from the outside of the ship.

"We need to go," Thomas said, holding Cynthia's quivering arm.

"Who are they fighting?" Cynthia asked. "How long have we been out?"

"I don't know," Thomas said, leading her out of the back

cabin door. "It can't be good."

They entered the next room where their backpacks and the crates Thomas had packed were lying on the floor. The crates had broken on impact. Thomas lifted the large backpack and strapped it over his shoulders. Cynthia followed suit, looking a little unstable as she did. Thomas picked the T-7 rifles out of the packs and handed one to her.

"These have the Magnesium shot in them," he said with a smile.

"Yeah yeah yeah. Maybe we can see what they do this time."

The next room was a gunnery room, full of cannons and machineguns poking out of the hull of the ship. Aside from three bodies strewn across the floor, the cabin was devoid of people. A large crack had split the side of the ship and while it amplified the fire fight outside, it also provided a way out.

They squeezed through the hole in the ship and stepped into the large mud pile the ship created during the crash landing. Everything smelled of engine oil and burnt rubber. A forest of dense trees at least thirty feet tall surrounded them in every direction, like giant guardians forbidding anyone to enter. The debris field from the crashed Jupiter looked like a smoldering junkyard. A huge propeller, separated from its engine, was stabbed half way in the dirt nearby and unrecognizable pieces of the ship were strewn everywhere. In the dark, muzzle flashes at the back of the airship briefly lit up the forest like random camera flash bulbs.

"Should we join the fight?" Cynthia asked, softly.

"I don't want to leave them, but I think we should. We have to complete the mission and I don't want you catching a bullet," Thomas said. "I have the Marine's map to the lab. It does no one any good if we are killed."

Huddling behind a large piece of debris next to the wreckage, Thomas pulled the map from his backpack.

"We don't even know where we are," Cynthia said.

Thomas rummaged through his pack again, pulling out a silver and copper rectangle that looked like a thick clipboard. The top was inlayed with several different rows of shapes, names and numbers etched in the corners.

"You brought the Magna Map," Cynthia exclaimed a little too loudly. "That's brilliant."

Thomas held the rectangle level and wound a lever on the side that resembled a music box winder. Instantly the rows of shapes began to move on the machine, quietly grinding and sliding over one another until they lined up and came to a stop. Thomas ran his forefinger over some of the markings on the top and bottom until they converged on a central location.

"Here we are. Well, here we approximately are."

He held the paper map up and compared the two. "We are far away from Maier's lab. At least twelve miles."

"Thomas, really, should we wait on the Marines?"

"I think we should go while the Lemurians are distracted. If you get captured or killed then everyone has died in vain," he said.

A fresh round of gunfire exploded from the battle on the other side of the ship. "The problem is we will have to go as far around them as we can. We have to go right through the fighting to get there. Hopefully, they won't have a big perimeter set up yet."

Cynthia nodded and they took off around the front of the crashed Jupiter hoping to avoid any contact with the fighting. Flares and gun blasts continued to light up the forest in waves, casting eerie shadows on the monstrous trees. As they circled the wreck, they saw the Marines, along with Captain Moore, hunkered down behind the enormous back ramp of The Jupiter that had been torn away in the crash. They took turns poking out from different angles and firing at unseen Lemurian soldiers who had taken up positions in the thick forest.

Thomas and Cynthia ran toward a particularly dark area where the trees seemed thickest. Several bullets streamed by them, buzzing like angry lead bees. They flattened themselves behind a large oak tree to catch their breath. More bullets flew in their direction, shredding the opposite side of the tree.

"They saw us," Thomas said grimly. "We've got to get out of here."

"Why would they shoot at their own people?" Cynthia asked. "We have their uniforms on."

"Maybe we look suspicious. Two dirty people running from the wreck. They probably don't care who we are."

A fresh volley of bullets slammed into the tree making Cynthia yelp. Thomas pulled his T-7 rifle off his shoulder, aimed toward the woods and fired off three shots. The rifle hissed and pressurized instantly after each shot and the blinding white magnesium bullets darted off into the night. One hit a tree and burned like a flare for several seconds, lighting up the enemy's position. Silhouetted bodies were running back and forth behind the trees trying to avoid being seen. The West Canvian Marines took advantage of the temporary sight and all fired at once.

"Now is our chance," Thomas said. "Run!"

He fired another round in the same direction, but before they could turn and run, a metal box flew out of the air and landed in front of the allied Marines. The lid of the box sprung open and a highly annoying metallic buzzing reverberated from the box. Small black dots raced out of the open box dipping and rising in every direction.

"What is that?" Cynthia asked, peering around the tree.

"It's bad," Thomas answered.

The dots randomly flew in the air until they honed in on the Marines behind the broken ramp. The dots seemed to swarm the Marines causing them to fire their weapons in the air. Explosive steam filled bullets, some with bright magnesium tracers were flying in every direction.

"Thomas! What's happening?"

Thomas just watched with his gun trained on the woods beyond the Marines.

"Shhh." Thomas hushed her as he stared down the barrel of his rifle.

The stray bullets made branches and twigs fall around them like raining kindling. Several bullets came close to Thomas and Cynthia, one smacking into the ground just inches from Thomas' foot.

"Thomas," Cynthia said with a dead seriousness in her voice. "You have to look at me right now."

Thomas lifted his rifle and pressed his back against the tree next to Cynthia.

"What is it?" he whispered angrily.

Cynthia held her arm out for him to inspect. Sitting on her sleeve was a small copper and gold bug. The size of a large coin, it looked like an oversized metal mosquito, its thin silver legs had a firm grip on Cynthia's sleeve, and its transparent copper webbed wings gently flapped as if it was enjoying the smell of the flesh under the jacket. The mechanical bug's long pointed proboscis was undulating as if it were going to suck Cynthia's blood any second.

"Don't move," Thomas said quietly. His voice was barely audible through the Marine's gun fire in the background. "It's a Sleep Mosca. If it bites you, it will put you out for hours."

"Slowly hold your arm up," Thomas said. "Slowly."

Cynthia looked at him, her eyes wide with concern.

"Trust me. Just hold your arm up slowly. If I grab it, the thing will sting one of us before I'm able to crush it," he said in a calm voice.

Cynthia bit her lip and held her arm out straight. The Sleep Mosca flapped its wings gently and tightened its grip. Thomas held his rifle up and pointed the muzzle inches away from the metal insect. Cynthia closed her eyes tightly. He fired one shot and Cynthia yelped in fright.

Her scream set off a new barrage of enemy gunfire from the far tree line.

"Run," Thomas said, grabbing Cynthia's arm and dragging

60

her further into the woods.

With bullets flashing by, tree branches swatting their faces, and the messy terrain crunching beneath their feet, they ran as fast as they could. After a few minutes Thomas stopped, leaning against a big tree to catch his breath.

"Did it sting you?" He asked between huffs.

"I don't know. I don't know." Cynthia replied in a panic.

She held her arm up again. The shot had singed her sleeve but hadn't ripped completely through the fabric. She rolled her sleeve up but there was no puncture wound. She sighed in relief.

"I think I'm okay," she said, studying her arm in the dark.

"They hurt," Thomas said. "I think you would know if it got you."

Distant gunfire was still raging back at The Jupiter.

"They are all going to be captured or killed aren't they?" Cynthia asked.

"It doesn't look good. Those Sleep Moscas are nasty."

Thomas sat on the leafy ground, reached in his backpack again and withdrew the Magna Map. He wound it with a lever on the bottom and the round part began to glow a light blue color. He sat on the ground and pulled out the Marine's map.

"We should be here," Thomas said, pointing to a spot on the black and white map. "The fastest way to Maier's lab is through this village called Silvertown."

"That's far." Cynthia bent down to get a look at the map. "We need to get going before those Moscas find us. Or worse the Lemurians."

"Agreed," Thomas said, hopping to his feet.

They raced toward the small dot on the map representing Silvertown, keeping a sharp ear and eye out for anything unusual. The forest was consistently dense, with trees eons old packed close together and towering endlessly into the night sky.

"I've felt weird ever since I woke up," Cynthia said, breaking the silence.

"Probably on account of the adrenaline."

"Well, that and something else. You'll think I'm crazy."

"Try me," Thomas said.

"Well, ever since I woke up, I can hear her."

"Hear her? Hear who?"

"Lillian," Cynthia replied. "She's in my head and she is talking. She is constantly talking and complaining. She can see everything just like I could when she was talking through me, but I can hear her now."

"That's annoying," Thomas said. "Tell her to shut up."

"She just told you to shut up."

"That's nice," Thomas said. "All the more reason to get to Maier's as quickly as possible."

"She says if you get me killed she will have you executed."

"That makes no sense. If you get killed, she dies with you."

"She isn't saying anything now," Cynthia said smiling. "I think you made her mad."

"Good."

"Wait. Stop." Cynthia suddenly held her arm out in front of Thomas.

Thomas froze in his tracks. "What?" he whispered. "Is her highness complaining again?"

Cynthia stared into the darkness. "No, something is in front of us. I can hear it."

They stood like statues for a full minute. "I don't hear anything," Thomas whispered.

Cynthia pursed her lips and shot him a dirty look. "Shut up and listen. It sounds like footsteps."

The faint sound of branches being snapped echoed in the distance. They both leveled their rifles and with a nod from Cynthia they cautiously walked forward, alternately watching the darkness in front of them as well as the forest floor so they wouldn't make too much noise themselves. They walked as quietly as they could until the random sound of the distant footsteps became louder.

"It sounds like a bunch of people," Thomas whispered.

"It could be an animal," Cynthia whispered back.

"That is a lot of animals, or a big animal."

In the distance a glimmer of light flickered in the darkness. They both aimed at the flash of light. Cynthia increased pressure on the trigger of her T-7 rifle to the point where if she pulled anymore, the gun would fire.

A silver object clomped out of the dark and into view. Thomas' eyebrow cocked in wonder. Not noticing them, a full grown replica of a male black bear came into view. It was completely robotic and finely made. Its head was sharply angled and its large body ornately decorated with gold filigree designs, its metal joints squeaked as if it had not been oiled in some time. Its eyes glowed a faint blue and it seemed to be innocently scanning the area as if foraging for food.

"What is that?" Cynthia asked.

"A bear," Thomas said.

"Umm, yes, but why is there a mechanical bear here?"

"It could be a patrol of some kind," Thomas said, ready to pull his trigger at any sign of aggression.

"It seems old," Cynthia said. "And it's so pretty. Whoever made it was a wonderful artist."

The bear stomped around until its pale blue eyes focused on Thomas and Cynthia. Something about it seemed non-threatening. While it was artfully made, it was a rotund and clumsy creature that didn't appear to be made to kill, stalk or spy. It seemed like a gadget that had gotten lost, a stray robot wandering through the woods.

"Its jaw doesn't open," Thomas said. "It has to be a patrol machine or someone lost their giant toy."

"What should we do? I hate to break something that gorgeous."

The mechanical bear stood there for another second, then disregarded them entirely. It plopped down on all fours and lumbered over to the nearest tree where it began scraping its front paws down the side, tearing of strips of bark. Thomas and

Cynthia followed it with their rifles.

"I don't think it's a threat," Thomas said. "I read a few years ago that people were making all types of animals and instilling certain behaviors in the machines. That's exactly what this looks like. It could be a machine for a fair or a zoo."

"A zoo robot?" Cynthia asked, with a twinge of sarcasm. "Don't they have any real animals here?"

The mechanized bear stopped scraping the tree and took a few cautious steps toward the darkness of the forest. It paused, curiously looking into the blackness.

"What's it doing?" Cynthia asked, looking down the barrel of her rifle.

"It's acting weird."

The unmistakable sound of steam being released from a large machine echoed in the distance, followed by the cracking and crashing of trees. The bear turned and looked at Thomas and Cynthia as if it was warning them of something, and with uncanny speed, it darted off in the opposite direction. Within seconds the metal animal had disappeared.

"This place is getting stranger by the minute," Cynthia said, still holding her rifle toward the oncoming sound. "I hope that's a logging machine."

"I don't think a logging machine would be working in the middle of the night."

Cynthia looked at him crossly, annoyed he didn't catch her attempt at comic relief. The sound of trees being felled got closer by the second. Whatever it was, it was surely making a mess of the forest.

"We need to get out of here," Cynthia said.

"Agreed, but too late," Thomas answered, as he used the barrel of his rifle to point at the visible tree tops falling within sight. "Quick, behind the big tree."

"Yeah, that's smart," Cynthia chided, as she followed him behind the thickest tree they could find.

They knelt down on either side with their rifles at the ready.

64

The thing got closer, literally uprooting and toppling huge trees in its path with great ease. The sound of releasing steam squealed and rushed loudly from the machine. Rumbling tracks, like those of an unearthly sized tank, growled and whined. Leaves and small branches were flying through the air obscuring the view. When it came closer, Thomas and Cynthia hugged the tree to avoid getting hit with falling debris.

The machine rumbled toward them, the deafening sound of metal on metal brakes screeching like a giant monster's deathly warning. The trees closest to Thomas and Cynthia cracked and crashed into the ground. They each dared a peek to discover the most massive machine they had ever seen.

6
SILVERTOWN

Sitting in front of Thomas and Cynthia was a twenty foot tall, black iron-clad steam tank. It had a heavily armored rounded front with four cannon ports. Its huge treads dug vast trenches in the ground as it groaned to a stop. It had four auxiliary wheels with heavy spokes on the sides. Twenty feet in the air was a deck with multiple metal machinegun bunkers. A fancy decorated guard rail surrounded the deck and a huge gold rimmed exhaust pipe jutted from the middle of the beast billowing dirty black steam into the night sky. From what they could see, the thing was ribbed with layers of spiky iron that overlapped one another like an armored beetle.

"How did it know we were here?" Cynthia whispered.

Even though it was stationary, the tank continued to clink and clank, causing a racket in the forest.

"Does it know we are here?" Thomas countered.

"Why would it have stopped?"

"We don't have anything even close to disabling it," Thomas said. "Maybe we can board it."

"There has to be a crew of at least twelve or more on that thing," Cynthia snapped back. "Did you see the machinegun ports on the top?"

"Was there anyone in them?"

"I didn't see anyone, but I didn't get a good look."

"If we could get an arc spinner in one of the hatches it would clear the whole thing out," Thomas pondered aloud.

"There could be ten compartments in that thing," Cynthia protested. "While I would like to take it on if I knew we could beat it, this thing is just too big."

"Well, here's the problem. If we run, and someone is watching us, they will cut us down for sure. If we attack it, we don't have very good odds of winning. If we sit here, we are right in its path and it will mow us over."

"The town we are looking for is that way right?" Cynthia asked, pointing to the left of the tank.

"I think so. I am not going to pull the map back out right now."

"Let's make a run for it," she said. "If it follows us, it has to make a ninety degree turn. As long as we can get far enough away from it, we can out maneuver it."

"I sure would like to take that thing down," Thomas said. "You're right. We have to complete the job. Are you ready?"

Cynthia nodded her head and gripped her rifle. The two took off running to the side of the tank. Immediately voices started yelling from inside the iron monster. Thomas and Cynthia never looked back. With adrenaline still providing energy, they sprinted in the opposite direction.

It was too late. The giant's engine restarted with a mighty roar and a huge pillar of discolored steam erupted from its smoke stack. The tracks began to roll and the mobile fortress lurched forward.

"It's coming," Cynthia said.

Thomas chanced a glace behind him. The tank had already begun to turn and a blur of men were taking positions on the top deck. Since the Lemurians could see them, Thomas stopped in his tracks, took one second to aim his rifle and squeezed off three magnesium shots toward the deck of the tank. He barely had time to see if he hit anything as he turned to catch up with Cynthia who had kept running.

The tank had lined itself up with them and was picking up speed, continuing to mow down trees like they were blades of grass.

"Don't do that again," Cynthia said as she ran.

"I just wanted to throw them off!"

"Stop talking and run," she huffed.

They dodged trees, low branches, and leapt over dead logs on the ground. They were not going to be able to keep their pace for long in this terrain. The tank roared as it gained on them. The machine guns blared from the top deck. Based on the sheer randomness of the shots, the men manning them obviously couldn't see Thomas and Cynthia, but every bullet was dangerous. One lucky shot and either of them could die instantly.

Neither of them was sure where they were going and it didn't matter. The tank was gaining on them and sooner or later they were going to get shot or they were going to run out of steam and have to slow down. In a rash decision, Thomas grabbed Cynthia's arm and yanked her to the ground behind a fallen tree.

"What are you doing?" she yelled in his face.

"Start shooting at the deck," he yelled back.

He stood up and ran around some trees to his left so that he was facing the flank of the tank. He saw Cynthia fire a few white hot magnesium rounds at the tank. They would do no good unless she was lucky enough to hit someone, but they drew the tank's attention to her. It righted itself on a straight course with her shots and she increased her fire. Sun-bright magnesium shots stuck to the tank, burning hot for a moment and then disappearing as they melted the tank's armor.

Thomas took a deep breath and ran toward the tank from the side. In the dark, and distracted by Cynthia's gun fire, no one on the deck saw or heard Thomas leap onto the back of the machine. The layered armor plates slid and moved freely under each other and Thomas balanced to the best of his ability on the monstrosity. Careful not to get his feet caught up in the moving parts, he ran up them like stairs, and within seconds the entire top deck was in view. The machinegun nests were small pill boxes, each with a long slit in the front, but exposed in the back.

Thomas knew he only had a few seconds to do something before the tank rolled over Cynthia. He hoped she had moved by now, but he couldn't take any chances. Still shaky on his feet, he ran up on the nearest pill box. All of the gunners were busy spraying the forest with bullets and the muzzles flickered like strobe lights inside their protective shells. Thomas stuck his rifle in the doorway and fired three rounds. They lit up the first pill box like a light house. That machinegun stopped. Somehow, the others didn't seem to notice, they continued to hold down their triggers and blast away into the night. He repeated his move, taking just a few steps to the next gunner. One, two, three shots and the inside of the nest burned bright.

"This is too easy," Thomas thought to himself as he made his way to the next gunner. Before he could reach him, the machine guns stopped. His second bright light must have been seen. The deck was as black as the clouded night sky, and on his way to the next pill box, his entire leg dropped into nothingness. Not only had the men been careless in their rush to get to the pillboxes, but they had left an entry hatch open. He heard voices nearby, and partially blinded by his own magnesium bullets, he could only see faint silhouettes popping out of the machinegun bunkers. Uncomfortable on his rear with one leg down the hatch, Thomas flipped a small switch on his rifle with his thumb. He pulled and held the trigger down as dozens of magnesium bullets flew from his T-7. He waved the rifle back and forth making a light show reminiscent of a fireworks display, hoping to hit anything standing on the deck. He heard men yelping and he heard muffled voices below him. The tank screamed as steam burst through the top pipe and the huge tank treads came to a dead stop. The thing was so massive it seemed to sink into the earth beneath it.

Cynthia fired two more shots from the darkness, sending the shots intentionally toward the sky like miniature comets.

Thomas hauled his aching leg out of the open hatch and waited a few seconds, looking for any other movement on the deck. One man moaned but he didn't seem like he was going to be in any position to return fire. Thomas raised his rifle and blasted two shots skyward in response.

As the idle engine hummed, Thomas heard voices echoing in the tank below him. Frantic soldiers shouted orders to one another and Thomas pointed his rifle down the open hatch he'd fallen halfway down. The hatch had a short ladder that led down to a small room lit only with a flickering gas light hanging above a door that led to another chamber.

Thomas reached in his backpack, felt around for a second and found the string of acid bullets that took up almost half the space. He ejected the magnesium bullet cartridge and fed one of the coin sized acid bullets into the chamber, while the rest hung on the side like a belt of machinegun bullets. Cocking the acid bullet in place, Thomas noticed movement below him. Without seeing exactly what it was, he squeezed the trigger three times. The bullets pounded against the metal floor of the tank, exploding on impact and instantly making the metal sizzle like a hot frying pan. Two male voices instantly began screaming in terror.

Thomas raised his gun out of the hatch and rolled flat on his back to the top deck of the tank. The terrible noises below him made his stomach turn. He, with Cynthia's help, had made these hideous bullets and the sounds below made him instantly feel empathy for his enemies who wouldn't hesitate to kill him. Thomas' intention in changing the bullets was to eat through the tank floor and hopefully into something that could help break the huge machine. The splatter from the acid bullets had apparently hit at least a few of the operators. One of the voices fell silent and the other turned into soft, delirious moans. After a few moments, he glanced around the top deck in search of Cynthia but she was nowhere to be seen in the darkness.

He took a quick peek over the top hatch and saw one of the men lying motionless on the floor, his body covered in corrosive acid, making Thomas wince at the results of his own invention. Just beside the dead man three ever-growing holes where the bullets had struck revealed portions of gears and tubes that drove the machine. He saw no sign of the second man, but Thomas could see the driving controls. There was no one manning anything in the control room. With his rifle at the ready in one hand, he lowered himself down the ladder, looking down into the small chamber below the entire way.

Once in the room, the smell of blood and chemicals almost overwhelmed him. He covered his face with his hand, vainly trying to divert the stench. A blood trail led through the round door and into another chamber in the tank. The next room was completely dark save for a red light that glowed dimly on the far wall. Thomas peeked quickly inside and noticed this was some kind of common area, equipped with stretchers, a table and a makeshift cooking area.

The next thing Thomas knew a cold piece of steel was pressed against the side of his head.

"Drop the gun," a ragged voice ordered.

"I can't," Thomas said.

"Drop it," the gruff voice ordered from the glowing red room.

Thomas could hear the man breathing heavily, each breath wheezing uncomfortably. He chanced a quick look at the figure in the darkness and could instantly tell that this was the other man that had been hit with the acid bullets. His silhouette was hunched over in pain and he seemed to be leaning heavily on one leg.

"I told you I can't drop it. The bullets might–"

"I don't care!" The man pressed the barrel of the gun harder against Thomas' head.

Thomas dropped the rifle and raised his foot in case one of the bullets cracked and spewed its corrosive contents. Footsteps clanked from the top deck meaning someone else had survived and was coming down. Even if Cynthia was able to get down into the compartment, he would surely be shot first by his captors.

"Who are you?" The Lemurian soldier asked.

72

The footsteps grew louder on the metal floors behind him.

"Raymond? Coleen? Who's up there?" The man called at the noise. He leaned close to Thomas' ear. "You're dead now."

"What is going on here?" Cynthia questioned in an arrogant voice as she descended the ladder to the lower compartment. "Whoever that is with the gun better put it down by my authority!"

"Who's there?" The soldier asked. "I don't know your voice. If you're with this guy, I swear I will kill him right now!"

"Not unless you enjoy torture," Cynthia barked. "Who are you soldier?"

Thomas stayed silent and felt the pressure of the rifle barrel ease away from his temple.

"I won't put down my weapon," the soldier's garbled voice said.

"This is Lieutenant Lucy Brewer of the Lemurian Special Operations unit. Whoever you are soldier; you are holding one of your own men at gun point. That's treason and punishable by death." Cynthia said in a strong and confident tone.

"I've been blinded and this guy's the one that did it." The soldier protested.

"Your tank violated a top secret zone. We were required to disable it," Cynthia lied.

"But…"

"But nothing," Cynthia interrupted, her voice echoing off the metal walls of the tank. "I am your superior officer and you'll have hell to pay if you hurt my platoon chief!"

From her view, Cynthia could only see the soldier's gun, but at her demands, the rifle lowered from Thomas' head. She quickly lunged forward, grabbing the barrel and pointing it away from Thomas.

Thomas reacted instantly, grabbing the soldier by the jacket and kicking him against the nearest wall. Cynthia swiveled around the door and fired several shots into the wounded soldier. Each shot was a grim snapshot of death as the muzzle of the rifle lit the room up for a brief second.

Cynthia's face was steely and emotionless as she fired, but as quickly as she reacted, the moment she stopped pulling the trigger her expression changed. She stepped back, dropping the rifle on the floor and threw her hands over her open mouth.

"I didn't know what to do Thomas," Cynthia babbled hysterically. "He could have hurt you, he could have had a knife or–or–or anything."

Thomas didn't say a word as he dragged the dying soldier into the lighted room with the ladder that led to the hatch, dropping his limp body next to his friend. The soldier hadn't lied about his injuries.

"Calm down," Thomas said seriously. "Just calm down. You did well."

Tears rolled down Cynthia's cheeks and she quickly wiped them away with her sleeve. "I've been through a lot. I didn't know what to do. I thought you might be dead, and then I saw the gun to your head. I just thought…"

Thomas smiled. "It's okay. Everything is fine, you did well," he said again as he embraced her. He could feel her trembling. After a few heavy sobs, she stiffened up, trying not to show any further sign of weakness.

"So you are my superior officer huh?" Thomas asked trying to lighten her mood.

"Of course I am," Cynthia said, wiping away any moisture left on her bruised face.

"Keep your voice down. There could be more soldiers in here someplace," Thomas said.

"I don't think so. I saw the gun rooms were empty. By the time you finished your little fireworks show on the deck, it was easy to hop on. There are a lot of bodies. I guess you caught the last of them hiding in here. Or he caught you," Cynthia said, looking at the soldier she just shot.

He was badly burned from Thomas' acid bullets. His face and throat, blistered and gory, accounted for his disturbing voice.

"Ew that's disgusting," Cynthia said, turning her head. "What do we do now?"

"No doubt they sent some kind of distress call. It won't be long before this area is teeming with Lemurians. We should get away quickly."

The two exited the tank, took another look at the map and headed in the direction of their original destination, Silvertown. Small Lemurian airships buzzed over the tree lines looking for their lost tank, but Thomas and Cynthia kept a fast pace despite the increasing pain in Thomas' leg. The night sky started to brighten and the duo decided they were probably far enough away from the tank to make a small camp for a few hours.

When Cynthia was collecting firewood, she discovered they were on the outskirts of Silvertown. "There are small houses in the distance, just around the foothills outside of the forest," she said happily, dropping the broken branches she'd cradled in her arms.

"Perfect. We will go through in the daylight. I'm exhausted."

"Me too," Cynthia agreed, plopping down in the dirt next to him.

The sun shone brightly in Thomas' eyes. The comforting black that his eyelids usually gave him was a bright red. Annoyed, he sat up. Cynthia lay next to him and beside her the bundle of fire wood had never been lit. Out of pure exhaustion, they'd fallen asleep on the ground.

Covered in engine oil, blood, dirt with all manner of scuffs, tears and stains, the Lemurian uniforms would not go very far in their current shape. It might get them through Silvertown, but they surely wouldn't fool Maier's guards.

Thomas stood up and the leg that had fallen down the tank hatch vibrated with pain. He knew he had done some damage to it, but he hoped it was just a bad bruise. His thigh throbbed like a giant heart had been implanted inside. He hobbled out of Cynthia's view in case she woke, then pulled his trousers down to examine the damage.

Never had he seen such colors on his skin before. His entire thigh was a mix of black, blue and red which made him think of an abstract painting. It was small comfort the skin wasn't broken and his bones seemed intact. It would just be painful to walk for quite some time. In any one second the night before, he'd cheated death dozens of times. He felt lucky, luckier than the assumed fate of the West Canvian Marines back at The Jupiter.

Thomas made his way back to Cynthia, whose uniform was as unsightly as his. Holding his stiff leg he gingerly limped over, sat next to her and shook her leg. She grumbled and rolled over.

Realizing she was lying on the cold hard ground Cynthia awoke and sat up immediately. She squinted at Thomas, who was looking back at her very peculiarly.

"What?" she asked groggily.

"You have the biggest shiner I have ever seen," he said, with a crack of a smile on his face.

Cynthia patted her face with her fingers, winced in pain and shot Thomas a dirty look. "And you think it's funny? I should give you one to match it!" She raised her fist and tried to stand, but as she moved she groaned and sat back down. "Oh...I am really sore."

"I am too. My leg is completely black and blue. At least you look tough," he said with a wink.

"Thomas Riley," she snapped. "I don't want to hear another word about it."

Thomas held up his hands in mock surrender.

Cynthia paused and looked around. "Thomas. What are we doing? We can't do this alone. We're all banged up and we aren't soldiers, we are scientists."

"Can you still hear her?" Thomas asked, coldly.

Cynthia looked at the ground. "Yes," she answered solemnly. "She won't shut up. Last night while I was in the tank, it took everything I had to try to block her out. She was screaming like she was being stabbed the entire time. When I close my eyes, she orders me to open them. When I walk, she wants to sit down. She's a bossy little thing." Cynthia paused and looked up at the cloudy morning sky. "See, she is telling me I am a popper and a harlot right now."

"That is why we're going to keep going. Anyway, you don't want to walk through the forest all the way back to West Canvia do you?"

Cynthia shook her head.

"Let's get a look at this town you spotted, huh?"

"I'll show you," Cynthia said. "I have the spy glass. As long as it isn't broken."

Cynthia led him to the edge of the forest. Beyond were rolling green hills as far as the eye could see. She pulled the spyglass out of her backpack and extended it.

Of course this version was custom made by Mercury Craft Industries. It magnified thirty times more than the commercial version and was shaped with a slight telescoping curve with a large round crystal bulb on the end. Tiny farm houses with smoking chimneys were clustered together at the base of the hills. It appeared there was a stream, probably man made, that wound through the town. Thomas could see a curved bridge at the entrance and a variety of people wandering about doing their daily chores.

The town was rural. Its homes were all made of stone and there were ruins of a silo and a place of worship in the rear of the town. This town had seen some action in the war. Craters and blackened walls were proof there had been some air raids by the West Canvians at some point. Other than the battle damage, the town seemed serene and relaxed.

Thomas didn't want to put the spyglass down. He was enjoying the peaceful view of normal life. He couldn't remember the last time he'd had a day to do nothing but enjoy the weather, a cup of tea, or a pint at a pub with friends. He'd actually lost touch with his old friends. The war had him and Cynthia working seven days a week.

Sure, he enjoyed his job and his fame. He thought he'd probably just roll over dead if he wasn't working, but there was a small part of him that wanted a taste of the simple life he was watching through the spyglass.

"Well?" Cynthia asked, interrupting his daydream. "What's the plan?"

Thomas sighed. "We don't look like very good Lemurian soldiers anymore, but we need to eat. Let's straighten ourselves out the best we can and march right into town."

Cynthia bit her lip again. "This sounds like a disaster waiting to happen. If you think we should, let's go."

They packed their belongings and shouldered their rifles. After some fruitless brushing at the dirt and mess of their uniforms, they started across the field toward the small town.

As they approached Silvertown, they saw it had been hit worse by his own country's air raids than Thomas had originally thought. He wondered why they had targeted such a small place. Possibly, there were soldiers here at one time, or maybe the town had been some kind of weapons depot.

There hadn't been much rebuilding. Only the essential buildings had been reconstructed. The town folk seemed to still use the silo despite its damage. Upon closer inspection, he saw they'd haphazardly boarded the damaged parts with rough pieces of wood. The town was only big enough for maybe two hundred inhabitants and there were a handful of people walking about in front of them. Every passerby looked at them like they were aliens. No one said anything, but they gave them fearful, angry stares.

"Try to look like you own the place," Thomas whispered.

Cynthia's eyes flickered over at him like he was crazy, but she straightened her shoulders and increased the precision of her gait.

The streets were grey cobblestone and the buildings had been constructed hundreds of years ago with cut stone. A few weathered, wooden signs dangled above doors and most of the empty storefronts appeared as though they hadn't been cared for in quite some time. The streets were narrow, only wide enough for a horse and buggy and maybe one pedestrian, but the town had a certain charm about it. When they came upon a sign for The Crown & The Dragon Inn and Pub Thomas stopped.

"Let's try this," he said, so only Cynthia could hear him.

"A pub?" She sighed. "All right."

The heavy wooden door creaked open to reveal a very old pub with only a few tables, six bar stools lining the bar, and a thick, finely carved shelf in the back with a smattering of bottles. The entire place smelled of old booze and musty wood. The bartender, who busily swept a narrow staircase, was the only person inside.

He stopped sweeping and looked at them nervously. "May I help you?" the man asked, squinting.

He was a rotund, weathered man in his sixties. He had a thick grey handlebar mustache that looked more like a caterpillar than hair. He was bald, save for a halo of grey hair that circled his head.

"We have seen some heavy action and were separated from our platoon," Thomas lied. "Can we get a few drinks and a place to stay for the night?"

The bartender leaned his broom against the wall and slowly ambled behind the bar.

"I can get you two drinks if you promise me you killed a good number of those Canvians," he said in a surly voice. "Martin Bartlow, at your service." The bartender extended his stubby hand.

"Captain Walker here killed one with her bare hands last night," Thomas said, waving his hand toward Cynthia. "That's where she got that badge of honor on her eye. Lieutenant Mayland." Thomas introduced himself.

The bartender smiled. "What'll it be ma'am?" he asked.

"Just water please," she replied.

"I'll take a beer," Thomas added.

"My pleasure," Bartlow said, as he waddled over to some large barrels and poured the drinks.

Thomas could feel Cynthia's eyes burning a hole in him for ordering a beer. He really didn't want one, but he wanted to appear like a rugged soldier. It seemed to work. Bartlow came back with a frothy beer and an extra tall stein of water for Cynthia.

"How much is a night's stay?" Thomas asked, taking a swig of his beer and wiping a small line of foam off his upper lip.

"War heroes stay for free in my place," Bartlow said. "Over the years we've taken quite a beating here, being only a few hours from the Canvian border and all."

Cynthia's eyebrows lifted in wonder, but she hid it by lifting her metal mug and taking a large gulp of water.

"Since the war started we have had over a hundred people die here. Skirmishes, random bombs, Canvian sympathizers, air raids. You name it; we have had it happen here," Bartlow explained as he rested his elbow on the bar top. "What was going on last night?"

Thomas bought himself a couple more seconds to get his story straight by lifting his beer and taking another sip.

"We were accompanying a tank along the outer edges of the forest last night when we were ambushed," Thomas said. "Captain Walker and I pursued two that were trying to retreat. It was nasty business, but we took care of them."

Bartlow's smile widened under his mustache and he declared, "It's good to have soldiers like you watching out for us."

He reached under the bar and produced two large skeleton keys on a brass loop. "Please take the back room. It's got two beds and it's the quietest one in the place. You both look pretty beat up."

Thomas smiled and thanked the man. When they finished their drinks, they headed upstairs with their backpacks and found there were only four rooms. The furthest was at the end of a single narrow hall. It was a modest place with two beds and clean looking sheets. There were no other accessories in the room besides a small, simple table between the beds and some tarnished brass hooks on the walls to hang clothes.

Even though they'd caught a couple hours of sleep in the forest just a few hours ago, both of them were still well beyond tired. Cynthia threw her back pack on the floor and collapsed on the nearest bed. Thomas followed suit on the far bed and within a few moments he was pleasantly asleep on top of the thin bedspread.

7

THE CROWN & THE DRAGON
INN AND PUB

A few hours after Thomas and Cynthia had retired to their room, Bartlow typed in numbers on his Narro Phone behind the bar. While being a gracious host, he knew the Lemurian army had to be searching for their lost soldiers. He thought it strange that they didn't ask to use his phone to call their commanders, but he chalked it up to their weary and ragged condition.

As a Lemurian, Bartlow was a war hawk. He knew too many people–friends, families, women and children–who'd died in the war to give any sympathy to the West Canvians. He thought the best thing was to call the local authorities and make sure any manpower being used to find the two missing officers in his inn could be diverted to more practical uses, like fighting the war against their neighbors.

The Narro Phone buzzed in Bartlow's ear. "Wartime Intelligence, Sergeant Clayton speaking," the tinny voice said through the earpiece.

"Hello. My name is Martin Bartlow, I am the keeper of The Crown & The Dragon Inn and Pub in Silvertown. I have two of your army officers here and I wanted to let you know in case you had a search party looking for them."

"Officers?" Sergeant Clayton asked.

"Yes," Bartlow replied. "By what they were wearing I would say some kind of special unit. They are a bit beat up."

"Hang on a second, sir," Sergeant Clayton said.

The Narro Phone crackled while Bartlow waited. His mind wandered, looking at the bar, prioritizing the next chore he needed to attend before the small crowd of regulars came in for the night.

"Sir?" Sergeant Clayton asked. "Your name is Barton?"

"Bartlow...Martin Bartlow of The Crown & The Dragon Inn and Pub in Silvertown," he replied eagerly.

"Are these officers a man and a woman?" Sergeant Clayton asked.

"Yes," Bartlow answered. "You have been looking for them right? They are here at my inn and they are safe."

"Listen closely," Sergeant Clayton said. "You will be held under the penalty of treason unless you do exactly as I say."

Bartlow shuddered. He was just trying to a favor for his country and its war heroes.

"You could be harboring spies and saboteurs." Sergeant Clayton's voice crackled as the Narro Phone's signal wavered.

"Are you sure?" Bartlow asked. "They were wearing official uniforms and–"

"Quiet," Sergeant Clayton interrupted. "You are to make sure they don't leave. We have soldiers on route now."

"Are they traitors?" Bartlow asked. "I will kill them myself."

"You will do no such thing Mr. Bortron."

"Bartlow," he corrected.

"Whatever," the sergeant replied sharply. "Make sure they do not leave. The only thing you can do to avoid the charge of treason is to keep them in your place of business."

"How long do I need to keep them here?" Bartlow asked. "What if they wake up? What am I supposed to do?"

"Stall them," Sergeant Clayton said. "I don't care if you have to use force, just don't kill them. I am watching the airship take off from my window. They will be there in about two hours. A tank will arrive shortly after. Do understand me Mr. Bortin?"

"Yes. Yes, sir," he replied.

"Keep a close watch on them and their room," Sergeant Clayton said, abruptly switching the Narro Phone off.

Bartlow scrambled under his bar top, fiddling with latches

until he produced a very long rifle. He snapped the bolt back and inserted two dusty shotgun shells. Then he went to the front door of the pub and locked it. Creeping up the stairs as quietly as he could, he peered down the hall on the second floor.

The door they had gone in was shut and no doubt locked. He wished he could shoot them himself and he felt his blood pressure rise in his head at his own ignorance. They'd been convincing enough, but that was no excuse. He was angry and it took every bit of his restraint not to burst into the room and blow them apart. Not only did he hate Canvians, but he had been fooled and what about that little story about the woman killing someone with her bare hands? Was that lie as well, or was the man telling of a Lemurian's death?

Bartlow slid down the wall, sat on the floor and waited. If they came out of their room, he would catch them. Maybe he would aim for their legs if given the opportunity. The only escape was the single window in their room, but they would have to know someone was after them in order to try it.

The two hours felt like two days to Bartlow, who had to keep shuffling his position as his legs continually fell asleep. Every ten minutes he had to move, which invariably made some kind of sound, making him paranoid that he would wake the fugitives. He couldn't shake the anger of being lied to by his country's enemies and despite his best intentions if his guests escaped he would be hauled in for treason. He ignored that bit of government irony and kept watch, sweating with his shotgun pointed at their door.

Finally, the faint sound of propellers and the gentle grumble of dirigible's engines emanated from outside. Bartlow wanted to go unlock the front door and direct the soldiers to the guest's room. He pushed as hard as he could and stood up. He took a step, but despite his attempt to keep moving while he'd waited, his legs were numb and collapsed beneath him. He crashed loudly to the old plank floor.

Paranoia raced through him. *Not now*, he thought. *Just a few more minutes.* He used his extra long shotgun as a cane and hauled himself to his feet. Gripping the old handrail at the narrow staircase, he cautiously went down the creaky stairs.

Something loud stirred Thomas from his sleep and he rolled over in bed. It seemed so foreign yet so comforting to be in a real bed for the first time since he'd left his lab. Surely it was the old inn keeper cleaning up downstairs. He noted it was still light outside, so he covered his head with the thin pillow to block out the remaining light. Just as he began to drift back to sleep, he heard something familiar that had him snapping upright. The continuous and unmistakable sounds of steam engines hummed in the air. There was nothing quite like the compression and release of steam in an engine. It seemed to fill the sky outside.

"Cynthia," Thomas whispered loudly.

He reached over and shook her. She mumbled something unintelligible and curled deeper into her bed. Thomas was already on his feet and spreading apart the thin drapes at the window. Within his view were two small Lemurian airships, normally used as fast troop carriers, landing simultaneously behind the inn.

"Cynthia! Wake up now," he said limping across the room.

She woke, but to make sure he got her attention, he pressed his fingers just under her black and blue eye.

"Ow," she yelled, jumping out of bed. "Thomas I shou–"

"Quiet," Thomas interrupted. "They've found us. There are two ships landing right now behind the inn. There are surely more in the front. Get your pack. We've got to get out of here right now."

Cynthia snatched up her backpack and slung it over her shoulder like it was weightless. She handed Thomas his pack.

"What are we going to do?" she asked, craning her neck for any view outside the window.

Thomas clipped the largest magazine of magnesium bullets into his rifle and Cynthia followed suit.

"Here," Thomas said, pulling an Arc Spinner from his pack.

He cracked open the door to the room, and found the hall empty. "Get out and see if any of the other rooms are unlocked."

Cynthia exited rifle point first. Thomas extended the rip cord from the Arc Spinner and wrapped it around the door handle. He stretched it as far as it would go without exploding and squeezed through the door with much difficulty.

"They're all locked." Cynthia said with desperation in her eyes.

Thomas didn't hesitate. He took two steps across the hall and with one kick; the door to an empty room flew inward. He stumbled as the bruise on his thigh protested the motion. He peered inside and made sure there was a window. There was.

"Here," he said, waving.

Cynthia went in first and he followed, closing the door behind them. Thomas could only hope that no one heard him break the door in, but he'd had to take the chance. Cynthia already picked up the small table from between the beds to jam against the broken door. That done, they rushed to the window. As they peered out, they heard the heavy booted footsteps of soldiers downstairs.

The view from this window was clear. It led to the side of the building where a tiny alley separated The Crown & The Dragon from the business next door. Thomas unlocked it and after a two tries to push it outward it finally gave way. Thomas nearly flew out with it. Instinctively, Cynthia grabbed his backpack and pulled him back in.

"Thanks," he said with wide eyes.

"We can't just hop down there," Cynthia said, looking out the window.

The sound of boots echoed from the stairs. It would be a matter of seconds before they entered the room across the hall and the Arc Spinner would explode.

"Sit in the window," Thomas ordered.

"What?"

"Just sit," he said, impatiently patting the dirty window sill.

Cynthia stuck her backpack out first and sat on the sill facing Thomas. He grabbed her wrists tightly and pushed her out of the window backwards. She blurted out a high pitched yelp, but Thomas was still gripping her as he hung out of the window. He reached as low as he could to get her closer to the ground. His arms strained with her weight and the window frame cracked under his belly.

"It's only about ten feet or so," Thomas said to the dangling Cynthia.

"That's more than ten feet Thomas," Cynthia protested.

"Bend your legs. Don't land stiff. Try to roll when you land."

"Try to–" Cynthia tried to repeat as Thomas let go of her wrists.

The landing shot sharp pains up her entire body, but she rolled as she hit just like Thomas suggested. A few seconds later she staggered and stood up.

"Come on," she said looking up at Thomas positioning himself in the window.

He gripped the edge of the window and lowered himself down as much as he could. Before he'd fully extended, the window sill snapped and sent him falling to the ground. He tried to twist and remain limp but the ground came faster than he anticipated. He smacked the ground with his shoulder, but luck was on his side as the brunt of the force was taken by the large backpack. He rolled in the dirt alley, gripping his shoulder. Cynthia hovered over him in an instant.

"Are you okay?"

Thomas moved his arm and smiled through the pain. "I think I am," he said. "Let's–"

The rapid popping sound of the Arc Spinner rattled from inside the inn. Seconds later thousands of tiny metal fragments shot out of the entire top floor of the inn, perforating every inch of the old and worn walls. Thomas and Cynthia ducked even though they were relatively safe on the ground. Pieces of termite-eaten wood rained down on them.

"Can you run?" Cynthia asked.

"Yes," Thomas answered, though he wasn't sure.

"Quickly then. Down the alley, maybe we can escape out a connecting alley. There's a really large ship in the front. Let's take our chances this way," Cynthia said.

Thomas stood and his heavily bruised leg screamed in pain. His face twisted in agony, but kept his lips together. They trotted down the alley and much to their dismay, there was no connecting alley. The two troop carriers were tethered to the ground with stakes and heavy anchors lopped over their sides. Thomas and Cynthia looked around the corner of the alley into the back area where the ships were parked. Men darted everywhere in confusion, but there were only two men standing guard at each ship.

"We go for the closest one. Don't fire until he sees us coming," Thomas said. "Ready?"

Cynthia rolled her eyes. "Ready."

They dashed as fast as they could toward the ship. The confusion of the Arc Spinner explosion helped them get closer to the guard. Cynthia was first to fire, burying a magnesium shot in the soldier's side. He spun around like a noiseless top and fell to the ground.

Cynthia ran into the airship, while Thomas approached the thick chain holding the anchor to the ship and shot it with his acid bullet side arm. Two shots from inside the ship burst through the cabin window. Seeing the magnesium flash, he was sure it was Cynthia who'd pulled the trigger. Thomas dashed up the ramp to the ship and with a quick assessment he found the cabin. Cynthia was already powering up the engine and re-inflating the balloon on top.

The gunfire gained the attention of several nearby Lemurian soldiers, already running to intercept them.

"Close the ramp! And man the side guns!" Cynthia barked

out orders.

Thomas rushed to the back of the ship, pulling the lever to close the ramp. Several Lemurian soldiers sprinted toward him. He fired two random shots with his hand gun just before the ramp shut. The airship started to rumble as Cynthia turned on the bottom propellers. Thomas gripped the handles of the nearest machine gun protruding from the side of the ship. Just as he looked through its sights, a deluge of enemy fire peppered the ship. Its mix of wood, iron and copper hull bent and shattered as the bullets impacted. Thomas squeezed the trigger and without looking waved the cannon sized machinegun left to right, hoping to hit anyone and anything in range.

The airship lurched upward. The rope and stake tethers temporarily held, but Cynthia increased the power, ripping them from the ground. At such high power, the ship burst upward, knocking Thomas off his feet. Bullets from the ground continued to pierce the ship's thin hull.

"Hit them," Cynthia shouted. "We have the high ground…high air now."

Thomas staggered to his feet again and grabbed the double handles of the gun. Pointing it downward, he let fly a barrage of ammunition. The men were no larger than toy soldiers now, but he could see them untying the other small airship. He paused, aimed carefully, and focused all of the machinegun's firepower on the top of the other airship. Tracers burned red every few shots, keeping him on target. He was sure some of his shots must be hitting his target and after a few seconds he saw the ship list and fall over, the dirigible on top flattening.

"Good work! Can you hit the big one?" Cynthia yelled.

"Big one?"

Thomas looked through his gun port but saw nothing else on the ground. He shifted to the machinegun opposite him, but still couldn't see what she was talking about.

"What big one?" he asked over the roar of the propellers.

"Come see!"

Thomas moved up to the cockpit. Cynthia had her goggles over her eyes, her untamed hair stuck up in all directions. The man Cynthia had shot was lying dead on the floor.

"Look," Cynthia said pointing out of the spider webbed window. She was right; a medium sized battle ship that had been parked on the opposite side of the inn was powering up and getting ready to chase them down.

"I can't hit it from where the guns are," Thomas said.

"Stupid Lemurians," Cynthia said in frustration. "We will just have to try to out run it."

"Once that thing gets off the ground, it'll catch us."

"I know. I know," Cynthia said, turning the steering wheel of the ship. "And it has much more firepower. Maybe even a fighter attached. Let's see how fast this thing can go."

Cynthia searched for a moment and found the main steam tank lever. She pulled it as far back as it would go and the needle on the pressure meter instantly began to rise. Yanking the controls starboard, Cynthia positioned the ship so Thomas could get an angle with the machineguns.

"It's going to take a few minutes to build full power," she said. "Take a look and see how that battle ship is coming along."

Thomas went back to the open gun ports and looked toward the ground. The ship was gone. As his eyes moved up, there it was in the air, about a thousand feet below them and gaining fast.

"It's already in the air," he yelled. "It won't be long before we're in range!"

He pulled a new box of ammunition up to the machinegun and loaded it. He knew they would be in the battleship's range long before it was in their range of fire, but he thought it best to be prepared.

Back in the cockpit, the steam pressure meter wasn't at its highest level, but under the circumstances, Cynthia blasted the engines with all the pressure that had built. The little ship howled as the propellers on the sides of the ship spun even faster. The wind through the gun ports was strong and cold on Thomas' hands. Despite the chill, he gripped the handles hard and kept the end of the gun focused on the approaching battleship.

"One gun against that thing?" he said to himself. "This will never work."

The battleship gaining on them was a monster compared to the smaller airship they were flying. It had two armored dirigibles on the top with two stacked wings and four propellers on each. Thick grey smoke flowed from two smoke stacks on the sides. Even with the distance between them, Thomas recognized the tiny sticks poking out from the sides and front of the battleship as gun ports. He was sure almost everyone was manned and ready to fire.

Their little troop transport buzzed as Cynthia tried to push it to maximum speed. Every moment was a tense one. Thomas wasn't sure how heavily their pursuer was armed, but he knew they would surely shoot first. He just held the gun as steady as he could in the wind, aiming above the oncoming ship in hopes that some of his bullets might find their mark.

A small puff of grey steam erupted from the battleship and a black dot sped toward them.

"Air torpedo," Thomas yelled.

Vainly, he fired the machinegun with a fool's chance of hitting the oncoming missile. The craft turned as sharply as Cynthia could manage in an attempt at evasive maneuvers. The ship was not designed for dodging missiles or dog fighting and gave a measly degree of slant. She cursed loudly at the airship's rigidness.

"Cyn," Thomas shouted. "Do something quick!" He let off another burst of machinegun fire.

"I'm trying," Cynthia yelled back, pulling the steering wheel as far to the side as it would go.

"It's on us!" Thomas was desperate.

Cynthia made a last ditch effort and threw the flaps completely down, sending the nose of the ship downward. At their maximum speed, the flaps on the small wings ripped off. The air torpedo rushed them, grazing the ribbed dirigible on top. The impact dropped the airship, but the torpedo sped on without detonating.

The little airship vibrated violently, blurring everything. The nose was pointing directly toward the earth. Thomas gripped the machinegun for stability. They were heading down once again and this time there was not much to protect them from a crash. Cynthia blew exhaust and excess steam out of the top ports. The small ship shuddered as if it was going to break apart and with another blast of steam, the ship started to right itself from its nose dive. Still on a grave downward trajectory, Cynthia tried anything she could to level the airship. Little was working, but she felt doing something was better than nothing.

Through the din of the rushing air and the engine grinding itself to death, distant pops and bangs sounded off from outside. The battleship let loose a salvo of gun fire, determined to bring the little ship down. Before either of them could react, several of the shots hit their mark. The troop transport rocked and clattered. Huge holes blasted through the hull and wings, sending pieces of debris flying through the ship. While the impacts doomed the failing vessel, it leveled its trajectory in the meantime. Black smoke poured from the back of the ship.

Thomas, still holding on to the machinegun, took the opportunity to aim and squeeze the trigger as hard as he could. The gun rattled until it ran out of bullets. Thomas knew he had hit the battle ship when several thin ribbons of smoke spewed off it. It didn't matter; it would take ten more boxes of ammunition to bring something that big down. As he reached for a fresh box of ammo, Cynthia screamed for him to come up to the cabin.

Thomas dropped the box and slid across the floor until he reached the cockpit.

"What?" he asked, trying to catch his breath.

"We're going to crash. No doubt. Get in the co-pilot seat, and strap in now! There's nothing I can do!"

Thomas took one look out of the window and jumped into the seat next to Cynthia. After fiddling with the seat belt, he managed to get his waist and shoulder harnesses fastened tightly. The tree line quickly closed in. They barreled over a large river with several large steam boats gently rolling along. Thomas took the millisecond to wish he was safely aboard one of those comfortable ships instead of this crashing wreck. The tops of the trees scraped the bottom of the airship. They were going to crash again, and this time there was no way they'd be as lucky as before.

8
A PARKSIDE MUGGING

Thomas' final act before they crashed was to reach up and pull his goggles over his eyes. He knew it wouldn't make any difference, but he did it out of habit more than protection. The battered troop carrier crashed through the tree tops, making deafening sounds and jolting with breakneck violence. Huge drops made them both sick and disoriented. Tree limbs smashed through the window, breaking all of the glass and bending the frames of the windshield. The craft slowed unexpectedly, then lurched forward, and stopped abruptly. The sound of cracking wood and the whine of bending metal rattled Thomas and Cynthia's eardrums.

A second later, with leaves and small splinters of the airship raining inside the cock pit, the ship grew silent. Thomas checked on Cynthia, who was already staring at him through her goggles. Thomas gently lifted his goggles to his forehead.

"Are you alright?" he asked quietly.

"I think so," she replied in a similar monotone. "What happened? We must be dead."

Thomas extended his left arm and poked Cynthia in the shoulder. "I don't think so."

He leaned over to look out the small port next to his head. A large branch had impaled itself directly through it and into his seat just inches from his head. There were branches everywhere. Cynthia lifted her goggles and looked out her side window.

"A tree caught us," she said soberly.

"You have to be kidding me. It's impossible."

"I can see the ground," Cynthia said looking out her side window. "We're hanging ten feet in the air."

Thomas looked behind him. The cabin that usually held troops and machineguns was compressed as if two giant fists had smashed the back of the airship together. Everything was littered with pieces of trees and broken glass. In front of them was a mess of odd tree limbs that seemed to grow down toward the ground. Thomas quietly unsnapped his safety harnesses. The nose of the ship was still facing down in a forty five degree angle, so he braced himself with his feet and stood to get a better look.

"It's a banyan tree," Thomas said, looking around. "Actually, it looks like a lot of banyan trees."

The stress overcame Thomas. He had no way of dealing with the situation besides laughing at their fortune. "Do you know how lucky we are? The past two days have been filled with nothing but luck," he said between bursts of laughter. Cynthia smiled and started giggling along with him. What was left of her red lipstick was smeared along the side of her face.

"The worst part is we are still in Lemuria and we haven't come close to finding Maier." She laughed harder.

"You know it won't take them long to send soldiers here?"

"Then I guess we're dead," Cynthia said, still laughing.

After the few insane moments of laughing through their stress, they threw their mangled backpacks out the front window and found a suitable limb to shimmy down. Once on the ground, they stared at the airship in amazement. It had made a path through the thick banyan treetops, slowing with every impact. The ship happened to end up in a particularly old and large tree with a V shaped top, which had grabbed the ship and squeezed the fuselage until it stopped.

"I can't believe it," Thomas said. "We really should be dead."

Cynthia gave him a light punch in the shoulder. "But we're not," she said, smiling. "Let's see what survived in our packs."

They laid out their packs and gently removed the contents. They salvaged the two backup custom hand guns Thomas packed. The last Arc Spinner was bent, but Thomas thought it still could work. Two boxes of explosive bullets and one box of acid bullets were also deemed okay, although the box was dented. They repacked the items into one backpack. Rope, their custom survival knives, two pre-packaged army rations, the damaged Arc Spinner, and the map the marines had given them were the only items worth keeping. Sadly, both of their T-7 rifles were twisted in the back cabin someplace beyond their reach. That also made the three magazines of Magnesium bullets useless.

"Where do we go?" Cynthia asked. "After surviving this much, I think our nine lives are running out and I don't want to be here when the soldiers show up."

"The Magna Map is completely broken," Thomas said. "I see the river we passed here on the map."

Thomas thought back to the moment before they crashed. "Let's head to the river. It's that way," he said pointing to the opposite end of the airship. "I saw a lot of fancy boats just before we… er, landed."

"Hey, at least you are still breathing."

Thomas hoisted the backpack on his shoulders. "No thanks to your flying skills."

"And no thanks to your gunnery skills either," she teased back.

"You know you look awful," Thomas said, chuckling as they walked.

"Aren't you the one to talk?" she said in an upbeat tone. "You look like the perfect gentlemen, with your ripped shirt, stained pants and grubby paws."

They looked like two animals in clothes they found in a morgue. They were dirty, beaten and worn, with only a few hours of sleep each. They couldn't even pass as transients in their Special Forces uniforms.

Trudging through the forest of banyan trees, they reached the river and just as Thomas promised, there were two large, ornate paddle wheel steam boats passing each other in opposite directions.

"Those are beautiful," Cynthia said.

"We will follow the river bank and hopefully we can find a dock or a coal station," Thomas said.

Cynthia nodded.

After half an hour of waking, the number of fancy steam ships on the river increased to the dozens. Huge white wooden ships with three story tall paddle wheels on the sides, all of them with gilded inlayed decoration floated serenely back and forth. Groups of well-dressed men and women congregated on their decks. They didn't seem to care that a war was going on. They strolled along the decks sipping their drinks while men died in the dirt just miles away. The fleet of boats appeared to be part of some kind of celebration.

"This is it," Thomas said, stopping at another banyan tree. "Look at all of the people."

He pointed toward a huge gathering of people massed around a large set of docks. Hundreds of people in clothes befitting a royal wedding were walking around a small park adjoining the docks. Some stood in circles of friends, talking with drinks in their hands. Some were groups of ladies in lace white dresses with ornately cut double topped parasols. Thomas and Cynthia moved tree to tree until they reached the edge of the park. They found a nice hedgerow they could hide behind without being seen by the Lemurian elite.

"You know what we have to do right?" Thomas whispered.

"Um, what's that?"

"We are going to have to get some clothes. And get on one of those ships."

Cynthia smirked. "You want to just nab a few of these people and take their clothes without anyone noticing?"

"That's exactly what I want to do," he said. "There are plenty of couples." He pointed to several easy targets close to the edge of the park.

Thomas and Cynthia felt like dogs watching the people socialize like they didn't have a care in the world. While Cynthia was dubious of everything that had been done in the last few days, she seemed to be handling whatever confronted her. She felt so ugly, dirty, and tired that this idea was a bit of relief in some strange vagabond kind of way.

"Okay then," she said. "Which ones do you want?"

"How about them?" Thomas asked, pointing at a nearby couple talking close to each other.

"Look at what she is wearing," Cynthia said in disgust. "I would rather walk out there looking like I do now.

Thomas sighed. "Fine, you pick."

"The two at the far end by the fence. I could fit into that nicely and I want her hat to hide my eye as much as possible."

The woman was sitting demurely on the top of a fence that bordered the far edge of the park. She wore a red, heavily ruffled dress, black riding boots, and an oversized hat that only a person of wealth could afford. Adding panache, she had tied her hair back with a bright blue ribbon that trailed from under the hat's curved brim. She held a double topped parasol, like many of the ladies in the park, which helped obscure not only the sun, but nosy people as well.

The man she was with looked swank in a red trench coat styled jacket with black lapels, a double breasted black vest, a maroon shirt and a shiny black tie. Overall, he seemed to compliment the lady's outfit save for her blue ribbon.

Thomas wanted to complain that there were people much closer, but he thought it best to yield to Cynthia's choice. He knew some of his impatience resulted from the trauma they'd been through and that in the end, this particular couple was as good as any other target.

"We go around the park then," Thomas said. "Here, I have the rope, this should help."

Thomas pulled the rope out from his back pack, and drew his gun. Cynthia grabbed his arm.

"I hardly think you're going to need that."

Thomas smiled. "I won't need it, but they need to think I do. How surly do you feel?"

"Pretty surly."

"Good. It's time to act desperate."

Cynthia let go of his arm and pulled her gun. She understood what Thomas was doing now. He wanted to look like the worst pair of derelicts. The more scared their victims were, the more likely they were to stay quiet.

Thomas and Cynthia managed their way through the thin tree line on outskirts of the park. Closing in, they noticed the woman had cocked her parasol to the side, shielding the couple as she kissed her suitor. To Thomas and Cynthia's advantage, the kissing seemed to go on forever. Intertwined behind the parasol, the fancy couple was lost in a world of privilege and passion.

"Could it get any more perfect?" Thomas whispered. "Make sure you play the part."

Again Cynthia knew exactly what he meant. To add to her dishevelment, Cynthia quickly cocked her dirty goggles to the side as if she had just fallen off of something. They tip toed up to the kissing couple and Thomas put his gun to the man's temple while Cynthia simultaneously jabbed her gun in the woman's back. With her free hand, she grabbed the parasol handle to hold it in place.

"'Ello kind sir," Thomas said with a convincing accent. "Why don't you treat the missus an' me to a bit o' company?"

The man opened his eyes wide and the woman opened her mouth to scream, but Cynthia jammed the gun harder into her back, almost pushing her off the fence.

"Now, now. We wouldn't wanna go makin' any noises would we?" Cynthia said, in her best accent. "Dem are de people that get holes in em."

"Come wit us all quiet like, an' we won't hurt ya," Thomas said.

The man looked utterly mystified as if he'd been woken

from a deep sleep. Cynthia gripped the parasol tightly and held it out so that most of the scene was blocked from the view of others in the park.

"Come on," Cynthia said. "Make it quick an' I promise we won't hurt ya."

The woman swung her legs over the fence and stood in front of Cynthia with a stiff but scared face. Cynthia tried to look even nastier.

"You too, govna," Thomas said, giving his gun a little wave. The man slipped over the fence and seemed to reach inside his vest when his back was to Thomas.

"Ah, ah, ah," Thomas said pushing the barrel of his gun hard into the man's back. "Wot we got 'ere?"

Thomas reached around the man, who was taller than he was, and patted his vest finding a small lump inside his pocket. He reached in from behind him and pulled out a tiny, one shot pistol.

"An' wot ya gonna do wit that?" Thomas said. "You gonna kill a little birdy? Get in da woods!"

He quickly marched their prisoners behind a few layers of banyan trees, and then ordered them to sit on the ground together.

"Do you know who I am?" the man asked, with a snootiness that matched his elegant clothes and face.

"No," Thomas said. "An' I don't care neither."

"We have money," The woman said. "All you want."

The man nedged her with his elbow and she shot him a desperately dirty look.

"Well that sounds nice," Cynthia said. "We'll be takin' that too."

"The only way we are gonna let you to live is if we can get your pretty clothes," Thomas said. "We been admiring them."

"Off wit dem my lady," Cynthia said. "Jus' that pretty dress an' your pocketbook."

The woman looked at her like she was crazy. "You…really

want…my dress?" she asked.

"That's right an' make it snappy or I will shoot Cap'n Goody here in da knee cap," she said with an extra dramatic flare.

The woman stood up, quivering, with her hands in the air. "Okay, okay. Just give me a second."

"Don't worry missus, I'll make sure he don't look," Cynthia said. "Look away Cap'n Goody!"

The woman disrobed down to her rather plain underwear.

"Wot is this?" Thomas asked the man. "Your lady friend seems to have more guts than you sir. Go on now, get strippin."

The man rolled his eyes, stood up, and began to disrobe.

"You can go on an look at 'im if you like Missus," Thomas joked to the nearly naked woman. "It's nuthin you ain't never seen before, eh?"

Thomas and Cynthia kept the big bundle of clothes on the ground in front of them. They ordered the two sit with their backs to the tree trunk, away from the view of the park. He tied them together and the woman started crying.

"Eh, there," Thomas said, tightening the rope. "I told ya I ain't goin to hurt ya if ya stay quiet. Let's not ruin dat huh?"

She bit her lip to hold back her tears.

Cynthia collected the all of the clothes, the parasol and the woman's pocketbook while Thomas knelt down in front of the couple.

"See, I am gonna be a man of me word," Thomas said, pulling his old socks out of his tattered jacket pocket. "I am gonna change into these nice duds right over there. If I 'ear a word from you, I will come back an' shoot ya for fun. Understand?"

The couple nodded in tandem.

"Good. It's almost all over. One last bit of nastiness. Open yer mouth," He said holding out his two dirty socks.

The couple looked more horrified now than they had when Thomas had the gun on them.

"Come on now. Don't make me kill ya over this."

Cynthia was already heading deeper in the woods with the clothes. The couple glanced at each other and the man opened his mouth. Thomas stuck the dirty sock in and patted him on the head. The woman followed suit.

"See, It ain't so bad now is it? Look, jus let me get away from 'ere, then you can scream your bloody heads off. Do we have a deal?"

The couple nodded again. Tears ran down the woman's face. She looked pathetic with the sock sticking out of her mouth. Thomas wondered if her tears were from being mugged or from the embarrassment of being found in such a state. A pang of guilt ran through him, but he had to do whatever it took to survive, even if it meant assaulting Lemurian aristocracy. Blanking out the feeling, he walked back into the woods, glancing randomly at the couple as he disappeared behind the banyan trees. Cynthia was standing behind one, already in the woman's red ruffled dress.

"That was quick," he said.

"I had to get out of that uniform. It's utterly disgusting."

After a moment of modest hesitation, Thomas figured Cynthia had seen him in a myriad of embarrassing situations so he stripped his torn uniform off and changed into the man's outfit. "This is nice. Oh, by the way, when did you become such a great actress? Brava!"

"I've watched you act with those weapons contractors a million times. Besides, I'm a young starlet," Cynthia said with a smirk.

"Hey! I am only four years older than you."

"Old man," Cynthia whispered, picking up the fancy black parasol and unsnapping the woman's pocketbook. "Figures. Just make up and a mirror. Great."

"Don't worry," Thomas said, holding the man's wallet out. "Look in Cap'n Goody's wallet. Where did you come up with that?"

"It just popped into my head," Cynthia said, giggling and

grabbing the wallet. "Oh, this is good. He has a wallet full of Lemurian money." She held up the wad and waved it in the air.

Thomas slipped the red trench coat over his shoulders. "How do I look?"

"Like a dirty guy that just stole a rich person's clothes."

"Really?"

"No. You look fine. How about me?" Cynthia said, tipping her hat so the brim covered part of her bruised face.

"Ravishing," Thomas said. "Black eye and all."

"Hey, you remember what I said I would do to Cap'n Goody right?"

"Yeah, yeah. Come on. We need to get on one of those boats."

They packed their goggles in the backpack and Thomas tried to carry it like a suitcase.

"That doesn't really fit the get up," Cynthia mumbled as they walked nonchalantly into the park.

"Well, I couldn't leave it behind. Just act like you own…well everything."

They walked out on the boat dock with only a few disapproving looks at the army green backpack. Groups of richly dressed people were all around laughing and talking, so it was slightly easier to move through the crowd without being noticed. Cynthia bent the brim of her hat down in an attempt to cover her black eye.

The dock split into two distinct sections with a sign in the middle:

The Crane Celebration
Lemuria City Right
Rudolfo Plantation Left

Thomas couldn't believe their luck. Not only was the ship going straight where they needed to go, but if all went well, they would travel first class. He was relieved a stress free ride awaited them. Both grand boats were waiting as people boarded via red carpeted loading ramps with fiery gilded railings.

They joined the line of people to the right, listening to their bland conversations. Thomas put his arm around Cynthia's waist and held her close as if they were a couple. He could feel her squirm awkwardly under his hand.

"Thom–"

"Just go with it."

Cynthia relaxed and strode onward with a seemingly confident gait. They boarded without a ticket or without spending one Lemurian cent. A snappily dressed greeter tipped his hat as everyone boarded. Neither of them knew what the Crane Celebration was, but they were happy to have safe passage to Lemuria's capital city.

On board, they kept to themselves. Thomas left Cynthia standing on the front deck of the magnificent ship with the backpack while he went to the cash bar for drinks. When he returned, he noticed she was leaning on the rail with a smile on her face. He handed her the drink, a fruity mix of cherry juice and Jenever. The brim of her hat flopped gently in the wind off the river.

"This is crazy, Thomas."

"I know, but this is the best way to get there, don't you think?"

"Of course," she said, looking away. "It's just crazy."

The boat lurched backward, steam billowed from the smoke stack, and the huge paddle wheels on the side of the ship began to turn. The crowd cheered as the boat backed slowly from the dock, the voices rising with excitement. The ship pivoted and within a few moments, Thomas and Cynthia were heading down the wide river with Lemuria's social elite, sipping glasses of fruit spiced spirits on the deck of a ship more fitted for a ball than for travel.

9
THE CRANE CELEBRATION

The paddle boat gently slapped and sloshed its way through the river. Thomas and Cynthia stood on the deck trying to look inconspicuous. Cynthia kept sneaking tugs on the back of the dress as the top portion was a bit constricting.

They stood on the bow deck surrounded by other well dressed couples and groups. The conversations ranged from which designer had made which dress to the fighting with West Canvia.

This subject fascinated Thomas the most. Although he and Cynthia were trying to look away from as many people as they could, he found himself turning his head whenever someone mentioned the war. They mostly complained about money: how much they were being taxed, how much they had donated to the cause, or how their company was involved in doing something for the war effort. They were nothing like the people of Silvertown. These people barely knew Silvertown existed.

The ship itself was three stories tall, just like the two wheels that moved it. The top deck jutted outward in a forty five degree angle and was made entirely of glass. Even from where they were standing, Thomas and Cynthia could see a giant wooden steering wheel through a window above them. A massive man with a short trimmed white beard stood behind it surveying the crowd below. He wore a traditional black captain's suit, complete with service medals and a black and white sea captain's hat.

"Would you mind getting me another?" Cynthia asked, holding her empty glass out.

Thomas looked at his half glass of beer. "Um, sure. Are you alright?"

"Yes, I'm fine. The alcohol actually helps Miss Lillian quiet down a bit."

Thomas took the glass and headed over to the line at the bar, keeping his head high as a man of confidence or arrogance would do. The air was thick with pockets of perfume and cologne. While he was dirty, he wasn't sure if they could smell him through the fresh clothes and the cloud of fragrance in the air.

His mind wandered back to the people they'd mugged for the clothes. He was most proud of Cynthia. She had done well through two airship crashes, escaping a group of Lemurian soldiers and piloting the airship amid little hope of escaping.

He knew she'd had fun taking the rich Lemurian's clothes. That was her devilish side showing though. She often played pranks on Thomas and their clients in the lab back home, altering a rifle to blow a balloon out of the barrel or filling a bomb casing with flower petals.

"Robert?" a man's voice said behind Thomas.

Thomas knew the voice was speaking to him, but he didn't turn around. After a few seconds the man behind him gently tapped him on the shoulder.

"Robert?" he asked again.

Thomas turned around to see a man about his age, a few inches taller, standing behind him.

"Oh, sorry ole chap," the man said. "You looked familiar."

"No problem," Thomas said, smiling. He turned away, hoping to end the conversation.

"Did Miss Claudia make that jacket?" the man behind him asked.

Thomas turned around again. "Why…yes she did," Thomas answered with a smile.

"My friend Robert has an identical jacket by Miss Claudia. It is so rare for her to make more than one of the same item," the man said. "How on earth did you get her to do it?"

Thomas paused, quickly thinking of a lie. "I asked her for a red trench coat and she showed me this design. I was unaware another had been made."

"Strange indeed," the man said. "I believe my friend is actually on this ship. What are the chances?"

"Small world."

"Yes it is. Arnold Blakely of the Blakely Food Supply Company," he added, holding his hand out.

"Thomas Marshall," Thomas said, not remembering the fake name he came up with before.

Thomas had heard of the Blakeley Food Supply Company. He had read that they were one of the suppliers of food rations for the Lemurian army. Arnold looked at him strangely for not announcing his trade.

"So, Thomas what do you do?"

"I deal in gold sales," Thomas lied. "The wife and I are here on business with the government. Actually Mister Blakeley, you may be able to help me. What do you know about the Alchemist Isaac Maier? I would like very much to meet him."

Arnold chuckled. "I bet you would. I heard Doctor Maier can turn ten different elements into gold."

"So you know him?" Thomas asked.

"We've met a few times, usually at parties. Between you and me, the man is brilliant, but completely off his rocker. I promise you, friend, you'll be lucky if he speaks to you. He's quite eccentric."

"Good thing I'm not afraid of eccentricity," Thomas said. "Can you tell me where his office located?"

Arnold held his hand up to his chin. "I don't remember the street name. It is somewhere in the Brayer borough of Lemuria City."

"Ah," Thomas said. "Brayer. It shouldn't be too hard to find then."

Arnold shot Thomas another funny look, as if he had said something wrong. The man in front of Thomas side-stepped, leaving him next in line for a drink. Thomas was never so happy to see a bartender in his life.

"A house beer and Jenever with cherry," Thomas said breaking the conversation with Arnold.

When presented with the drinks, he turned to Arnold and nodded his head. "Wonderful to meet you Mister Blakeley."

"And you as well," Arnold said.

Thomas smiled and walked off, hoping his stories didn't raise any suspicion. He waded his way through the crowd, finding Cynthia still on the front deck with her back to the crowd and the backpack full of weapons next to her feet.

"What happened? Did they have to distill the alcohol?"

"I wish that was all. Someone started talking to me. Apparently I am wearing a one of a kind coat. He knew the guy we took it from."

Cynthia looked at him sharply. "How did you get out of it?"

"I said the designer offered me this coat. I don't know. I had to make something up."

Cynthia grabbed the ruby red drink from Thomas, and took a quick sip.

"I did get the name of the area of town where we can find Maier. It's called Brayer."

Cynthia smiled at the rhyme. "Well that's good. Was he suspicious?"

"I don't know. Maybe a little. I think we're fine."

After thirty more minutes of travel, the tops of the tall buildings that crammed the center of downtown Lemuria City popped over the horizon. Thomas and Cynthia tensed as the city came into view, nervously sipping their drinks, Cynthia again finished hers first.

As the boat pulled closer to the city, thousands of people had gathered on the docks and the long, grassy waterfront. Colorful tents created patterns of bold, vertical stripes among the throng.

"What have we gotten into?" Cynthia asked, bending the brim of her hat again to obscure her eyes.

110

As they sailed closer, a scene of pure merriment came into focus. Thousands of party goers bumbled around the waterfront with heavy mugs in their hands and packs of people sung traditional Lemurian songs reminiscent of gypsy tunes Thomas had heard in the past. As they approached the dock, the rumble of the crowd blended with the sound of the ship's engine. It seemed everyone was intoxicated and having the time of their lives.

Thomas wondered how they could afford such luxury with a war going on. The only sign of the war was a group of soldiers acting as policemen and three anti-airship cannons placed on the edges of the waterfront slope.

West Canvia was very different. They would never have parties like this, especially not outside where they were vulnerable to attack. Of course, West Canvia never attacked civilian targets as the Lemurians often did. It was this laxness that made Thomas believe West Canvia could win the war.

The boat was roped to pilings and amid a few gawkers the boarding ramp was lowered to the dock. Thomas and Cynthia blended with the first crowd exiting the ship. Cynthia strained to hold the oversized backpack like a purse at her side.

"What are they celebrating?" Cynthia mumbled.

"I have no idea," Thomas replied.

"What do you mean?" a voice behind them said. "You have to be a sponsor to be here."

Thomas and Cynthia turned around to see a woman with her head tipped sideways. She wore an ugly hat that looked like it had a crooked black saucer on the top. Her eyes glared at them through her green tinted glasses.

"Excuse me," Thomas said. "My lady friend has had a bit too much alcohol."

"She has a black eye," the woman said in a snooty voice. "And you said you have no idea what they are celebrating as well do you?" Her eyebrows raised above her glasses in a scolding expression a master might level at a slave.

People started to disembark the paddle boat, their voices loud and full of excitement. Thomas grabbed Cynthia's wrist and they took a step forward, putting other people between them and the nosy woman.

"Excuse me," the woman called loudly. "Sir! Excuse me!"

With Cynthia in tow, Thomas picked up his pace, excusing himself between people until they were on the dock and mixing with the masses on the waterfront.

"I don't think they are sponsors," The woman announced. "Why are they on this ship?"

Thomas went for the thickest group of people close to them, dodging and weaving until they were out of earshot of the woman. Thomas glanced back at their accuser. Men on the boat raised custom spyglasses looking for them, not only on the dock but from the ship as well.

"We need to get out of here. Take off your hat."

Cynthia removed the large hat, and her filthy blond hair and black eye contrasted with her sparkling outfit.

They quickly made their way to the shelter of one of the tents exclusively selling beer. Large ceramic mugs were changing hands so quickly; it looked like they were giving it away for free.

"They'll never find us now," Cynthia said, pulling free of Thomas' grip and leaning against the table where servers were passing frothy beers to the massive crowd.

"This probably isn't the best place to stop," Thomas said, looking at all the people clamoring around them.

"Ah, we're fine."

A short man turned with his mug of beer and bumped into Thomas, spilling creamy white foam on his jacket.

"Sorry, sir," the man said with an inebriated smile.

"Oh," the man replied, stopping short. "Thanks to you both!" The man's filthy goggles atop his bald head, the brown leather apron, and dirty work books gave away his status in Lemurian society.

"For what?" Thomas asked.

"For the beer of course. It makes everything a little better."

"Wait," Thomas said, reaching out as the man turned to leave. "I don't understand. We didn't give you the beer."

The man flashed them a discolored, toothy smile and sidled up closer to Thomas. "Well of course you did, sir," he said. "I know you for a sponsor in those clothes."

Thomas gave him a confused look. "Tell me, what is this all about?"

The man mirrored the expression. "Oh, this is a test, huh? If you want to play games, I can play. Anything for a sponsor."

The man took a step back and lifted his beer to take a large sip. "We will never forget the people who make this war bearable by providing loyal citizens like myself beer in these monthly crane festivals. May we soar like the cranes to victory over the Canvian dogs. And let me assure you, Sir and Madame, the festivals do give us hope."

Realizing what the man was talking about, Thomas quickly reached into his vest pocket, pulling out a random Lemurian bill and handing it to the man. "Well done, sir. You are a loyal citizen and I am glad we have such outstanding men as yourself working hard every day."

The man's eyes almost popped out of his head when he glanced at the bill. He looked up at Thomas, his eyes filling with tears as if he would cry. "God bless you, sir! Thank you! I will work hard every day. I will. I promise."

Thomas smiled at the man and nodded his head like he thought Lemurian nobility might. "Please, go enjoy your beer. Oh, but don't tell anyone about our little test or the money, okay?"

The man nodded quickly. "Of course, sir. Not a word. I swear on my life."

He bowed as he walked backwards, his steps light as if Thomas had set him free with the single, stolen Lemurian bill.

"Do you know how much that was?" Cynthia asked with a

sly look on her face.

"I have no idea. It could have been a hundred dollars, I didn't look."

"It was five hundred dollars," Cynthia said rolling her eyes and turning to the table. "Two beers please!"

A large serving woman noticed Cynthia's command and quickly produced two messy and frothy beers.

"We're going to need these if you are going to give everyone five hundred dollar bills," she said, lifting her beer and taking a swig.

Thomas grabbed his, lifted it in a quick toast and drank. "At least we know the rich are feeding the citizens with beer in order to keep their support."

"You did well. But please let's get going before I turn into an alcoholic trying to keep Lillian quiet."

When the beers were finished, they waded through the crowd and away from the waterfront. The soldiers acting as policemen stood at the gated exits watching the crowd, thicker groups of them mingled around the anti-aircraft guns. Thomas and Cynthia followed a thin line of citizens who were leaving. The gates were left open with only one guard at each exit. Without making eye contact with the guards, Thomas and Cynthia walked freely into Lemuria City.

On the streets of Lemuria City the buildings towered over them, some so high it was difficult to see the tops. In typical Lemurian architecture, they were all tall boxes stretching upward, competing for the city's height record. All the business and government buildings had no style or sense of art. Everything down to the smallest shop was a plain box, each with simple signs that stated the name of the business. Even the wording of the businesses was in the same banal print. The only noticeable difference was the background colors of the signs. One blue, one yellow, one green and so on, they stretched endlessly in the same efficient but depressing style.

Down the street and into the heart of the city, Thomas and

Cynthia looked like rich tourists staring at the buildings. Cynthia put her hat back on, half to hide her identity and half to hide the black eye that seemed to draw extra glances from passersby. Hundreds of three-wheeled cycles flew by them on the streets. Surprisingly, only a few steam cars and water combustible engine motorcycles huffed by. Most of the traffic was bikes and pedestrians, many of them heading to the Crane Festival at the river.

"I have never been to Lemuria," Cynthia said. "We have been at war with them almost since I was born."

"I was very young when it started. I came with my parents when I was just a baby, but I don't remember it," Thomas said quietly as they walked down enemy streets. "They have changed the reasons to fight so many times. Originally it had something to do with West Canvian officials getting assassinated, but then both sides warped it into border disputes over resources, then it turned into a religious conflict."

"It's crazy," Cynthia said. "I make weapons with you to kill these people, but I make them because now if we don't win, we'll be killed or forced into slavery."

"Yep. I do it for my parents as well."

"I know," Cynthia said solemnly.

They walked silently down the sidewalk of the busy street until they passed the majority of the soaring buildings.

"Brayer," Thomas said at last. "We need to find Brayer."

They continued to walk. Thomas had extracted the map from the backpack and studied it as they strolled. "I think we are headed in the right direction."

Cynthia stopped a man in grubby clothes. "Kind sir. Which way to the Brayer borough?"

Mesmerized by her appearance, the man stopped and gave them directions. They seemed quite easy, five blocks straight ahead then left for two blocks, followed by another six blocks to the left. A short while later they arrived in the Brayer borough, the location made obvious by several businesses named after the town. Thomas and Cynthia passed The Duke's Brayer Tavern, The Brayer Steam Works, and The Brayer Apothecary.

"We're here," Thomas announced unnecessarily.

Cynthia wanted to laugh at him, as she saw the same signs, but her exhaustion and the alcohol she had earlier kept her quiet.

"Now to find Maier's lab. And how do we do that?" she asked. "Shall I ask someone else?"

"I am not sure. It's on this map, but there is no address. I guess the Marines would have known. Besides we've come in from the opposite direction."

The boxy buildings remained the same everywhere they went. It wasn't until they saw a spiraled and turreted building poking up from the flat roof tops a block ahead that they had an idea.

"You don't think that's it do you?" Thomas asked. "But the man on the boat said Maier was crazy right? Why shouldn't he have the most ornate building in the city? Let's give it a look. It's probably just an old church."

They found the building embellished with faded gold accents and as they got closer the church-like structure proved even more wonky than they'd originally thought. It had five turrets with pointed tops, stained glass windows and a multitude of small and large balconies peeking out from every angle.

As they approached the unusual edifice, they saw an undeveloped span of land about an acre square showing the unmistakable wear of weapon testing. Charred grass, a variety of holes, and battered targets were scattered about as if an attacker was satisfied with the results. Excited, they walked around to the front where hanging from the entryway was a large silver sign with the words, *Lemurian Progress House* etched in metal. A formidable iron fence surrounded a small strip of grass, a few neatly manicured shrubs, and Maier's distinctive lab.

Everything was decorated like some old master had put their touch on the building. Gargoyles perched on every corner and above the doors. Statues of ancient gods stood on the

116

grounds and a large Roman numeral clock ticked away on the front of the building. A single soldier stood watch at the front doorstep.

"This is it," Thomas said.

"We can't just walk in," Cynthia said. "Look at the size of that place. And it has a guard; there have to be more like the Marines said, as well as the platoon down the street that they mentioned."

The two tried their best to case the place for weaknesses without being noticed, walking around the building several times.

"I have an idea," Thomas said, "but we will have to wait."

"Wait where?"

Thomas looked around. Behind the battered acre of weapons-tested land was a row of seemingly abandoned brick buildings, none with windows and all of them black with dirt and grime that apparently hadn't been cleaned for decades.

"In there," he said pointing. "We can get some sleep and then try to get inside in the middle of the night when there are hopefully fewer guards."

"But there is only one guard now," Cynthia said.

"Surely there are more inside."

"Agreed, and I can sleep just about anywhere right now."

They found their way to the old service structure that looked like a hollowed out apartment building and gained entrance without incident. The burned brick building proved nastier than either of them thought. Obviously Maier had used the structure as his personal shooting gallery. Pockmarked walls and fire-scorched floors looked eerily familiar from tests Thomas and Cynthia had done in their lab back in West Canvia. Everything was trashed, looted, and only pieces of glass from broken windows remained scattered on the floors. There was nothing left but the skeleton of the building and its rooms.

They found a room where they could see the back of Maier's lab. After ensuring that they could sufficiently hide from the back windows of the lab they ate some of their military rations which Cynthia abhorred. After the meager meal, she fell asleep as promised on the cold and dirty floor.

Thomas, assured of her slumber took the first shift as lookout. He knew when they woke it would be time to do the impossible. They would either perform the Lifeblood Alchemy on Cynthia there, or kidnap Isaac Maier and take him back to West Canvia.

10
THE NEFARIOUS DOCTOR

Taking three hour shifts of one sleeping and one standing guard, Thomas and Cynthia spent the rest of the day in the abandoned building. Filled with anxiety, they barely spoke to each other. By midnight they had gotten enough rest to continue with their plans.

There was no sign of the platoon of soldiers the West Canvian marines had mentioned, the only sign of activity was a changing of the lone guard that Cynthia saw during her lookout shift at dusk. From Thomas and Cynthia's view, only one light glowed from an insignificant little window that appeared to lead to the basement. As the large moon reached its peak the sky, Thomas woke Cynthia, gave her time to clear her head and told her his ideas to gain entrance to the building.

Leaving their trash in the room, Thomas and Cynthia dashed across the testing yard with the craters and broken targets to the unprotected back of the laboratory. Finely carved stairs greeted them, leading up to a back door, but it was the row of lead lined stained glass windows that intrigued Thomas. He wondered what the building used to be. It was too grand and artfully designed to be an old government building, and it was too odd to have been a church. He imagined that it must have been an old residence or second home for some past royal Lemurian.

With their pistols in hand loaded with acid shot, Thomas rummaged quietly through the backpack while Cynthia pressed herself against the wall acting as a lookout. He pulled a single acid round out of the box and examined it in the dim moonlight. The bullet was a little bigger than his thumb, and held enough hyperactive acid to eat through several feet of concrete. He extracted one of the knives from the pack, and placing the bullet on the ground, he gently stuck the tip on the knife on the round where the acid was housed. This was dangerous work, if the bullet cracked; he could easily have his hand eaten away or fatal holes burned into his body. He scooted the bullet to the end of the window and pressed harder. Cynthia took two extra steps away from him in case of disaster.

Thomas twisted the knife against the polymer portion of the bullet like he was unscrewing the tiny bolts on a pair of spectacles, taking his time and making sure his hand didn't slip.

"That's ridiculously dangerous," Cynthia whispered sharply, taking yet another step back. "Do you think this is the wisest course of action?"

Thomas glanced up at her. "No, but if it works we can get in without making much noise."

After a short time, a tiny hissing sound came from the bullet. He had punctured the bullet with the smallest hole, but it was the tip of the knife that was sizzling. When he held it in the light, the once pointed tip was already sufficiently rounded. Thomas scooped the bullet on the flat end of the knife and wedged it against the middle section of the window. Scraping the projectile gently along the stained glass, a tiny stream of acid poured from the pin hole in the bullet, making the window hiss as it burned away. Cynthia's head swiveled as she looked from side to side for any sign of movement.

The window started to disappear under the corrosion, bubbling and liquefying until holes started to form. Thomas did his best to evenly spread the stuff, but it wasn't long before the entire knife blade had fallen part and the bullet fell on the ground. Thomas and Cynthia stepped back and watched the window disappear before their eyes. When the acid seemed to lose its potency, the bottom half of the window was gone, leaving a daunting menagerie of jagged stained glass hanging from the frame like a guillotine. They waited a few minutes longer to make sure the acid would not rub off on them when they shimmied through the hole. Thomas stuck his head in to take a look at a dark room. Only a conveniently placed desk under the basement window was visible.

Feet first, Thomas backed into the window, his legs dangling until his boots touched the desk below. He felt some kind of office accessory under his right foot. He kneeled on the desktop and patted around with his hand to clear off anything else that might make noise. Cynthia followed him through the window and into the black room.

It didn't take long for their eyes to adjust to the low light and they realized they were in some kind of library. Shelves of books lined the walls while stacks of books that would not fit were stacked on the floor like literary headstones. A single door led out. With guns drawn, they crept quietly across the wood floor. The door opened into a finely decorated hall. Oil paintings hung on the walls, a plush carpet ran down the middle of the floor, and at the end a door stood open to a staircase leading to a lower level. Gas lit sconces offered a little light and a yellow glow emanated from the stairs in front of them.

Thomas jerked his head forward in a silent signal to keep moving. Clicking sounds echoed off the old masonry and the glow from below grew brighter as they descended. Someone or something was down there. The sounds could have been a machine, but Thomas deduced they were random enough to be a human. He gave Cynthia a cautionary look and then he gingerly took a step down. It seemed solid enough, but on the second step, the wood creaked under his boot. He froze, holding a hand back to keep Cynthia from following. The clicking sounds continued uninterrupted, so he dared another step. Again, the next stair groaned under his weight. He held his hand up again and stood silently, trying not to breathe. Surely if someone was down there, they would have known there was an intruder on the stairs. He took another step, then another, ignoring the moan of the wood. When he arrived at the final step, he crouched down and peered around the corner.

What greeted Thomas was the most impressive collection of scientific artifacts and gadgets he'd ever seen. It appeared to be a single room, spanning the entire width and breadth of the house above. On one side were rows of shelving full of labeled boxes and endless rows of books. Extinguished gas lamps hung from a ceiling cluttered by dozens of machines strung up to the beams like exhibits in a museum. There were mechanical birds, propellers, airship parts, and a mess of metal inventions. The huge room was a maze of large and small gadgets and prototypes, some looking abandoned and some looked deadly and ready to move. Silent robots with square faces lined the left wall. It appeared that they were all being fitted with an array of deadly looking attachments. The center of the room was dominated by an oversized science table with a shelf running above the entire length. It was so grand it could have held twenty or more scientists working at once like a giant triage. The surface was covered in all manner of glassware, tubes and fluid containers. A single source of light came from a large gas lamp with a circular mirror attached to the back side, reflecting the light on a long desk piled high with machine parts and tools. The light focused like a spotlight on a man in a black jacket with his back to Thomas, his wiry white hair stuck up as if he had been hit by lightning. He seemed to be tinkering with a small device creating the clicking sounds.

Cynthia came down the stairs with the same racket that Thomas made, but the man took no notice. Thomas couldn't believe it. Maybe Maier was deaf, or engrossed in his work. Either way it was going to work to their advantage.

"Oh my god," Cynthia mouthed as she got an eyeful of the endless space.

He gave Cynthia a bewildered look, left the backpack with her and stepped down on the stone floor of the basement. He held his handgun forward and walked on the edge of his feet as he crept up behind Maier. His felt as though he could hear his heart beating in his head. The light blaring down on Maier was so hot Thomas felt the warmth from several feet away. How did this old man take the heat? Maier had a copper colored strap around his head with two telescoping goggles that were fully extended over his eyes. The old man had a dirty red handkerchief wrapped around his neck and a copper brace attached to his right arm. A cup of aromatic tea steamed next to him.

One thing hit Thomas like a ton of bricks as he stared at the mission objective. The drugs. The entire plan was to drug Maier to make him cooperate and Thomas had not checked the inside pockets of the backpack. He wasn't sure if he had retrieved the correct one from the crashed airship. It was of no matter now; he was barely three feet away from Isaac Maier with a gun in his hand. Thomas stepped into the light and pressed the barrel of the gun to the back of Maier's head.

"Doctor Isaac Maier?" he said as he touched the old man's head with the gun.

"Yes?" Maier confirmed confidently. He didn't flinch or even look back. The man didn't seem surprised at all.

"I will need you to come with me," Thomas said, completely thrown off by the old man's nonchalance.

"I can't do that. There's work to be done."

"I don't think you understand the situation Doctor," Thomas said with authority.

Maier held a metal ball with several open compartments in his hands. It was the size of a grapefruit, with some of its mechanical innards showing through the openings. He tilted his head to the side and with a flick of his thumb, the ball snapped opened like a flower. Something cold and wet hit Thomas in the face knocking him backwards. He stumbled over his own feet, fell to the ground and dropped his gun. Fear jumped through him. Maier was famous for his molecular weapons, and for a moment, Thomas was sure he was a dead man. He put his hands to his face, hurriedly wiping the slimy goo from his eyes.

"Gotcha," Maier exclaimed, choking and coughing with

laughter.

"Cynthia," Thomas cried out.

"Oh, Miss Basset is here as well?" Maier said, turning in his chair and standing up. "Where is she?"

Thomas continued to try to clean his face. Something about the goo was familiar and as his brain flipped through what pathogen it could possibly be, he struggled back to his feet.

"Miss Basset," Maier called out. "I am so glad you came! I have been meaning to offer you a job ever since you made those bloody lamp bombs. That was quite an ingenious little device. Where are you my dear?"

Thomas spit some of the goo out of his mouth. There was something about the flavor that was familiar as well. He couldn't remember which poison tasted like this.

"You are a poor scientist, Mister Riley," Maier said, lifting his long goggles off of his face and pointing the most ridiculous looking hand gun at Thomas.

The gun had a small tank on top with three circular sights attached to the end. It had two triggers and an extra handle on the side that seemed to have no purpose.

"Miss Basset?" Maier called out again, his beady eyes darting around the basement. "Please come out, I would hate to turn Mister Riley's head into liquid."

Thomas wiped another glob of the goo out of his eyes and looked at his fingers. It wasn't anything diabolical at all. It was a chicken egg. Maier began laughing uncontrollably, which made Thomas even more nervous as his hand was shaking with that crazy gun pointed straight at him.

"See, Mister Riley. Foiled by an egg. My portable egg incubator has a faulty spring. Seemed funny enough at the time. Pretty punny isn't it? Egg on your face?"

Maier laughed so hard he looked like he was going to fall over dead. Besides being completely embarrassed, Thomas steamed with anger. Somehow Maier was right; he had been foiled by an egg. It was the last thing in the world Thomas would

124

have expected.

Finally, Maier's laughter died down.

"Okay," he announced, his voice bouncing off the stone walls. "Miss Basset, come out from wherever you are hiding right now. Don't make me have to count, I may forget a number. Oh and this is your last chance for that job offer."

"All right," Cynthia said appearing from the other side of the table. "Don't hurt him. We're not here to hurt you."

"Then I guess I'm here to hurt you," Maier quipped. "Nice try you little minx, but I know this room like the inside of my eyelids. I have to hand it to you though, you got pretty close. Oh and I am impressed with the formal clothes. The black eye is not so becoming though."

He waved his hand for Cynthia to join Thomas in front of him. Reluctantly walking around the table, she looked ashamed that she had been discovered. Maier sat back on his table with a smug look on his face.

"Do you know what they are offering for you two alive? It's like winning the lottery. Even if I shot you both dead, I could get a year's pay. I can't wait to hear all that juicy information from the interrogators."

Maier paused. "Mister Riley, you're looking a bit chicken."

Maier exploded with laughter at his own bad joke. He coughed and hacked so much his face began to turn red. He reached for his cup of tea and took a hearty swig, patting his chest until he calmed down again. "So what shall we talk about before I get the soldiers? I have so many questions. I don't know where to start. How about...why are you here?"

Thomas looked down. "We needed your help."

Maier's smile grew unnaturally wide. "You, needed my help? First off, how much mercury have you been using in your experiments? Apparently way too much. What on earth possessed you to think I would help you?"

"We had a problem with Lifeblood. We thought you were the most brilliant Alchemist around," Cynthia said, trying to stoke Maier's ego.

"Well, I am. But let me inform you of something Miss Basset. Just so you know, our two countries have been at war for over two decades, and in case you forgot, we both make weapons for our respective sides. You better have some mighty powerful potions to convince me to help you with anything, especially Lifeblood. Whose idiotic idea was that anyway?"

"I did it," Cynthia lied. "I was trying to help someone and now they are locked inside of me."

The delighted expression on Maier's face looked as though he had never had a better time in his life. He sat on the table top with the gun still trained on Thomas and Cynthia and took another gleeful sip of his tea.

"I will never understand how you make such brilliant weapons. Either of you! You realize not only are you two going to be the laughingstock of the entire world, but that life as you know it has now ended. I mean can you see it? I can read the headlines now. 'Canvian Weapons Makers Caught Asking Enemy for Help'. Or, 'Canvian Boobs Doom The War'. I hope Mister Riley here gave you that black eye for trying to use Lifeblood," Maier spewed.

"Well," he continued, "you've made your bed, no matter how stupid it was. Now you have to lie in it."

Maier hopped off the table to alert the guard and as his feet touched the ground, his knees gave out from under him. He flopped to the ground like a rag doll, dropping the gun. Thomas didn't hesitate, snatching it up along with his own gun he had left on the ground.

"All right you arrogant old goat," Thomas said, pointing both guns at Maier.

"What is the day time cow bell?" Maier said with slurred words.

"What?" Thomas asked. "Another lame trick? This time no eggs, and no games. I will shoot you in the arm every time you say anything stupid."

126

"A tempura grenade. I told him that was funny."

"That's it," Thomas said.

"No wait," Cynthia yelled, "I put the drugs in his tea. He's going to be a mess for at least twelve hours."

Amazed, Thomas turned and threw his arms around Cynthia. "How did you do it?"

"I dropped it in when you were on the floor."

"Brilliant! Absolutely brilliant! How much did you give him?"

"The entire packet."

Thomas began to laugh. "He'll be out for longer than twelve hours. I put double the dose in those packets. I hope the old guy doesn't overdose. Wow, I was so worried we had left the drugs on the airship."

"We were lucky then," Cynthia said. "When you went gallivanting off the stairs over there, I couldn't get your attention about the drugs."

"We've been very lucky," Thomas said. "I want to get this over with before our luck runs out."

"How are we going to get him out?"

Maier wiggled slowly on the floor, mumbling before he passed out. Thomas reached down and checked his pulse. He looked up at Cynthia with a furrowed brow.

"Okay, he's out. His pulse is slow. I really hope we didn't just kill him."

"It's funny really. A week ago we would have given our right arms to have this guy die from an overdose," Cynthia added.

Thomas set about the room, gathering random materials to carry Maier's limp body out of the lab. He pulled a long sheet of copper from a pallet and a length of rope to tie Maier to the sheet and to wrap around himself. Cynthia, still captivated by the impressive laboratory helped gather anything she thought might make the homemade sled easier to glide. She was constructing thin runners on the bottom of the sled when logic hit her.

"Thomas?"

"Yes?" he asked from the far corner of the lab.

"You know this is stupid and impossible right? There is no way we are going to be able to drag this man back to West Canvia. Even if we were able to do it this sled would leave huge tracks."

"That's why you are going to carry him."

Cynthia felt her blood pressure increase until Thomas started laughing.

"Yeah funny. Good one," she said, staring at the sled.

Thomas kept laughing.

"It isn't that funny."

"No?" he asked. "How about this?" Thomas emerged from the corner of the lab rolling a rickety homemade air ship in front of him.

Cynthia's eyes lit up. "Can it hold all of us?"

Thomas inspected the ship. "It only has two seats, but it has a balsa wood cargo compartment. I am sure Doctor Maier wouldn't mind sitting in there."

The ship had a small deflated dirigible sagging on its skeletal frame. Underneath was a pole framed cockpit that resembled a glider more than an actual flying machine. It only had one pair of wings, which were folded back for storage. The machine had two propellers, a large one in front and a smaller one on the back for added thrust. A small semi-automatic grenade launcher was welded roughly on the passenger side. Maier had made this machine by hand–possibly as a scouting prototype for the army.

"There is no way that thing flies," Cynthia said.

Thomas leaned into the machine, wheeling it close to the long row of gas tanks Maier had lined up against the wall. There were two large wooden doors with iron rivets on the opposite side of the lab that would accommodate the passage of such a large object.

"Well, the only way to find out is to give it a try," Thomas

128

said. "I hope there's a lift behind those doors."

He fastened a hose to the helium tank and turned the valve. The semi-rigid air ship began to inflate, its separate compartments filling one at a time like lungs breathing in oxygen after being submerged under water. Cynthia sat on the floor next to the pieces of the sled they were going to make, her eyes filled with concern.

"I'm impressed," she said. "At least the balloons are filled. Now we just have to hope the wings are sturdy, the engine works, and the thing can fly. He made that himself you know. I've never seen anything like it. It's like a go cart with a balloon on top."

She stood up, unable to resist inspecting the airship. She extended the wings as far as possible in the lab and turned Maier's gas lamp with the mirror attached toward the engine. Thomas opened the large double doors, revealing a dark ramp that appeared to lead outside, but there was no light from the stars or the moon.

After following the length of it, he came back excited. "It leads right out to the back. There's a huge trap door under one of the targets. The big hay bale is completely fake. We can open it and this thing will rise straight up and out."

"Well, I have to say the engine looks like it will work," Cynthia said, still looking under the machine. "He might be a nut, but he's quite good at what he does. I mean, we knew that before, but being here, seeing all of this is a chance of a lifetime, especially for us."

Thomas nodded, taking a moment to look around the room. "Keep checking that engine, I am going to look for rounds for that launcher."

"My pleasure."

Cynthia reveled in getting her hands dirty, while Thomas was the more complex math and science kind of man. They were the perfect balance in the laboratory, the grease monkey and the engineer.

"This guy has everything," Thomas said as he perused the shelves of labeled boxes. "Rubber tubes, copper wire, rubber balls, ball bearings, shrunken heads? I don't want to know."

"No ammo?"

"Hold your horses, there are hundreds of boxes. Here's one labeled bat wings."

Cynthia filled the tank and tested the heater, which seemed to be operational. "This could actually work. I admit I'm surprised, but I'm not complaining. I would say this engine could travel about two hundred miles without a refill."

"That should get us pretty close," Thomas said. "As long as we can find a lake or river, we can make it to West Canvian air space pretty safely."

"Ah," Thomas interrupted himself. "Ammo! And lots of it. Smoke, incendiary... probably magnesium, the old man probably stole that from us. There's shrapnel and puncture rounds too. I'm going to grab a few of each."

After loading the grenades on the floorboard of the passenger seat, they lifted the unconscious Maier and placed him in the cargo box in the back of the ship. It wasn't made for a human to fit inside of, so they jammed his legs in the best they could and slid the simple lock shut. Cynthia loaded their backpack in as well, which gave her no leg room, but it was a discomfort she was happy to deal with.

"Let's try it," Thomas said.

They pushed the airship up the ramp to the secret exit under the fake hay bale. Cynthia slipped her goggles on and crammed herself into the passenger seat. She grabbed two random rounds and loaded them into the launcher. Thomas located a crank on the wall and wound it counter clockwise. The faux hay bale creaked as it opened revealing the night sky above them.

Thomas jumped into the driver's seat. After tossing the sand bags off the side, the airship instantly started to rise. It was slow at first, but once they were a few feet off of the ground Thomas pulled the primitive cord and on its first try the engine loudly cranked up. Both propellers began to spin. The ship rose another ten feet when Cynthia noticed a man rounding the side if the building. It was the guard from the front door with a gun in one hand and some kind of communication device in the other.

"Shoot him," Thomas yelled over the engine noise.

Cynthia grabbed the launcher and aimed at the man. A second later she fired. The round smacked the ground next to him and exploded with a large cloud of black smoke.

"That was a smoke round," he yelled, "shoot him!"

Cynthia fired a second time and again a plume of dark smoke billowed from the ground. She let out a string of expletives at her poor choice of ammunition. The guard fired toward the ship. One round hit the wing, sending bits of wood flying in every direction. Cynthia screamed.

Thomas looked at her. "Where are you hit?"

"A couple of places, just shrapnel," she yelled. "I'm fine, just fly!"

Thomas throttled the engine making the propellers roar. Cynthia pulled a revolver from the backpack and shot all three acid rounds into the smoke below them. She wasn't sure if she hit the guard, but he'd stopped firing. The airship rose and lurched forward, sputtering and buzzing in the air. They had done it. They had captured Isaac Maier and were actually in an airship en route to West Canvia.

"I hope this thing will make it," Cynthia yelled over the engine while inspecting her wounds.

She loaded two more rounds in the launcher and held her shoulder.

"Are you sure you are alright?" Thomas asked.

"Yeah. They're small pieces; they just sting like the devil."

The air ship was airborne and heading west, the tall boxy buildings of downtown Lemuria City loomed around them. Thomas silently worried about what was ahead of them. Surely the army knew of the abduction and soon someone would give chase.

11
THE PYRE'S FORTUNE

The little airship rattled in the cool night sky. It was as simple as a flying machine could get. Its light frame shook violently in the slightest breeze.

Thomas kept the ship at a semi low altitude–just high enough to skim over the tall buildings, but low enough the integrity of the craft would not be jeopardized. Remembering the anti-airship guns on the waterfront, Thomas steered the craft away from the city, opting to make a large semicircle around it. The night air was cold and the thick cloud cover above threatened rain.

"Do you think this heap of bolts will make it back home?" Cynthia yelled over the sound of the engine.

"So far so good."

Thomas felt a rush of importance when thinking about the last few days. They had avoided death more times than he could count and they had successfully captured Lemuria's top weapon's designer. He felt like this entire mission was not just a lucky string of events, but part of him and Cynthia's destiny.

They passed the downtown area, then the river without being seen. When it began to rain, Cynthia donned her big hat and held it to her head to shelter herself from the icy rain drops. As they passed over the outskirts of Lemuria City, Thomas gazed at the thousands of tiny lights from the houses below.

The air around the ship rumbled with a heavy *woosh*. It was a quick burst of noise, but alarming enough to make Thomas to stop daydreaming about the people below and glance behind him. Something round, about the size of a basketball flew just over the air ship from behind. It passed them at incredible speed and as it reached about thirty feet beyond the little ship, it exploded with white steam and light. The shockwave sent Maier's airship plunging downward.

Cynthia gripped the sides of the ship and Thomas gripped the steering bars with white knuckles, bearing down as hard as he could. The ship was so flimsy the vibration almost shook the two out of the ship. After losing a hundred feet of altitude Thomas stabilized the craft.

"No! No! No! Not again," Cynthia yelled. "What was that? Anti-airship guns?"

She grabbed the launcher mounted next to her. The wind had blown her hat off and her hair flew straight back from her face.

"No. Something is in the air. Probably a fighter! That blast was meant to stop our engine!"

"Do they know we have Maier?"

"I don't know! Keep a look out, they're probably above us now!"

Cynthia looked up through the poles that made a roll cage on the top of the air ship. She gasped as three Lemurian fighters darted through the clouds.

"They're up there! At least three."

She yanked the launcher and tried to aim it directly up, but the angle wouldn't allow her to aim that high. Thomas pulled the controls to the right, making the ship turn hard to starboard.

"Don't shoot unless you have a really good shot," Thomas yelled against the wind. "Those things are only impact rounds, so you have to hit the fighters directly!"

"I might as well throw rocks at them," Cynthia said as she scanned the night sky for the enemy.

As if she willed them out of the darkness, two of the fighters burst out of the storm clouds heading right for them. They were cone shaped, with double stacked forward swept wings, and two rudders that stuck out of the back like twin shark fins. While it was invisible from where Thomas and Cynthia sat

134

a giant propeller on the back end powered the fighters to high velocity.

"There is no way I can hit them. Two are coming right down on us," Cynthia screamed.

Thomas responded by pulling back on the controls, forcing the homemade flaps up and jerking the fragile craft. Thomas made this maneuver to counter the angle that the fighters were bearing down on them. Cynthia aimed the launcher, but the fighters dove past her in the blink of an eye. Thomas continued to climb into the sky testing the little ship's integrity at a heavy angle.

"What are you doing?" Cynthia yelled.

"Going to get us in the clouds!"

Cynthia didn't want to argue with Thomas and her throat stung from yelling over the engine and the wind. Thomas knew the dangers of going into the clouds, especially storm clouds. Besides the obvious risk of lighting, there was the incredible turbulence that could shake their little airship apart. But the way the fighters were flying, she knew the only way to lose them was to try to hide in the thick clouds.

The fighters already swung around and were angling back toward them when Thomas got the ship inside the clouds. Despite the danger, being inside of a cloud provided a surreal feeling. There was zero visibility, the air was bumpier and the clouds had a slight chemical smell–like a mild household cleaner. The turbulence shook the airship like a toy, but it held together despite the vibrations.

Without warning, the airship popped out of the cloud and into open air. For a second, there was no rain and the stars were visible above. Another thick cloud bank floated ahead, but it would take a few minutes to reach it.

"Turn around," Cynthia ordered. "We're sitting ducks!"

Thomas silently agreed and shifted the stick, but as the ship began to turn back all three Lemurian fighters broke through the same clouds.

Cynthia panicked. "Don't turn around. Don't turn around."

She jerked the launcher and trained it on the lead fighter while Thomas tried to correct his turn and head toward the next cloud bank. He ended up making a three-hundred-sixty degree turn.

Then the fighters were upon them. From cannons on their underbelly, two of the fighters launched the steam compression balls.

Cynthia fired the launcher, and with a tube echoed *thoomp* sound, a shrapnel round burst out of the end. It whizzed just between the fighters and Cynthia cursed loudly.

The metal compression balls didn't hit their target either, one going over them and one to the side of the small airship. They both exploded almost simultaneously sending steam-driven shockwaves crashing against Maier's airship from two angles. The compartment in the rear of the dirigible burst, dropping the back of the craft downward. The back propeller was completely shredded and the engine ground to a halt. The ship had only forward momentum as it hung in the air with only two inflated compartments on top. Cynthia loaded another round and repositioned the launcher.

"That's what they wanted," Thomas said, pulling his hand gun from his pocket. "They must know we have Maier. Those things are made to make airship engines fail."

Maier's ship slowly lost altitude. The fighters made several fly bys to make sure the damage was sufficient. Cynthia popped off another round, but missed again.

"They got us," Thomas said. "There's no way we can fix that engine now."

The cloudbank ahead rumbled violently as if a huge thunderstorm was going to explode from it at any second. It was a strange, unnatural sound that Thomas could only chalk up to their altitude. As the Lemurian fighters made another swing around them, the cloudbank roared again, and emerging from it like a cloaked titan was a huge warship. Ribbons of dark clouds rolled and twisted around the gigantic ship's masts. It looked like a Man O' War naval battleship had been attached to the underside of an armored dirigible with giant propellers on the back.

The ship slung to its port side, and without hesitation, let off a huge volley of cannon fire from twenty gun ports. The flashes lit up the sky like a lightning storm. Two of the Lemurian fighters burst into flames and dropped like giant flares. The last fighter pulled away just in time to avoid the attack. The battleship let off a volley of smaller shots that came from the top deck in response. Glowing red tracer rounds and dozens of steam shockwave rounds flew up into the night sky, popping and crackling like a fireworks display. The Lemurian fighter twisted and dodged, avoiding the onslaught as it climbed out of sight.

Thomas and Cynthia felt like gnats in Maier's tiny sinking ship. From their view, the battleship looked to be at least two hundred feet long with three lower decks where cannons protruded. Of course, Thomas and Cynthia had seen these ships before, but this one was quite menacing.

It was an older make of battleship used for power rather than speed. Originally this sort of ship was made for water and later adapted to take to the air by using steam. With the help of reinforced fabrics, the side sails could capture the strong wind currents in the atmosphere.

Thomas sat helplessly in the pilot's seat while Cynthia stared at the battleship, continuing to hold on to the launcher as if it provided some measure of safety. The battleship lumbered fully out of the clouds and Thomas saw the black flag at the tip of its highest mast. A Jolly Roger flapped violently in the gusty wind, the white skull and crossbones glowing with an eerie green tint in the night.

"Cyn. I think we have another problem. I am pretty sure that's the ship that downed The Jupiter."

Cynthia cocked her head to get a better look. Her mouth fell open when she recognized it.

"It is. Out of the frying pan huh?"

"Yeah."

The pirate ship slowed down and slid next to Maier's craft. The deck of the pirate ship was busy with men scurrying about, some hunkering down with small cannon and some clearing barrels and huge coils of rope from the wide top deck. Two men with oil lamps walked out from a cabin door escorting a third man dressed in a long black trench coat and a black three-cornered hat. The trio walked to the side rail and the man in the middle held up a metal, telescoping bullhorn.

"Ahoy," he yelled. "We do not intend to hurt you. But you do have a choice! You may land on our deck or we will take you by force!"

Thomas looked at Cynthia. "That's not much of a choice."

Cynthia grimaced. "Aboard we go."

Thomas cupped his hands around his mouth and yelled into the wind, "Please clear the deck! We wish to come aboard!"

Despite the howling wind, the man in the trench coat understood Thomas, stepped back and waved his hand in the air. It was some kind of signal to his crew to maneuver the ship and not take hostile action. A release of steam poured from the sides of the pirate ship and it slowly lost altitude to get under Maier's ship. With their dirigible damaged, Thomas and Cynthia continued to float down until they hit the wide-planked deck.

The man with the trench coat strode forward, his lamp-handling minions still flanking him. Thomas noticed they each had identical hand guns drawn.

"Mister Riley and Miss Basset, welcome aboard The Pyre's Fortune," The trench coated man said proudly. "I am Lieutenant Sam Burges. We're honored to have such distinguished guests on our humble ship."

"How do you know who we are?" Cynthia asked as she exited Maier's air ship.

"Fortunately we intercepted reports that you two had made an escape from Doctor Maier's Laboratory. With fighters en route, we thought it might be in our best interests to lend a helping hand."

Sam Burges was a tall man in his mid twenties, in peak physical condition and clean-shaven. He didn't look like a pirate in the least. If Thomas bumped into him on the street, he would have guessed the man was some kind of young dignitary.

Cynthia was immediately struck by Burges' appearance. She hid her immediate attraction to the man by telling herself she was his prisoner. To maintain a tough façade, she kept her goggles over her eyes and held her face in a blank expression.

"I take it Doctor Maier didn't make it?" Sam asked.

Thomas couldn't help cracking a smile. "Actually he's in the cargo chest on the air ship."

"Dead I assume?"

"On the contrary," Thomas answered, "he's heavily sedated."

"Bravo, Mister Riley," Sam said with a bit of drama. "I knew you two were quite the engineers, but I see your prowess for action is strong as well."

"Please remove Doctor Maier from the cargo trunk and place him in the brig," Sam told his men.

With haste, his men rushed forward and unlatched the trunk, then hauled the still unconscious Isaac Maier out of his cramped quarters.

"So, what would drive two of West Canvia's most celebrated engineers to sneak into Lemuria and kidnap their rival?"

Thomas and Cynthia looked at each other.

"Maier has superior Alchemic knowledge and we need his assistance," Thomas said.

Sam looked at Thomas and Cynthia with an arrogant lift of his eyebrow. "Dare I ask why?"

"His knowledge is vitally important to Cynthia's health."

"You're not sick are you Miss Basset?"

Cynthia shook her head.

Sam smiled. "That's fine. You can keep your secret for now. Anyway, I'm pleased to say that Captain Swan is taking a late supper and insists that you both join him."

"How can we refuse?" Thomas asked. "You've saved our lives. I am sure the good Captain has as many questions for us as we do for him."

Sam bowed. "Excellent. We'll have dry clothes delivered to you in the guest quarters."

Thomas and Cynthia followed Sam off the deck. Out of the cold and wet, the narrow wood paneled passage was a warm relief. He led them aft to rooms directly across the hall from each other.

They kept the doors open as they explored the guest quarters. Each room had a compact bed protruding from the wall, a sealed porthole window, and a tiny cabinet with a mirror on the inside of the door. The only place to store personal items was under the bed which stood a few inches off of the floor.

After a few moments alone, a short man, unshaven for several days, delivered fresh clothes to Thomas and Cynthia, bowing as if he was addressing royalty. Thomas thought about tipping the man, but realizing he was on a pirate ship, he thought better of it.

Cynthia gladly accepted a long sleeved white blouse, a black cotton vest, and matching black trousers. She was happy with the foreign clothes and she was surprised they fit her perfectly.

They quickly changed into the dry, clean clothes and–almost as if they were being watched–a knock sounded at their doors just as they finished dressing.

The short man returned to collect them for the meal with the captain and his officers. Famished, Thomas and Cynthia bolted out of their rooms and followed him eagerly.

Walking side by side, Thomas and Cynthia let the short man lead the way through the narrow corridors of the ship. They marveled at the workmanship of the ship's interior. Everything was covered in a lustrous dark wood, the moldings and door frames were carved with flowers and sea creatures. Only the wealthiest person could have afforded this as a sailing ship, much less an airship.

With the short pirate leading them, they wound through the corridors and up a spiral staircase. At the top was a large wooden door with two lion heads carved on the front. The short man knocked gently.

"Enter," a gruff man's voice said.

The short man opened the door revealing a lavishly decorated room and a table packed with domed silver platters. The various aromas scenting the air promised a wonderful meal and the room itself was a feast for the eyes.

The walls exploded with carved reliefs and oil paintings. The floor was covered with red carpet and the entire back of the room was a wall of windows exhibiting the puffy grey clouds of the night sky.

At the head of the table stood a bearded man in his fifties with salt and pepper hair. He wore traditional airship captain's garb with a gold embroidered white hat with a black brim, a large navy blue double-breasted jacket with gold buttons and a stiff high collared white shirt with a double Windsor knotted black tie.

Flanking him were Sam Burges and a woman Thomas and Cynthia had not seen yet. She looked a few years younger than Cynthia and her shiny black hair fell past her shoulders. She wore a thick black and white striped jacket and a loosely buttoned white blouse. Her eyelids were heavy with black eyeliner and she wore powder white makeup and maroon red lipstick, making her look like an angry doll.

"Welcome," the captain said, holding his arms out. "I am Captain Charles Swan."

Thomas and Cynthia each chose a separate side of the table to be courteous. Despite the woman's sly face, Cynthia sat next to her, shaking her hand as she approached.

"Please make yourselves at home. Lieutenant Burges informed me of your harrowing journey," Captain Swan said. "This is Ensign Ann Read, my third in command."

Ensign Read smiled pleasantly at her introduction. The table had several covered trays which the Lieutenant and Ensign removed displaying a small feast of steaming hot food. Their noses did not deceive them; on the trays were stuffed Cornish Hens, a large platter of cut potatoes, loaves of hard bread, and a kettle with thick brown soup. Ensign Read poured generous portions of bourbon in crystal glasses for everyone at the table.

"Please, enjoy yourselves," Captain Swan said. "It's an honor to have you two aboard."

The captain raised his glass, everyone mimicked him, and they all took a sip of the drink. Thomas wanted to laugh knowing that bourbon was one of Cynthia's least favorite drinks, but she didn't show any sign of aversion.

"Lieutenant Burges tells me you sneaked into Lemuria to kidnap Maier because he has superior alchemic knowledge. Is this correct?" Captain Swan said, as he took a large swig of his bourbon.

"That is correct sir," Thomas answered.

"How did you get so far behind the lines without being detected?" he asked.

"To be honest sir, we were very lucky," Thomas answered. "We originally came in on a West Canvian ship." Thomas paused, feeling Cynthia's eyes staring at him. "We were on a ship called the H.M.S Jupiter that I believe was shot down by your ship."

Captain Swan and his officers were caught off guard, but only for a few seconds.

"So you were in that monstrosity?" Captain Swan asked. "How embarrassing. I do apologize, a ship of that size posed a threat and we had no idea you were on a kidnapping mission. Well, it seems all has turned out well."

Cynthia fought back her anger. Nothing had turned out well

142

Dozens of people had died on that ship and any survivors were surely prisoners of war.

"Well, we have accomplished our mission so far," Thomas said.

"I need to ask," the Captain began, "why were you in need of Doctor Maier's alchemic knowledge?"

Thomas played with his Cornish Hen hoping the question might go away, but it was a futile act that bought him only a few seconds. "I will be honest with you Captain Swan. The Duke's daughter was mortally wounded in a skirmish in West Canvia. She was brought to me and I was ordered to use Lifeblood alchemy on her before she died. When I did, her soul was lodged in Miss Basset here."

The Captain's eyes lit up with intrigue. "Really?"

"So you survived an airship crash, and made it all the way to Lemuria City where you captured Doctor Maier?" Ann asked Cynthia.

"We had some…difficulties on the way, but yes that is how it worked out," Cynthia answered.

"I'm impressed. You two are as crafty as the newspapers say you are," Ann said.

"I appreciate your honesty, Mister Riley," Captain Swan said. "I will return the favor to you both. The Pyre's Fortune has been the most dominant ship in the skies for three years now. We make a lucrative living off your country's war. We raid Canvian ships, and we raid Lemurian ships. We don't discriminate when it comes to power and money. Whatever is ripe for the taking, we do the taking.

"We're not nearsighted, though. We are looking to expand. There are hundreds if not thousands of targets that can and will be exploited while this war goes on. Now the opportunity to help you and Miss Basset has arrived and we hold some of the greatest minds in this corner of the world on board our ship."

"We appreciate your help and your kindness," Cynthia chimed in.

This earned her a smile from Captain Swan and Sam, but a suspicious look from Ann Read.

"We do what we can, Miss Basset," Captain Swan said.

"So we have a dilemma," Captain Swan continued. "I'll leave this up to you. Please understand that the crew must benefit from your rescue and surely the destruction of the Lemurian fighters has landed us on someone's most wanted list. Originally we wanted to intercept you because your ransom is worth a fortune, but now other opportunities present themselves. We can continue with our original plan to sell you to the highest bidder or, you two can join the crew of this ship as Chief Officer Weapons Designers."

Thomas and Cynthia were speechless. All of this generosity and lavishness was just to entice them to join the crew. Their fate seemed bleak, whatever choice they made.

"I assure you, you will have your own quarters, and quality food every day. The general crew makes a bountiful living. Each man typically stays aboard the ship for two years then he most often retires as a rich man," Captain Swan added.

Cynthia lost her appetite and gently put her fork on the plate.

"That presents a difficult choice," Thomas said. "We are loyal West Canvians, so it makes it impossible to join your crew. On the other hand, we have Duke William's daughter here in the room with us, so we can't allow the Lemurian's to get their hands on us or her."

Captain Swan had already cleaned the bones of his Cornish Hen. He looked at Thomas expectantly. "Given the choices, which will surely end with death if we are handed to the Lemurians, Miss Basset and I will work aboard your ship to our best ability. I propose an agreement," Thomas added.

"I am open to all suggestions," Captain Swan said.

"We will work for you for two years with regular pay and we are to be released seven hundred thirty days from today. When Maier recovers from his drugs he is to perform the

144

necessary alchemy to remove Duke William's Daughter from Cynthia and her soul is to be delivered back to West Canvia."

Captain Swan leaned forward and picked up his glass of bourbon as if to toast them. "Welcome aboard The Pyre's Fortune, Mr. Riley and Miss Basset. You have a deal."

12
THE LIFE OF A PIRATE

For a week, they flew through the air without any action or discomfort. They were able to catch up on their sleep and, as promised, they were well fed, eating finely prepared meals more worthy of an elite restaurant than an airborne attack vessel.

The two spent the week going over the ship's numerous and complex weapons. The Pyre's Fortune was armed to the teeth with over sixty air to air and air to ground steam cannons. The pirates seemed to have a large supply and a large variety of ammunition in storage as well. Most of the ammunition was high impact and high explosive in nature, giving the ship nothing less than a brutal and unforgiving nature when it came to battle.

One of Captain Swan's biggest complaints was when they raided a ship they often damaged it beyond repair, or sent it crashing to the earth before they could board it. Showing good will, Thomas and Cynthia made vast notes on the ship and how it could be improved with less lethal weapons. Thomas had gone as far as drawing sketches of new, custom weapons which would improve the ship's looting capabilities.

Within the week, Captain Swan approved Thomas' first design, an eight foot long crossbow that could swivel on the ship's top deck. The crossbow would launch a projectile into an opposing ship's dirigible. With a sharpened end like an arrow, once it penetrated the opposing ship, it would inject the gas hexafluoride, which would sink the cambers that keep most large airships afloat.

Thomas also had ideas about making smaller hand held crossbows of this nature to add to the mayhem, but he first wanted to make the large scale weapon to better impress the

Captain. This sizable addition to the ship's weapons system would eliminate much of the broad side barrage that often happened when one large ship met another large ship in battle. One hit with this crossbow and the opposing ship would lose altitude within seconds of impact, denying them any advantage.

Twenty-four hours a day, Thomas and Cynthia were escorted by armed guards. They had no way of verbally communicating their true feelings of Thomas' decision to sign them up as pirates for the next two years. When they were working or eating, they only felt comfortable talking about trivial things as guards ate with them and were stationed outside their quarters at night. As new and unwilling conscripts, Captain Swan wanted to make sure Thomas and Cynthia weren't planning anything dubious as they studied the ships strengths and weaknesses.

With no privacy, Thomas devised a simple code where numbers he wrote in his notes would take the place of letters, therefore making it possible to speak freely with Cynthia as they passed the notes back and forth for study. He disguised the numbers with fake variables and mathematical marks so their communication would not be discovered.

After Cynthia understood what Thomas was doing with the code, his first note read simply. "All right, let me have it."

Cynthia's note the next day read *You have to be insane. If the Lemurian's don't kill you, then I will. This woman in my head is driving me crazy. She's reading this through my eyes and she understands it because she has access to my thoughts. She constantly complains and she's currently complaining about me complaining about her. We need to find a way off of this ship as quickly as we can. This is madness.*

There were already indications that the deal they made was going sour. Captain Swan would still not let them see Isaac Maier. They had not made port yet, but they were kept away from him for 'health' reasons.

Thomas and Cynthia were suspicious, knowing Captain

147

Swan was up to something. They had agreed as soon as Maier had recovered from the drugs that he was to be allowed to perform a proper Lifeblood procedure on Cynthia. This continued denial of access was further clouded by a mandate from Captain Swan that the ship's main priority had shifted to hunting another pirate ship in the area.

Via their guards, Captain Swan called Thomas and Cynthia into his quarters to discuss their progress. With stacks of notations, suggestions and sketches, they were brought up to the room where they had eaten dinner with him their first night on board. Again, Ann Read and Sam Burges flanked the captain at his large dining table. The trio of officers stood as they entered.

"Ah," Captain Swan said. "Our brightest crew members have arrived."

Thomas and Cynthia settled into the same seats they had taken before and arranged their papers as if preparing for a board meeting.

"First, let's hear what has been done so far," Captain Swan said.

Thomas shuffled his papers. "We checked the maintenance records on all the cannon and with only a rare exception, the men seem to being doing a good job with their cleaning and ammunition checks. We found no deficiencies there. We did make slight pressure modifications to the largest and smallest cannons. The largest cannons now have more pressure per square inch for an added range of one hundred meters."

"Aren't the cannons at maximum safe capacity as is?" Ann asked. "The last thing we need is for the weapons to fail and explode during a battle."

Thomas smiled. "We measured the density and the resilience of metals used on the cannons, and it is our opinion that they have been underutilized."

"That's why you are the scientists," Ann said with a snippet of annoyance in her voice.

"The smaller cannons have had their pressure reduced nine

percent to maximize the impact of the ammunition. We found that with slightly less pressure, the shells will not penetrate decks as well and will in turn do more damage to personnel as they were intended," Thomas continued.

"Excellent," Captain Swan said. "I've reviewed your plans and the materials needed for the crossbow weapon and we will need to make port in order to get many of your items. I have scheduled a stop tomorrow at the neutral island port of the Seychelles Islands. We can pick up everything we need there. Once the materials are on board, what's the time frame for construction?"

Thomas scanned his notes. "We can have a working prototype ready in about four days."

"Very good," Captain Swan said, stroking his short beard. "Be aware we are tracking a rival ship called The Blood Countess which we intend on making our next target. She is as big as The Pyre's Fortune and she has as many men. Having this weapon in place could be the tipping point of the seizure."

Ann seemed put out that she even had to sit there, and Cynthia was trying to hold back Lillian who was screaming inside her head about how improving the pirate ship would lead to more West Canvian deaths and was therefore treason. Cynthia could barely hear the conversation through the din in her mind. When the meeting ended, everyone stood and Sam wandered around the table.

"Would you like to take a walk with me on the top deck?" He asked Cynthia. "You look like you could use some air."

Cynthia bit her lip, ashamed that he noticed her discomfort. "Um, sure," she said with a half-hearted smile.

Ann rolled her eyes and exited the captain's quarters. Thomas was shocked by the advance. Sam's lack of subtlety was equally as surprising as Cynthia's agreement. Just because they were essentially the pirate's prisoners didn't mean Cynthia was fair game for courting.

Thomas returned to his room where he sat on his bed,

angrily thumbing through his notes on the crossbow. While he stared at the sketches and dimensions, his mind wandered. He was half angry and half jealous that Cynthia was off palling around with the pirate who kidnapped them and forced them to become part of the crew. After what seemed like hours, he heard Cynthia's door open across the hall. He opened his door, catching Cynthia as she stepped into her room. The two guards looked surprised at her appearance. Thomas reached across the hall and thrust two pieces of paper toward her.

"While you were off having a good time, I took some more notes on the crossbow. I think you should check my math to make sure it is correct."

Cynthia's eyes narrowed. "Thomas Riley. How dare you accuse me of having a good time?" She said abruptly grabbing the papers. "It is hard enough with this crazy woman in my head constantly commenting on whatever's happening." Cynthia paused for a second. "Yes I called you crazy," she snapped, looking at the ceiling. "Sorry, but sometimes it's nice to be treated like a lady."

"A lady?" Thomas asked angrily. "Ladies don't go cavorting with their captors."

Cynthia's angry expression turned into shock. She turned her back and slammed her door.

The guards smiled, snorting as they tried to hold back their laughter. "Good evening gentlemen," Thomas snapped, closing the door behind him.

Thomas lay back on his bed already regretting the confrontation. Who was he to reprimand Cynthia? If she liked a pirate, she liked a pirate and there was nothing he could do about it. She wasn't his girlfriend by any means. They had always had a professional relationship. He fought the urge to go and apologize.

Cynthia threw the papers on the floor. Close to tears, she pressed her hands to her head, trying to stifle Lillian's constant commentary. It did no good. She regretted yelling at Thomas

They were supposed to be a team and she felt like she had let him down by going out with Sam. Sure it was a pleasant walk and she wasn't going to deny she enjoyed his company, but she was in fact a prisoner.

What kind of man was Sam anyway? Why was he a Lieutenant on a pirate ship? He seemed more like a successful business man or some wealthy son of royalty than a murderous pirate. She couldn't imagine he had actually fired a weapon in malice.

The next morning Cynthia was fixing her hair so her goggles would rest correctly on her head when she felt the ship rock forward slightly and stop. A knock came at her door.

"Cyn?" Thomas' muffled voice said from the hall. "We've made port."

She stood up and opened her cabin door. Thomas stood between two new guards with an apologetic smile on his face. She returned the smile and joined him.

"Sorry about last night," Thomas said in a low voice.

"Me too. All of this is just getting to me. I literally have too much on my mind."

"No need to explain. We have both been under a lot of stress. Let's make the best of it okay?"

"Absolutely."

She was going to say more. She was going to tell him how a good night's sleep had made her feel better and how Lillian was wonderfully quiet this morning, but they stepped on the top deck of the ship and into sight of the glistening port at the Seychelles Islands.

It was a perfect tropical scene and delightfully hot. They had been in the cold air for so long, this was like a replenishing sun bath. There were small puffy white clouds roaming in the blue sky. The port was huge, with massive docks and decks that protruded out from the white sand beaches. Hundreds of people were walking about the docks. Several other ships, all waterborne, were moored at the port as well, their masts protruding into the skyline. The sapphire blue water was picturesque, only the calmest little waves lapped up on shore.

A long stretch of small buildings sat just beyond the first sand dunes, each with its own personality and design. For the most part they looked like homemade shelters, constructed out of local materials. To odd effect, all of them had some kind of modern technology connected to the bamboo and coconut tree exteriors. Long pipes protruded from roofs and wrapped around in all directions, small wind turbines whirled in circles, and puffs of white steam huffed from dozens of vents and smoke stacks making the organic little merchant town look like a small industrial city.

Beyond the buildings everything was a dense, lush green. Foliage packed every inch of space beyond the beach, giving the hilly landscape in the distance an organic pillow-soft appearance that swayed in the trade winds like a massive living creature.

Sam and Ann were waiting by the ship's ramp, already lowered to the dock. Sam had a pencil and a long piece of paper in his hands. "Welcome to the Seychelles Islands. It's one of my favorite places to make port."

The scorching sun reflected off of his round tinted glasses giving him a more mysterious look. Thomas felt a pang of jealousy run through him. The four of them walked down the ramp and toward the steamy merchant village.

"Believe it or not, the Seychelles Islands have everything an airship could want," Ann said, as they went. "They're a neutral land, mainly set up for the exchange of wealth rather than the progression of a country. I have to warn you, this place can get a little rough if you're not careful. Everyone that flies or sails comes here, so meeting an enemy is not uncommon."

"Is that our list for the crossbow?" Cynthia asked Sam.

"Yes," he replied with a smile. "It's quite a long list. I hope it works."

They made their way up the docks and into the small ramshackle city; the variety of shops and goods offered were overwhelming. There were items hand carved from giant maldivica seeds, guns of all kinds, and complex engine parts. Unusual, randomly placed plants lined the well-trod dirt road with green leaves shaped like butterfly wings. In the middle of the leaves, tiny white flowers protruded as if fairies were hitching a ride on the butterfly.

Each shop differed in appearance. Some were simple open-air buildings with thatched or tin roofs. Others were elaborate structures with multiple rooms and levels. Homemade awnings and signs hung from every store giving the impression of a tropical, Wild West town.

The store owners looked every bit the part Ann had described. They were all weathered looking men and women, most of them sporting old, dirty clothes. Depending on what they were selling, they wore a different array of surprisingly new technology. Thomas noticed a large, deeply tanned man with a food shop wearing a powered meat saw on his forearm, something he'd only previously seen in large warehouse operations. Each shop owner seemed to know Sam and Ann, greeting them with smiles and accommodating service. Obviously the crew of The Pyre's Fortune had done much business on these islands.

"We need wood, brass for the fittings, bolts, rivets, and the alloy for the projectiles," Ann said. "We'll also need an additional pressure tank and the last stop will be the hexafluoride tanks at the fuel station."

Ann was all business. She wore a black pointed army dress hat, her black hair in two pony tails wrapped tightly with a wide, shiny black ribbon. She had overdressed intentionally with her favorite grey dress pants with red stripes down the side and freshly polished knee high black riding boots. A sheathed cutlass hung from her thick belt. Her blouse was stark white with a pointed collar and big grey buttons down the front. Among the locals she stuck out like an obvious foreigner with her bold make up and crisp clothes.

153

A warm wind blew through the thick foliage, perfuming the air with the scent of flowers. As they found the materials they needed Sam would pay for the goods and delivery, write the store name and number, and set off for the next item on the list.

By mid-afternoon, Sam insisted on buying drinks at his favorite bar which he made a point to visit every time they made port here. The unimpressive hut was nothing more than an open air bar with a thick bamboo roof. A long wooden sign hung above the bar that read "Poseidon's Elixir" in black paint. Aged stools, dark with years of grime, surrounded the bar while copper oil lamps hung from the round rafters above. Several patrons sat around, most were seafaring men and women from the boats docked off shore. The man behind the bar had a handlebar mustache and clean, bald head.

"Meester Burges," the barkeep said happily, seeing Sam. "And Miss Read. It has been a while, young lady."

Sam shook the man's hand and Ann curtseyed with a big, genuine smile. "Good to see you Cale," Ann said hopping up on a bar stool.

Sam leaned on the bar. "Cale these are our newest crew members, Thomas and Cynthia. Thomas and Cynthia, Cale Charters."

They exchanged handshakes. Cale's hands were as big as both of Cynthia's put together. He gave them a pleasant smile and turned to Sam. "Slibovitz?" he asked.

"Yes, sir," Ann chirped.

Cale shot her a smile. In the week they had been aboard the ship, they had never seen Ann so happy. She went from a bossy Ensign to a giddy school girl in the matter of ten seconds.

"What is Slibovitz?" Thomas asked.

Cale chuckled as he lifted a cloth-wrapped bottle off the bar. "Think of it as a plum brandy. It's made in the mainland up North and it's been a favorite drink of the islanders for hundreds of years."

Cale put four short glasses half filled with pale yellow

154

liquid on the bar. "Luck!" He grunted with a smile.

"Luck," Sam hollered back as he took the glass and drank half of the contents.

Ann followed suit but Thomas and Cynthia hesitated to drink something they had never heard of before. It was thick and sickly sweet with a blast of straight alcohol that made both of them shiver as they swallowed.

Cale noticed their discomfort and chuckled. "Welcome to the islands."

Thomas and Cynthia sipped the next round, while Ann and Sam downed theirs and ordered more. Cynthia liked the effect because Slibovitz, like the Jenever on the boat, quieted Lillian's motor mouth. A third drink later, Thomas and Cynthia were happy to keep to themselves while Sam and Ann drank like the liquid was a life extender.

Sam and Ann reminisced about past times with Cale, which left Thomas and Cynthia out of the conversation. While it was a nice enough environment, both of them wanted to leave. The bar grew more crowded and a new group of men with nautical star patches on their arms continually bumped into Cynthia as she sat at the bar. Although she was not a socialite in West Canvia, she knew the attention getting games men played at bars.

One of the men from the group turned and put his elbows on the bar next to her. He wore a black three cornered hat and a navy jacket with gold stripes in his shoulder indicating some kind of rank. Noticing Cynthia, he nervously stroked his shoulder length greasy hair. "Hello little bird."

"Hello." Cynthia mumbled.

"Where do I know you from? I've seen you before. I swear it."

"Probably someone that just looks like me."

She turned her back to the man, trying to listen to Sam and Ann talk about some Northern pilot who had challenged Ann to a drinking game and lost, but she could feel the strange man staring at her from behind. She knew it was crazy, but this was the one time she wished she could hear Lillian's opinion. What would she have done in an uncomfortable situation like this? It didn't matter; Lillian was quite silent by now. Cynthia nudged Thomas with her elbow and shot him a concerned look. Thomas glanced behind her, meeting the other man's eyes.

"Wait a minute," the man said, putting his hand on Cynthia's shoulder and spinning her around. "I do know you. I know both of you. Hey fellas!"

Three men in his group turned sharply. They were all wearing matching jackets but with different symbols on the shoulders.

"You won't believe this," the man announced. "These are the two gun makers from Canvia. The ones the Lemurians are looking for."

One of the men in the back craned his neck to get a better look. "Well I think they should come with us right away."

"I would have to agree," the first man said.

Sam stood up. "I think it's in your best interest to take your hand off the lady and walk on out of the bar."

"And who are you to say what's me and my crew's best interest?" the man asked, pulling out a tarnished silver handgun from his holster. "If you're smart, we'll leave you and your girlfriend alive to tell the tale."

"Why don't we all go then?" Sam asked.

Sam reached into his vest and pulled out a round grenade the size of a plum with a pressure gauge on top. With his other hand, he withdrew his handgun and aimed it dead center at the man's head. Ann slid off the wooden stool and unsheathed her cutlass. The bar fell completely silent.

"You don't want to make this interesting," the man said, pressing the end of the gun against Cynthia's back.

Cale ducked under the bar. With unexpected speed he produced an enormous gun the size of his leg and slammed it on the top of the bar. "I think you should do what the man says and leave my bar."

Thomas sprang to his feet next to the frozen Cynthia. He instinctively reached for his gun, forgetting the pirates had confiscated it. He saw the man's eyes twitch in his head, darting from the guns in front of him to his men behind him. Thomas could tell he wanted to walk away, but he didn't want to look like a coward in front of his crew.

Thomas put his hands up and looked the man closest to Cynthia in the eyes. "Seeing as though we were all going to die in this scrum, why don't we call it a draw and live to fight tomorrow?"

The man looked at him nervously, but didn't speak. Thomas softly reached toward the gun and pushed it away from Cynthia. "Well played. Nothing wrong with a draw when everyone is still alive, right?"

"Right," the sea captain said, taking a step back and readjusting his hat.

His crew grabbed him by the arm and hurriedly scooted out of the bar.

Sam looked around the bar. "Cale, I appreciate your hospitality."

"Anytime," Cale said, his hand still on the giant weapon.

Sam put the little grenade back in his pocket and shuffled around for a second, before pulling out a handful of gold coins and placing them on the bar. "I think that's our cue to return to the ship. Are you alright, Cynthia?"

Cynthia nodded her head yes, but clearly was lying.

"You are quite the soldier and the diplomat, Mister Riley." Sam said, patting him on the shoulder. "I would have taken his head clean off."

"Thank you," Thomas replied.

After checking for a possible ambush in the street, they walked back to the docks and up the ship's ramp.

A guard greeted them. "I trust you had a good day sir?"

"The usual," Sam replied handing the guard the material list. "Please send someone to the fuel station to pick up the last items on this list. It's a gas in canisters."

"Yes, sir."

Sam turned to Cynthia. "You have had an exciting day. Please get some rest. If you need anything let me know."

"That's a good idea." Cynthia answered drearily.

Cynthia followed a guard down to her cabin while Thomas stayed topside with Sam. "It may be best if we're trusted with weapons for expeditions like this, Sam."

"I think you are correct, Mister Riley. The things that are coming will require you to have one."

13
THE BLOOD COUNTESS

The Pyres Fortune took off from the Seychelles Islands fully loaded with provisions and materials for Thomas's deck-mounted crossbow. Cynthia had spent the rest of the afternoon and all of the evening recovering in her cabin after the confrontation at the bar. Thomas took inventory of the materials by himself and arranged them in the cargo hold. Neither Sam nor Ann had told anyone about the near-deadly encounter. Judging from what Sam told the guard, either this was a secret he wanted kept quiet, or no one would have thought it an unusual occurrence. One thing was certain, despite the island's beauty; neither Thomas nor Cynthia had any desire to return to the Seychelles Islands.

The next morning Thomas woke up early. He dressed and opened his door to find a box waiting at his feet. The sleepy guard at his door nodded good morning. Cynthia's guard was missing from his post, but Thomas assumed he had dashed off to relieve himself.

Thomas took the box into his room and opened it. Inside he and Cynthia's handguns were cushioned in brown paper with the boxes of shells they had brought with them. He was glad to have one of his requests honored in a timely manner. He fastened his holster on his belt and slipped Cynthia's handgun into his pocket. Thomas figured if trouble found them at Sam Burges' favorite bar on the Seychelles Islands, then it could find them anywhere. He headed down to the cargo hold to start putting the first pieces of the crossbow together. His guard lazily followed him.

At the cargo hold, he found Cynthia's guard standing by the door like a shoddily dressed toy soldier. Thomas nodded as he walked inside to find Cynthia sitting on the floor with the crossbow plans scattered all around her. Dressed in her work clothes, the familiar sight made him long for the Mercury Craft Industries lab back in West Canvia.

"Good morning Thomas. I slept for most of the afternoon and I couldn't get back to sleep at night."

She had sorted all of the materials for the crossbow on the floor and already cut and assembled the rotation base that would be bolted to the ship's top deck. Everything was scattered around her in neat piles as if she was assembling a giant puzzle.

Thomas was impressed. "Well done. How long have you been working on this?"

Cynthia cocked her head and rubbed at her neck. "About five hours."

"It looks great. How are you feeling after yesterday?"

Cynthia paused, looking up at him. "I suppose I'm all right. I can't get over how close we have come to dying since we left West Canvia. It's a miracle we're alive."

"I know. Somehow I am starting to feel like we have some kind of destiny that has to be played out. Does that make sense?"

Cynthia bit her bottom lip. "Yeah, it makes a lot of sense. I just wish we knew where all of this was taking us."

"I guess we will see."

"Yeah I guess."

"Anyway, excellent work on the crossbow! I thought I'd beat you down here by showing up early, but I guess you had the same idea," Thomas said, breaking the awkward silence. "I can't believe that only took five hours. It looks great."

"Your plans are solid. I just need to put the ball bearings in and attach the top piece and the entire base will be done." Cynthia said proudly.

Thomas sat next to Cynthia on the cargo hold floor and shuffled some of his plans to see where she was in the process. He slid Cynthia's gun to her. "After yesterday, I asked Sam to give us our guns back so we could defend ourselves in any other unpleasant situations."

Cynthia smiled. "Yeah, that might have come in handy yesterday. Well, at least they did one thing we asked that doesn't benefit them."

"I was thinking the same thing!"

"This problem with Maier is really getting on my nerves," Cynthia said. "We know he's fine. We haven't even been allowed to see him. What are they hiding?"

"I don't know but–"

"But what?"

"Well, I was going to suggest you ask Sam," Thomas said sheepishly.

"I thought about it, but I figured I would give it a little time, you know?"

"I think he might be our best route speaking with Maier."

"I agree. This has gone on long enough," Cynthia said. "I will make a date for tonight. Maybe then Sam can steer us in the right direction for once."

Thomas smiled. He knew Cynthia's feelings for Sam couldn't have been entirely real. Cynthia's comments lifted an annoying weight off of his back. Thomas happily jumped in and gave his full attention to working on the crossbow with Cynthia. They assembled the rotation circle in the base of the crossbow and began inserting the pneumatic pressure pipes that would make it swivel with the switch of a lever.

Engrossed in their work, both Cynthia and Thomas had skipped breakfast that morning. Thomas' stomach was growling and just as he opened his mouth to suggest they take a break, an ear-blistering, high pitched squawking blared through the entire ship.

Thomas and Cynthia jumped to their feet. Cynthia picked her gun up off of the floor. "What the–"

The door to the cargo hold flew open and both personal guards charged in with rifles in hand.

"We are under attack," one of the guards yelled. "Come

161

with us now!"

Thomas and Cynthia didn't need another reason to follow. In a heartbeat they were out of the cargo hold and running down the hall toward the spiral staircase.

"What's attacking us?" Thomas yelled at one of the guards.

"I have no idea," the guard huffed, already out of breath. "Whatever it is, it is serious!"

The four of them ran up the spiral stairs, their feet banging and clanking all the way. They twisted until they reached the bridge. Cynthia and Thomas had not yet seen the bridge of the ship. It was a huge room with a captain's seat in the middle with windows and separate stations for all manner of control positions lining the walls.

There were at least fifteen people in the room and all of them were yelling information back and forth. The entire bridge was chaos as the alarm blared. Airmen focused on their jobs, and barked status reports to Captain Swan who stood in front of his seat. The room flashed with hundreds of lights, a cacophony of small personal alarms yelped at each station, and hundreds of round gauges turned and spun from the dashboards all around the room.

"Prepare for broadside," Captain Swan shouted.

Out of the windows the sky was a cheery blue. Fluffy white clouds sped past the windows as the ship had taken a dive to avoid contact with an enemy ship.

"Bogey is mirroring on port side at one hundred meters and closing," a man cried from the control bank.

Captain Swan pulled a lever connected to his seat and the alarm fell silent. He picked up a hand-sized metal cone with a ribbed tube and held it up to his mouth. "This is Captain Swan! All guns on port side prepare to fire! Recon drone prepare to launch!"

After sitting Thomas and Cynthia down in two chairs by the bridge door, the guards exited to assist the rest of the crew in the impending battle.

"Bogey at fifty meters port side," the man yelled again.

"They're going to try to board," Captain Swan exclaimed. "Hard to starboard!"

The Pyre's Fortune groaned as the main pilot, who sat front and center of the bridge spun a large wheel like one would see on a sailing ship. The ship responded by turning to the right, but the ship was so large, it had a bulky turning radius. Shifting to the right, through the bridge windows, Thomas saw another ship burst out of the clouds. It was a menacing airship, painted black, cannons protruding from three decks, just like The Pyre's Fortune. It had two dirigibles on top covered with some type of black mesh armor. Thomas noticed the enemy ship had twice as many masts and two very large wind fueled propellers mounted on the back. It mimicked The Pyre's movement, staying in sight and holding exactly parallel. The enemy ship crept closer in the air as if it was going to sideswipe them.

"What are they doing?" Cynthia asked.

"I don't know. There's no way they board a ship at this speed."

The Pyre's Fortune barreled through the sky as the black ship came closer with every second.

"Identity confirmed," a woman in the front row said. "It is The Blood Countess!"

"Try to contact them again, this time with an urgent warning. Tell Captain Benická this will not be tolerated." Captain Swan growled.

A moment of sober silence washed through the bridge. Everyone focused on their assigned duty. No one looked back towards the captain. They sat flipping switches, pulling levers and reading the dials that were jerking back and forth in their casings.

"No response from The Blood Countess," The woman yelled.

"Increase speed," Captain Swan ordered. "Full ahead!"

The crew responded quickly and The Pyre's Fortune lurched

forward, picking up air speed. The Blood Countess was right next to them before they could gain any distance. Without warning three giant spike tipped arms swung like giant hammers from the top deck of The Blood Countess. Within seconds, three impacts slammed into The Pyre's Fortune, rocking the ship and dropping the vessel fifty feet in attitude. Thomas and Cynthia, who had no means of keeping themselves in their seats, flew into the air, then crashed to the bridge floor like rocks.

"They have latched on," Captain Swan yelled from the floor where he was sprawled. "Prepare for counter measures!"

The captain crawled to his chair and grabbed the modified Narro Phone. "All crew prepare to repel! The enemy is boarding! Port gun commander! Fire all port guns at will!"

The Pyre's Fortune instantly rattled as if it was in the middle of a volcanic eruption. The vibration of the ship felt like it was going to disintegrate around them. Thomas couldn't remember when he'd had such a violent shaking in his life; it was enough to make him instantly sick to his stomach.

Several uncomfortable seconds went by before one of the ships officers yelled. "The Port volley has been aborted. We have been hit with a counter broadside!"

The Blood Countess had fired all of its starboard guns in unison nullifying or eliminating The Pyre's Fortune attack before it even happened. Captain Swan's orders were seconds too late.

"Pull away," Captain Swan yelled into the Narro Phone. "Hard starboard!"

Again The Pyre's Fortune groaned at the pilot's movement. The wheel spun and the engines howled as they fought against the three arms that had embedded themselves in the top deck, but despite a deafening tearing sound, the ship stayed attached to The Blood Countess. The ships flew through the sky attached by spiked claws, and as The Blood Countess took control of the flight, men appeared on the deck of the black ship.

Like spiders descending their webs, the crew of The Blood Countess leaped from the deck of the black ship, repelling cords spinning out behind them. Dozens of men hit the side of The Pyre's Fortune and dug in with spiked tools resembling pick axes. They all wore leather helmets covering their faces and green tinted goggles over their eyes. Another series of thunderous explosions hit The Pyre's Fortune. These explosions were deep and violent, sounding like they had pried the bottom of the ship clean off.

"Boarding drillers," Captain Swan said.

He scrambled for the Narro Phone and held it up to his mouth. "They're aboard the ship. Hand to hand!"

Small arms gunfire popped and cracked throughout the ship. Thomas grabbed Cynthia's wrist and pulled her close to him. "We have to hide ourselves. Back to the Cargo hold! Bring your gun!"

Cynthia gripped her handgun and they stood up. Before they could exit, half of the crew on the bridge had snatched up some kind of weapon and were barreling out to engage their attackers.

Thomas and Cynthia followed them as other crew members struggled with controls in a vain attempt to free the ship from the huge claws stuck in the ship's deck. The invading crew seemed to be concentrated on the top decks and toward the back of the ship at the moment. This gave Thomas and Cynthia an opportunity to retreat to a safer place. They knew the invader's first objective would be to take over the bridge. With guns drawn, they scrambled down the spiral stairs. They descended three stories, stopping when they saw multiple flashes of gunfire down the hall. The mess hall was on this level.

"Stop," Cynthia yelled, grabbing Thomas' sleeve. "They have someone trapped!"

Somehow the invaders had made it down into the deep reaches of the ship and had cornered someone in the mess hall where they were shooting like mad men into the room.

"Their backs are to us," Cynthia said. "Let's hit them!"

Without any rationalization, Cynthia ran down the hall with her gun aimed forward. She didn't say a word; she just started firing as she dashed down the wood carved corridor. Three nasty, acid filled shots impacted around the invaders. They screamed in agony as Cynthia's shots splashed them. All three crumpled to the floor frantically trying to wipe the burning acid from their bodies. As Cynthia got closer, she fired again. This time all three of her bullets hit the men straight on. It wasn't long before they gave up their struggles and expired on the spot.

"Who's in there?" Thomas yelled inside the mess hall door. "Don't shoot, the men attacking are dead!"

"This is Lieutenant Burges," a voice said from the back of the mess hall.

"Sam?" Thomas and Cynthia said in unison.

"Cynthia?" Sam echoed.

"Yes!"

"I have two wounded men in here. I need some assistance quick."

Thomas and Cynthia rushed in to find Sam and two other men on the mess hall floor behind a mass of tables and chairs they had heaped into a pile as a barrier. One man had been hit in his right arm, which was covered in blood. The other man was on the ground fading out of consciousness holding his bleeding torso. Thomas straddled the man with the torso wound and moved his hands out of the way. Thomas sighed loudly. "Cyn. I need some help! Get me some kitchen tongs, a thin knife, water and as many towels as you can find!"

Cynthia sprang up and began rummaging through the debris on the floor and flinging kitchen cabinets open to find the supplies. Thomas ripped open the wounded man's shirt and put his hand over the wound to compress the bleeding.

He had been shot with barbed shot, a cruel bullet designed to unravel after it entered a person's body. If it didn't hit a vital part of the body, its barbs would spring open in time, reaching into the body, doing more damage and lodging itself deeper.

"Sam," Thomas said as his hands turned scarlet. "Keep watch on that door. We don't need anyone else coming in shooting. I am going to do my best to save this man."

Sam didn't need further instructions. He cocked his gun and positioned himself so that he could get a clear shot at anyone coming close to the mess hall door. Cynthia scurried back with a few of the items Thomas had requested and threw them next to him. In a flash, she was off looking for the others. A knife and some salad tongs was all she brought, but it would be good enough to start. Thomas thought about the cleanliness of the instruments only for a second, he knew that if he didn't start working, the barbed projectile would kill the man for sure. Thomas wiped the blood away with his hand and picked up the tongs. A loud explosion rumbled from a far off part of the ship. It sounded like a grenade, but Thomas focused on the task at hand. He reached into the man's wound with the tongs and a few inches down he felt metal touch metal.

"Cynthia! I need water and towels now!"

Panic stricken, Cynthia knocked over a stack of pans. "I'm looking!"

"If you can find a light of some kind that would be handy too."

Thomas fished around in the unconscious man trying to feel the edges of the projectile. He couldn't see it, but at least he knew where it was lodged. Cynthia banged around in the background frantically looking for anything that could help.

"How long has he had this in him?" Thomas asked Sam.

"About five minutes before you came," he replied soberly, his eye and gun still trained on the door.

Thomas dug his fingers deeper in the wound. "That means it has at least two barbs out by now."

Cynthia burst out of the kitchen with an arm full of kitchen towels and a bucket of water slung over her arm. She slid next to him on her knees sloshing some of the water on the floor. "What can I do to help? I didn't see any kind of portable light back there."

"Wet a few of those towels and keep the blood clear so I can at least see what I am doing."

Cynthia went to work, clearing the wound as best she could, while Thomas gently twisted the tongs to find the end of the projectile. The man with the wounded arm dragged himself closer. "Let me know what I can do as well."

Thomas glanced up at him. "Just be ready for anything, okay?"

The man nodded. Thomas focused on the wound, getting as close as he could without laying his head on the man's chest. As gently as possible, Thomas clamped the tongs on the bullet and pulled to see how badly it was imbedded. It gave a little resistance, but there was nothing else Thomas could do. He pulled harder making a wet, fleshy, ripping sound. Thomas gripped the tongs until they bent in his hand and yanked as hard as he could. With more nasty sounds followed by a sizeable volume of blood, Thomas pulled the bullet from the man. Cynthia worked wildly, wiping away the blood. Directly after Thomas had removed the thing, she applied pressure to stem the bleeding.

The bullet itself looked menacing. It was a copper ball, the size of a shooter marble with thin silver strands of serrated tentacles dangling off the sides. Thomas held it up for a second to see if any of the tentacles had broken off, but all seemed well. He tossed the bullet aside and put his bloody hands over Cynthia's to increase the pressure.

Sam let off three rounds from his rifle.

"What is it?" Thomas asked, still pushing on the wounded man's chest.

"There are at least two by the door," Sam said quietly. "I don't think I hit anyone."

Sam jumped up from behind the mass of tables and ran to the side of the door where he pressed his back against the wall. Thomas continued to apply pressure to the wounded man, but poked his head up to assess the situation.

Sam bobbed his head and rifle barrel around the door frame

and let off two blind shots down the hall. Seconds later, rapid fire returned from the hall, making Swiss cheese of the mess hall wall. Sam fell to his knees but only out of shock. Miraculously he wasn't shot.

Thomas looked Cynthia in the eyes. "Keep pressure on the wound until the bleeding slows. Do you understand?"

Cynthia shot him a concerned look. "Yes but–"

Thomas let go of the man and ran around the piled tables. He pressed his back against the wall directly next to Sam. "Are you okay?"

"Yeah. Yeah I'm fine, just a little startled."

"I'll shoot first," Thomas said. "Four rounds. When I fire number three, you come around and fire four more. Got it?"

"Yeah."

Thomas whirled around the door frame and fired. Like clockwork, Sam knelt beside him and squeezed off four more rounds just as Thomas retreated.

"There are at least six of them. I am sure I got one," Thomas said.

"I did too."

The invaders were screaming instructions. It sounded like they were moving furniture with the bumps and thuds coming from the hall. Thomas heard a dragging sound. He peeked around and fired two more shots in their direction. From the one second of sight he gained, he saw all of the men running or limping down the hall, two of them were dragging their wounded pirate companions behind them.

"They're running," Thomas said excitedly.

"Let's go," Sam said.

"Cynthia," Thomas called, "I will be right back with help! Stay here with that man!"

"Thom–" Cynthia snapped.

It was too late. Thomas had already rounded the door with Sam behind him. The intruders had made it to the spiral staircase and the ones not burdened with the wounded had dashed up to the second deck before Thomas and Sam saw them. Those dragging the injured men were barely up the stairs when Thomas and Sam unloaded their guns. The two wounded and the ones carrying them collapsed, dead on the spot.

"Thanks for giving us our guns back." Thomas said.

"I'd be dead if I hadn't."

The gunfire around the ship faded, becoming more and more sporadic as Thomas and Sam pursued the invaders up the stairs. They skipped over the bodies and Thomas warned Sam not to touch the rails as there could be acid splattered on them. The tide of the battle had turned, but in whose direction was yet to be determined.

When they reached the open air of the top deck, a man was slumped over the open hatch. Thomas pushed the dead man's body out of the way and peered out. Destruction and carnage was everywhere. Three arms the size of cranes protruded from The Blood Countess' deck and remained firmly stuck into the top deck of The Pyre's Fortune. Like conjoined twins, the huge black ship was locked against the side of The Pyre's Fortune. The ships moved slowly as The Blood Countess had adjusted their airspeed to help get her men board. There were pockets of men fighting on the deck mostly with handguns, but some were locked in hand to hand battles with swords and knives. In the confusion, Thomas couldn't tell the battling men apart.

"Get up here Sam," Thomas said. "I don't know who is from which ship."

Sam pushed Thomas out of the way. He put his hand to his brow to keep the sun out of his eyes and when he locked onto a close fight, he slipped the goggles on his forehead over his eyes and pointed.

"There's Ann," he said, with his arm outstretched. "Follow me."

"But I–" Thomas tried to explain he only had two extra shots left on him, then he noticed the rifle from the dead man by the exit hatch. He grabbed it and followed Sam.

Ann was locked in a nasty fight with two men. She had withdrawn her cutlass and was swinging wildly at both of her attackers. Her black hair flapped in the wind and she had pulled her red scarf over her nose and mouth so she looked like a bandit.

Sam sprinted toward the men and tackled one as if he were a human cannon ball. They crashed to the ground, Ann's attacker stunned to be blindsided so harshly. Thomas raised his handgun, but thought twice about it, not wanting acid to splatter Ann. He holstered his gun and lifted the enemy rifle. With one shot, he pegged Ann's other attacker in the hip, sending him to the ground like a horse had kicked him. Ann hardly seemed to notice. By the time her attacker had hit the ground, she was on top of him hacking the man to bits. Sam had dispatched the man he tackled with a gruesome point blank shot and Ann helped him to his feet.

With Thomas following, Sam and Ann dashed off to the next skirmish where they quickly overwhelmed three men attacking three from The Pyre's Fortune. Pirates were dropping to the deck like scattered dominoes. A loud victory cheer rang out from the crew as only the last hand to hand battles ended.

Some of the invading pirates were trying to scurry back over the boarding arms, but too many of The Pyre's Fortune crew had gained control of the escape route, kicking the retreating enemies off and into the sky.

"Follow me," Sam yelled at Thomas.

Caught up in the emotion of the fight and the strange sense of camaraderie, Thomas ran behind Sam who leaped onto the boarding arm and dashed across to continue the fight on the deck of The Blood Countess. Thomas was half way across with his commandeered rifle and his handgun when he saw the hordes of men locked in a bloody melee on the enemy ship.

14
BATTLE IN THE SKY

Thomas paused only for a moment as he stood on the enormous boarding arm locked into the deck of The Pyre's Fortune. He glanced to his right to see only clouds underneath him and patches of green and brown earth thousands of feet below. The ships were still cruising through the sky but the arms had a railing system that gave Thomas something to hold as he stood on the space between the two ships. For a second he thought about going back, but he was spurred forward by another six men running along the arm to board The Blood Countess. Reluctantly he ran the whole distance, finally hopping off the arm and onto the deck of the enemy ship.

The Blood Countess was intimidating even on its own deck. With the exception of the fittings and rivets, everything was either painted black or made of some kind of black material, even the sails and the twin dirigibles were dyed black. Several dozen men were locked in ugly hand to hand combat on the deck with The Pyre's Fortune crew that had counter-boarded the ship. Cutlasses banged together, close quarters gun fire blasted away and when they seemed to have a clear shot, a small cannon from The Pyre's Fortune would cherry pick groups of The Blood Countess' crew.

Thomas saw Sam withdraw the tiny grenade he had flashed at the bar on the Seychelles Islands and tossed it into a group of enemy pirates. The explosion started with a high pitched squeal and ended with a thunderous bang as steam pressure mixed with some kind of combustible and sent two men flying over the side of the deck and five more collapsing face first.

Thomas had made his choice, he was here to fight, and now

he could tell the men apart due to their positions on the deck. He fired at a pack of men clumsily loading and pressurizing their water driven muskets. He got off three shots before the stolen rifle ran out of ammunition. He withdrew his handgun and fired a shot at two men who were running down some upper deck stairs. The bullet didn't strike them, but it didn't need to. His handcrafted acid bullet slammed into the wooden deck spraying the men's legs with ultra pure hydrofluoric acid. They stopped in their tracks, falling to the ground and gripping their furiously burning wounds.

Another dozen men and women had crossed over the boarding arms and joined the fray. With only one acid bullet left, Thomas holstered his gun and picked up a bloody cutlass lying nearby. He charged into a mass of men who fought like it was the Middle Ages on board an old sailing ship. He got a few nasty slices in, but he was in the back of the Pyre's Fortune group by the time he arrived. Sam and two other men pushed through the enemy pirates, splitting the group in half.

One large pirate with a glossy bald head and some kind of cutting device attached to his forearm kicked Sam to the ground and out of the pack. He was tall and well built, his muscles rippling beneath his torn shirt that flapped in the high wind of the sky. The huge man was on Sam in an instant, hacking away as Sam defended himself on the ground with a thin sword. After only a few strikes, Sam's sword had bent under the weight and strength of the bald man's arm machine. Thomas couldn't help noticing it had to be a custom made hand to hand weapon and for a millisecond he wondered who had made it.

Thomas shook off the momentary scientific pondering, raised his cutlass and charged the bald man at a full sprint. The bald man saw Thomas' running charge. He took one more swing at Sam, jamming the point of Sam's sword into the deck of the ship, and took a few steps back so that he could deal with Thomas properly.

Thomas swung the cutlass when he was close enough to the

174

pirate and even with the fast paced swing, Thomas' blade struck the pirate's arm and glanced off with a terrible clank. He could tell it hurt the man, but the machine on his arm remained intact and working order. Thomas brought his cutlass up for another swing when he noticed a large dent in the sharpened end of the sword. It didn't matter, it could still kill and that was all he needed. He swung again, but the bald man parried and dodged the blade. Thomas lost his footing and stumbled forward.

Sam dislodged the end of his bent sword from the deck and as the bald man stepped forward to take a swipe at Thomas, he jabbed the end of the wonky sword into the bald man's calf. The blow instantly buckled the massive pirate's leg and sent him to the ground like a wounded gladiator. Sam jumped to his feet and pushed the man onto his back. On his way down, the bald man swept Sam's legs, sending both of them crashing to the deck. Even wounded, the bald man could have pummeled Sam with his bare hands, so Thomas stepped in, and with one swing over his head, he slashed the bald man across the back. The bald pirate grunted, rolling face down against the deck. Sam scrambled out from under the big man and stood again.

"Thank you," he huffed. "Again."

Thomas gave him a quick nod, but the fight raged on behind them. A mass of bodies was piling up in the melee and it seemed to get uglier by the second. Several more of the Pyre's Fortune Crew had come aboard to assist in the counter-takeover and many of them were just waiting for their turn or a space to get into the fight.

Sam grabbed Thomas by the sleeve and pulled him aside. "We have to get those boarding arms separated from The Pyre. If Captain Benická chooses, she can rip half the Pyre's deck clean off."

Thomas wanted to debate the wisdom of this idea, but there was no time. Men were dying around them and if what Sam was saying was true, then Cynthia and everyone aboard The Pyre's Fortune could be sent crashing to the ground.

They trotted to the base of one of the boarding arms, a giant multi-layered wooden disk with brass fittings and wrought iron rivets holding it together. The arm was designed to flip overboard and impale the other ship, but there was no mechanism for retraction that Thomas could see. It was a daunting task, but Sam yelled at a few men crossing the bridge to assist in the fight and soon they were all hacking at the arm's base.

Thomas grabbed Sam. "Keep everyone away from the second one."

Sam yelled the orders for everyone to stay away from the middle arm but to continue chopping at the first one. Thomas ran to the base of the second arm, examined it for a moment, and shot the weakest part with his last acid round. The impact made dull thud and it instantly sizzled under the corrosive chemical. When Thomas looked back four more men were chopping at the first boarding arm while their comrades continued to win the fight on the deck.

Thomas joined the men hacking at the base of the first boarding arm. There was hardly enough room to get into the crowd, but he managed to find a spot. Surprisingly, it wasn't long before half of the arm had been chopped apart. Each man was taking turns splitting the wood and prying the fittings off.

The fighting at the other end of the deck had stopped. Either The Blood Countess' crew was slaughtered or they surrendered realizing there was no way to win. The sight was a gruesome one, with piles of corpses and wounded pirates from both ships lying on the shiny, blood covered deck. The remaining uninjured Pyre's Fortune allies started going through the ship. The first battle was won, but there were surely pockets of resistance in the lower decks.

Someone had found a construction blowtorch on the ship and added its power to separating the first boarding arm from the ship. Within minutes the base of the arm cracked loose from its connection. The men cheered again as the final piece broke

They migrated to the middle arm that Thomas had previously shot with his acid bullet. They hacked away at the spot that was already full of holes and brittle from the corrosion, but before they could make any real damage, the deck of The Blood Countess groaned under the pressure. It sounded like an oak tree snapping in half. In one violent motion, the middle arm ripped itself from its base and the back of the boarding arm launched upward sending three of the closest men flying over the side of the ship. The Blood Countess' engines were still going, while The Pyre's Fortune had stopped in order to make its attacker work that much harder. With only the back of the three arms left holding the ships together, The Blood Countess continued moving and The Pyre's Fortune stayed relatively still in the sky. Making a thunderous crack, The Blood Countess surged forward and the last arm stretched and pulled out of its fittings tearing a sizeable portion of the top deck with it.

Huge chunks of wood speared upward from the deck as the last boarding arm dragged down the back of the ship. The Pyre's Fortune crew scrambled like ants away from the sliding arm as it plunged toward the earth. The part that impaled The Pyre's Fortune also came loose, making the huge ship list to the side. The Blood Countess rocked like it was on water and Thomas was gripping a nearby railing so he wouldn't slide off the deck. The ship swayed in the air and The Pyre's Fortune drifted off into a cloud bank with black smoke billowing from its wounds.

When The Blood Countess righted itself the victorious crew gathered the remainder of The Blood Countess' crew. The prisoners huddled in a group of about two dozen on the main deck looking defeated and humiliated. Next to them were the scattered bodies from the fight. It was in fact their own attack that had led to their demise, so the crew of The Pyre's Fortune was even more proud they had repelled them and taken over their ship.

Sam stepped forward to sort out the prisoners, and to direct what was to be done with the wounded or dying. It was hard not to notice Sam's nearly psychopathic side when it came to fighting and battle. He twirled a bloody cutlass he had picked up from the deck and strode proudly to the prisoners. As he opened his mouth to address them a single shot rang out from the back of the ship. Sam spun like a top and slammed front first on the deck of the ship. A high pitched cackle came from the raised quarterdeck on the rear of the ship.

Standing with one booted foot on the railing was Captain Kathleen Benická. She was a dark skinned woman with two high ponytails that stuck up on top of her head and wide black goggles over her eyes. Her long gloved hands gripped a large pewter colored rifle with an oversized scope and magnifying glasses on top. Two tubes protruded from the sides into a pressure canister she had sitting on the deck next to her. The gun was so long, she had it resting on the rail next to her foot. Thomas had never seen such a crude, yet intimidating rifle.

"Who's next?" she yelled, swiveling the end of the rifle from one man to the next. "The captain has to go down with her ship! So why not take a few along with me?"

Everyone on deck fell silent. Only the howling of the wind through the sails rumbled over the open deck. Every man and woman from The Pyre's Fortune knew they could overtake her, but she would surely bring down several of the first to rush her. Sam was writhing on the ground, gripping his right shoulder, and a sizeable pool of blood was growing underneath him.

"I knew none of you had the courage to stand up to me," she taunted, still shifting the rifle around.

Thomas wasn't going to be insulted anymore, nor was he going to let her shoot people at random. On an angry impulse he held his cutlass forward and ran toward the stairs that led to the top of the quarterdeck screaming at the top of his lungs. Within two seconds he heard a large group behind him, their voices adding to his as they joined the blitz. Just before he reached the first step, Captain Benická trained her rifle on him and in a flash, she fired. The cannon-like report of the gun was matched only by

178

the sound of the bullet that missed Thomas' head by mere inches. He felt the whoosh of air on his face and he heard the projectile smack into his cutlass with the bang of metal breaking metal. His hand stung from the vibration and the cutlass went flying over the side of the ship.

He only slowed his pace for a second before he charged up the stairs unarmed. The quarterdeck had a row of stairs leading to the top on each side and a multitude of men were dashing up them. They would be on her in seconds, but Thomas was ahead of them all. He ran up the stairs, taking two or three at a time, until he reached the level part of the deck. Captain Benická abandoned her rifle and ran to the back of her ship. Thomas was faster and within a few feet of her, he jumped to tackle her but she dodged him, leaping on the back railing. Thomas slid on his stomach, missing the edge of her dress by inches.

Crouching on the rail as if preparing to jump, Captain Benická turned and sneered at Thomas. "I won't forget your face," she snarled.

She glanced down and then jumped off the back of the ship.

Thomas scrambled to his feet, gripped the rail and looked over the edge. The other men joined him, hoping they'd just watched their enemy commit suicide.

Captain Benická freefell until she was just a speck flying toward the ground. A small round shape popped up indicating she had opened a parachute. She was over water at the time so she would have to be rescued soon or she wouldn't survive long in the ocean. Thomas didn't care. It seemed the majority of his perils were done for the moment. He was most concerned with Cynthia and Sam now.

Thomas ran back down the quarterdeck stairs where some of the men had already propped Sam against a wall. His entire right arm was stained red and two men were inspecting the large wound on his shoulder. Thomas knelt in front of him.

"I think it came out the other side," one of the men said.

"If it did, it was lead shot," Thomas said.

He gently pushed Sam forward to look at his back. Sam gritted his teeth. There was an exit would.

"Someone fetch me that gun," Thomas asked the men on the quarterdeck.

"I can't move my arm at all."

"It probably broke some bones," Thomas said.

"The surgeon can decide that," Sam said defiantly.

Two men hauled Captain Benická's gun and tank down the stairs and set it next to Thomas. He picked it up and looked in the chamber to find six more round shot bullets. Another man with a sharp white goatee and round glasses tended Sam's wound.

"Are you a doctor?" Thomas asked.

"I'm the doctor's assistant. Wilfred Donnelly. I'm not sure our main surgeon is still alive. He was on The Pyre."

"Well, it's simple lead shot. So there are no poisons or devices the bullet could have left behind," Thomas explained.

Donnelly looked closely at the wound. "It looks like the top of the humerus could be shattered. This is going to be a problem. We need to make port as soon as possible."

"Not until we get our orders from Captain Swan," Sam growled in pain.

"Sir, this could kill you," Donnelly said. "At the best, if not properly treated, you might not have use of this arm again."

Sam tried to stand but three men around him kept him still. He shot them all dirty looks.

"You have to stay still," Thomas said. "You might bleed to death."

"Where is The Pyre?" Sam asked angrily.

"She floated away at least ten minutes ago," Donnelly said. "She was hit bad and billowing smoke."

"Someone find the communication room," Sam demanded desperately. "I need to get our orders."

Several bystanders went off in search of the communication room. While the wound was a bad one, Thomas had seen worse

180

and he had high hopes Sam would survive as long as he didn't bleed to death. In all of the excitement and adrenaline, he hadn't had much time to worry about Cynthia on The Pyre's Fortune. He had no clue if she was safe, or even alive. She was always in the back of his mind, but the battle had shifted his priorities. Sam's eyelids began to flicker, once again changing Thomas' focus.

"Don't touch him," Donnelly barked. "Let me at least stop the bleeding, and then we need to move him to a bed. He needs to lie down and rest. I will watch over him."

Eventually, Sam was moved to the Captain's cabin. Captain Benická had ransacked it before she left, turning over furniture and rifling drawers to take whatever small treasures she could with her.

Thomas took the liberty to tour the ship. The massive ship was much like The Pyre's Fortune, but with a much darker and more menacing décor.

Apparently these pirates lived a more sinister life than The Pyre's Fortune crew. The ship's interior was made of carved ebony that smelled of rum and dust. The carvings that adorned the moldings and door frames were relief scenes of armies marching into battle and of kings stepping on their conquered enemies. There were twice as many decorations on The Blood Countess as The Pyre's Fortune, making the walls look more like a museum than a war ship. How anyone was able to confiscate these kinds of air ships was beyond Thomas' comprehension. Something this grand and ornate would easily be the flagship of any nation's air force.

The rest of the ship had been taken without further bloodshed. Most of the captured pirates offered their services as loyal subjects to Captain Swan. This was the usual custom of pirates–to fight to the death until they realized they were on the losing side. When defeat was inevitable, they were happy to surrender and swear loyalty to the winner.

The communication room Sam asked about happened to be

located just under the last boarding arm that tore from the deck by sheer force. The room was completely exposed and most of the instruments were smashed to bits. Vital components had been ripped and flung overboard with the arm. There was no way of technological communication with any ship or port.

There was also the issue of who would captain the ship. Being Captain Swan's Lieutenant, Sam was next in line to direct the newly taken vessel, but due to his current condition, he wasn't even conscious to give orders. The new crew made it a point to work together to repair the ship as best they could in the air and be ready for wherever they would go next. The tears in the sails and a few broken chains would be an easy fix, but the majority of the damage was to the top deck and the communications room underneath it. The fear was that if the ship had to build significant speed more of the deck might rip apart, causing other parts of the ship to give way.

The crew decided to travel back to the Seychelles Islands at the slowest possible speed, using the air currents as the main method of movement. Thomas claimed an empty cabin while they crept along in the sky. The room was similar to his cabin on The Pyre, but it had a built-in closet for hanging clothes. It lacked a porthole like his last room, but there was a large oil lamp on a small end table bolted down next to the bunk.

Two full days of traveling passed before The Blood Countess was in sight of the Seychelles Islands. To Thomas surprise the two crews gelled quickly. The Blood Countess crew, no matter how seasoned they might be, received the worst jobs on the ship while the conquerors enjoyed better food, and lighter work. Despite this difference, and that forty eight hours earlier they would have hacked each other to pieces, the two groups didn't seem to harbor much animosity.

During the voyage, Sam had gone in and out of consciousness for the first day but awoke as they closed in on the port. Groggy and fatigued, he gave orders as best he could from his bed. The doctor's assistant deemed his wound was thus far

182

not infected, but he would probably have limited use of his right arm for the rest of his life. With Thomas' help, Donnelly constructed a moveable copper brace that held his arm in place, but could be modified later to give support when the arm healed.

Thomas stood on the bow of The Blood Countess with his goggles over his eyes as they reached the tiny islands that surrounded the main Seychelles Island port. The wind was brisk and it blew his hair straight back as he gripped the front rail. He hoped The Pyre's Fortune had had the same idea and gone back to the port for repairs, but as they approached there were only two water ships in the docks. Looking at the busy waterways of the islands, Thomas hoped for some news of The Pyre's whereabouts from the locals.

The Blood Countess landed in the water dock and was swarmed by a number of laborers who thrived on assisting anything from food delivery to repairs when the ships came in. Since his last excursion off of the ship, Thomas elected to stay on board for the duration of the repairs. This time he had no guide and no protection so he waited for the local workers to come to him.

Another half day went by and the crew had gathered fifty additional men to repair the ship, including the fittings for new boarding arms. A small team of rather grubby looking communication workers set to repairing the radios, signaling machine and the air to air telegraph. Thomas assisted the workers as best he could but with so much of the equipment missing he would have to wait for replacement parts to finish the repairs. He spent the time in the communication room questioning the workers.

"Have you heard any information about the air ship The Pyre's Fortune?" Thomas asked one of the men installing a shiny new copper tapper on the telegraph.

"I don't know. Several people have asked that same question. I could have made a small fortune by now if I did have information."

The man was short and tan from the island sun. He wore a beige jumpsuit covered with construction instruments hanging from loops on his clothes and a large black leather tool belt.

"How long to do you think it will take to repair the communication room?"

"You'll be able to send telegraphs in about two days," the man said. "I'm waiting for a shipment with the acid batteries to come in for the power supply."

"Do you have something back at your shop or home that I could use to send a message?" Thomas asked.

The man smiled. "No, but I can find you one to use for two hundred gold."

"I don't have gold."

"Surely you have something of value."

"What else are you interested in?" Thomas asked.

"Guns, ammunition, alcohol."

"Well now we're talking," Thomas said. "I have the high pressure lead shot rifle from the former captain of this ship. It has ammo and the tank is practically full."

The man's eyes lit up. "Bring it to me, I'll make sure it's legitimate and that it works and I'll take you to a telegraph tomorrow."

Thomas turned and left the communication room in search of the bulky rifle Captain Benická used to shoot Sam. He found it in her cabin where Sam was still resting on her bed.

"I need this," Thomas said, picking up the long rifle and tank that was attached.

"I was going to keep it as a trophy," Sam replied groggily.

"I can trade it for use of a telegraph within twenty-four hours. We can contact The Pyre."

Sam sighed. "Twenty-four hours, huh? Take it."

Thomas smiled and nodded. "How are you feeling?"

"It hurts to breathe. But they say I'll live. Go make your deal. We need to know where The Pyre is located. In her condition, she's very vulnerable."

Thomas nodded again and took the rifle to the communication room where the man was still installing the telegraph tapper. He turned around as Thomas entered.

"Is that it?" The man asked with a toothy grin.

"It is. Tomorrow, what time shall we meet?"

"I'll be back here mid-afternoon," the man said. "You can come with me to contact your ship when I am sure the gun is in working order."

The man stuck out a filthy hand, which Thomas shook without hesitation. "I trust your word."

"And I yours."

Thomas went back to his cabin to try to sleep the day away. He was so full of anxiety he could hardly close his eyes, so after two long hours of rolling around in his bunk, he got up and decided it might be better to occupy his time with something constructive. He took another tour of The Blood Countess, this time checking the weapons systems just as he had done with The Pyre's Fortune.

Thomas' understanding of pirate ships had grown tenfold since he and Cynthia had been taken aboard. He found The Blood Countess possessed almost identical weaponry as The Pyre's Fortune, but it had ten more extra-large cannons that could decimate ships at a much further range. They were primarily made for wounding other ships, but they all had more than enough firepower to obliterate enemies if needed.

As night came, Thomas' attempts to exhaust himself failed. He thought he could work and try to get his mind off Cynthia and The Pyre's Fortune, but as he lay back in his bunk, he spent most of the night staring at the ceiling of his cabin, going through every possible scenario of Cynthia's fate.

Skipping breakfast, and then lunch, Thomas sat on the side rail of The Blood Countess for most of the morning waiting for the repairman to show up and take him to a working telegraph. He was ashamed that in his excitement he hadn't even asked the man's name. He felt rude asking after they'd made their deal. He

185

also had not tested the rifle and worried that it might have been damaged after it was used to shoot Sam.

Thomas visited Sam again in the captain's cabin to get the air to air telegraph coordinates to The Pyre's Fortune. Sam also gave Thomas his personal codename, HECATE, ensuring the message was taken seriously.

Thomas sat on the rail of the ship, watching every new person who emerged from down the dock or the market like a loyal dog hoping to see its master appear out of the crowd. The wind from the ocean blew through Thomas' black hair, getting it twisted in the goggles on his forehead. He found a lead shot handgun on the ship that he brought with him as he refused to enter market with no one but the worker to protect him. The gun was huge and heavy with a small tank attached to the back. The cylinder was as big as his fist and the bullets were the crude old-style round balls rather than the aerodynamic bullets the military used. It definitely was a layman's gun, but it would do its job in a pinch.

By mid afternoon, Thomas' stomach growled with hunger, but just as he was about to dash into the mess hall and get something quick to eat he saw the man walking up the docks. His heart almost jumped out of his chest. It looked like he was wearing the same thing as the day before, but he had a mail bag strapped around his shoulder. The man stopped at the bottom of the ramp and waved to Thomas at the other end of the deck.

"Well come on," he hollered. "I have to be in there working in an hour!"

Thomas hurried down the ramp. "It worked well didn't it?"

"It shattered the coconuts I tried it on. That's good enough," the man said with a menacing smile. "Follow me."

Thomas walked with the man off the dock and into the market, with his right hand on the handle of the gun. The last thing he needed was trouble from anyone. Thomas followed the workman silently, trying to appear that he was staring at the ~nd when in fact, his eyes were darting from side to side examining everyone they passed.

Ten minutes into the trek, Thomas became nervous. Although the market stretched for miles, his guide was taking him through shady alleys that were nothing more than dirty stretches of land between shops and other roads.

When they arrived, the building was less than impressive. A simple shack made of bamboo walls, with a copper roof that had been oxidized to the moldy shade of green, the structure looked more like an overflowing garage than a store. The top of the shack had dozens of antennas, pipes and cubes protruding from the top, appearing heavy enough to collapse the sad structure in a light breeze.

The small man parted a brown grass curtain that hung where a door should have been. He said something in a different language to someone and Thomas followed him inside. The tiny room was completely cluttered with a variety of old pieces of technology from floor to ceiling. It smelled of engine oil and steam.

An old man sat on a stool. Like most of the islanders, he was very tan and wrinkled from years of exposure to the intense island sun. He wore wire framed multi-spectacles, with four sets of lenses hanging off the sides like rear view mirrors. They could slide over the eyes when extra magnification was needed and slide away when the work was done. Behind the spectacles, the man's grey eyes were dulled with a haze Thomas recognized as an ocular ailment.

"This is the man?" the old man asked, standing up and extending his wrinkled hand.

Thomas shook it. "Yes sir. Thomas Riley."

The old man's eyes opened wide. "The scientist?"

"Yes, sir," Thomas said, his eyes darting around for any trouble. "Is that okay?"

"Of course it is," the old man said, still gripping Thomas' hand. "I've heard of you. My name is Niccolo Cabeo. Do you know your coordinates?"

"Yes, sir."

Thomas pulled out a piece of paper with fifteen numbers written in sequence and Sam's code word HECATE at the bottom.

"Come this way," Cabeo said.

He cleared space on a desktop covered with all types of tin boxes with dials and pressure gauges sticking out of them. He dragged a wooden box with a gold telegraph tapper to the front. Reaching over to a wood cabinet with metal fittings around the edges, he pulled a knob out and turned a large dust-covered dial. The slight, high pitched whistle of steam came from the back of the box and it hummed as energy pulsed through it. A round, dull yellow light illuminated on the front.

Cabeo looked up from the telegraph. "I assume you can use one of these."

"Yes, sir, of course."

"Have at it then," Cabeo said, gesturing toward his little stool.

Thomas sat down in front of the telegraph and laid the piece of paper on the dirty desk. Dialing the coordinates was done with a series of knobs that lined the front of the telegraph. The process was much like dialing the combination of a safe. He tapped out the message.

"HECATE: URGENT. NEED WHEREABOUTS OF PYRE'S FORTUNE. THE BLOOD COUNTESS AT SEYCHELLES ISLANDS FOR REPAIRS. WHAT IS YOUR STATUS? END."

Several minutes went by as Cabeo and the worker from the ship conversed in a different language. Thomas became worried when the machine did not respond. He had his finger on the tapper to repeat the message when the wooden box vibrated. A long piece of paper jerked out of a thin slit on the side. When it was done moving, Thomas ripped the piece of paper out of the machine and read the message.

"EN ROUTE TO LEMURIA FOR REPAIRS. MADE

DEAL FOR CANVIAN PRISONER AND LEMURIAN DOCTOR. WHEN CAN YOU RENDEVOUS? GLAD YOU ARE WELL SAM. END."

Thomas began to breathe hard as he concentrated on the tapper.

"WHERE IS THE RENDEVOUS DESTINATION? END"

Again, several minutes went by which enveloped Thomas in fear. His heart beat so fast he was afraid it might stop all together. The paper rattled out of the machine

"LEMURIA CITY. ROYAL DOCKS. END."

Thomas ripped the paper off of the machine and pulled his gun. Cabeo and the worker yelped in fright, but Thomas was off the stool, through the grass curtain door and into the streets running full speed toward the docks.

Even at an adrenaline fueled sprint, it took him longer than he thought to wind his way through the market and locate the dock. When he saw it, his legs seemed to move even faster. He was up the ramp and down the stairs heading toward the captain's cabin. He didn't even knock when he reached the door; he just burst in unaware he still had his gun drawn.

The doctor's assistant started, and stood, appalled by the intrusion.

Sam painfully straightened himself in bed. "What are you doing, man?"

Thomas panted hard. "Captain Swan is selling Cynthia and Maier to the Lemurians!" He trotted to the bedside and showed Sam the telegraph papers. Sam read them a few times and looked at the doctor's assistant.

Sam's lips tightened and his brow furrowed. "Get the ship ready to leave as soon as possible. I don't care what shape she's in, just make sure she is fully armed. We're going to Lemuria."

15
HECATE AND ATHENA

Men double-timed as they ran all over The Blood Countess' decks. It looked like a stampede of ants dashing up and down the ramp to the dock and throughout the galleys of the ship. Large wooden crates filled with expensive armaments and materials thundered up the ramp and were lowered by a huge hook and pulley down to the gun decks.

Meanwhile, the constant banging of hammers and the soft rumble of blowtorches continued without hesitation from every damaged portion of the ship. There was some plunder aboard the ship, but not enough to pay for the massive amounts of materials being loaded. Whatever deal Sam's envoys had struck with the locals must have been a promising one.

Directly after his short meeting with Sam Thomas gathered a host of weaponry, which included the cutlass he had taken when he boarded, the lead shot handgun, and a small grenade launcher which he found in the captain's cabin propped behind the door. The little monster was triple-barreled and used oxygen propulsion to fire tiny explosives the size of walnuts. Next to the launcher was a full box of thirty rounds. Depending on their explosiveness, this many grenades could wipe out an entire ship of men. He loaded the launcher and put the remaining rounds in a backpack. Sam's idea was to intercept The Pyre's Fortune before they reached Lemuria City and rescue Cynthia and Maier by diplomacy or force. Either way, Sam's life as a pirate was going to change drastically.

Even though he was part of the group that tore the boarding arms off the deck of The Blood Countess, Thomas wished they still had them. If they had to board The Pyre's Fortune, it would now have to be done with grappling hooks and zip lines while the ships were in motion.

He knew The Pyre's Fortune could not have made many repairs since escaping The Blood Countess, but he also knew the ship had hardly fired a shot during that conflict. There had been significant damage to the gun cabins, but he didn't know what might be superficial and what might be a real problem.

Time was of the essence. In effect, The Pyre's Fortune was a sitting duck with a skeleton crew, but the trick would be intercepting her before she landed to make the trade. Going into Lemuria with a damaged ship was alarming enough. He was sure they would encounter Lemurian battleships and fighters. They were facing the prospect of fighting the Lemurian air force and engaging in another battle with The Pyre's Fortune.

By the middle of the evening, the ship was ready for the twenty-four hour journey to Lemuria. Full of anxiety, Thomas went down to the communication room to see what progress had been made. The place still looked like a bomb had hit it. While some of the large instruments were flashing and humming, others were still in complete shambles.

Three men from the crew were diligently working on the open machines. Wires, tubes and vacuum tubes were laid out and scattered all over the floor. He noticed one man hovering over the new telegraph that still needed a battery for power. Then something odd on the floor caught his eye. It looked like a black bread box with two copper posts sticking through the top. Thomas walked over with his brow furrowed. "Excuse me. I that a battery for the telegraph?"

The crewman turned. "Yeah."

"How did we get that? It wasn't supposed to be here."

"The guy who was working on this room. You know some islander got it fast. He got a pretty penny for it too."

Thomas sighed. The islanders were really all about money and goods. No price was too high for the right deal. They would sell their fingers if they could.

192

"Is the telegraph operational?"

"Not yet. I have to get the transmitter up and running first. It should take a few hours or so. I have to go out to the blasted crow's nest to install it."

Thomas paced around the room. He noticed a mass of gears, gauges and wires lying in the corner. "Are you using these parts for the repairs?"

"That's all junk," the crewman said. "We pulled all that out and replaced it."

"So can I have some of the pieces?" Thomas asked.

"Yeah. Like I said, it's junk."

Thomas sifted through the pile, filled his arms with the most promising parts, and took them back to his cabin.

He dumped the communication parts on the floor and separated them into piles of like components. Gears, an empty tank, wires, a bent antenna, gauges and malleable tubes and small steel pipes filled his cabin floor. Sitting back, he examined the pieces, evaluating the possibilities as the ship's engines cranked up. Moments later the Blood Countess lifted out of port and into the night sky.

Thomas figured the time would pass more quickly if he put his mind to doing something constructive. With an idea in mind, he made a trip to the galley where he rifled through the spices. Finding three jumbo sized cans of red and black pepper he absconded with them, taking them back to his cabin.

Thomas feared some kind of confrontation with The Pyre's Fortune and it might be advantageous to have something that could cause a distraction without killing anyone. Thomas tinkered with the pressurized tank and hoses. Mixing the peppers together, he carefully packed the irritant into the tank. His eyes watered and his nose twitched, but he managed to fashion an electric fuse that ran down the side of the tank. From there, he ventured out on the deck in search of a power source. He had never been on deck at night. The entire top deck and the masts were aglow with maroon lights, making it look like Hell's own flagship.

The Blood Countess' Jolly Roger featured a white sickle that glowed a light green in the dark sky. Pirates were always so proud of their flags and they used a clever, incandescent paint to absorb the sunlight making their flags glow brightly through the night.

The wind in the sky was so cold it was almost unbearable to stand on deck, but Thomas saw several things he could use. He wrapped his arms around himself and investigated the power sources for the lights. The lights were powered by individual, unconventional batteries that drew power from the motion of the ship and the wind that blew through slits on the battery's sides. It was old technology, but it was free energy that put no drain on the ship's main fuel supply. What made this particularly attractive to Thomas was that power was derived from the friction of a small copper coil that rubbed against a metal casing inside the battery.

Choosing a random light on the back of the deck he shut the battery off with a cold metal switch that separated the connection of the wires to the power source. Looking around nervously, he unsheathed his cutlass and slipped it behind the battery fittings. It was hard work, but after a few minutes he pried the screws loose from the wooden railing. The wood cracked and the chunky cylindrical battery fell to the deck with a heavy clunk. Thomas' head darted back and forth. He wasn't actually stealing as the ship partially belonged to him, but he was sure that some of the crew would not appreciate him vandalizing the lights. The few scattered crew members outside took no notice, probably because of the heavy din from the high altitude winds. Thomas cut the wires that fed into the light and returned to his warm room below decks.

Back in his cabin, Thomas strapped the battery to the tank filled with pepper using pieces of rubber tubing. He connected the battery to the wires that led into the tank, and realized he needed only one more component.

He took his contraption to the aft engine room. All airship engine rooms had auxiliary and emergency steam pressure generators and this one was no exception. Stinking of warm copper and oil, the room was the largest room on the ship, spanning all three stories of the ship and lit with dozens of dim yellow gas lamps. Tubes and pipes stretched in every direction like a bizarre, overgrown tree. With the deafening generator going at full power, the room was moist and sticky.

A man and a woman were monitoring the gauges, making sure nothing went wrong while the ship blasted through the sky toward Lemuria. They didn't seem to care that Thomas had brought what looked like a homemade bomb to the engine room and that concerned him. He nodded at them as he walked to one of the smaller generators and hooked the hose to the top of his pressure tank.

It was an old fashioned hand cranked generator, but he didn't need much steam, so he whirled the crank creating a metal on metal whine. As he gyrated, he saw the small gauge on his tank twitch and the needle slowly began to slide to the right. He got it up to seventy-five percent of its capacity and stopped. If he had to use it, he didn't want the thing to burst and send copper shrapnel flying.

After unhooking the hose from the generator, he waved politely to the engine room attendants and left for his room. Thomas spent several more hours tinkering with his homemade pepper spray, adding a wax seal to the nozzle and thoroughly checking the connections and battery. In theory, he should be able to shake the tank and battery like a champagne bottle and throw it. With enough friction and wind power, it would send a charge through the tank blowing the wax seal off, and spraying pepper in a compressed jet of steam.

Finished Thomas sat back on his bunk. Despite his best efforts to keep himself occupied and wear himself out, he was still wide awake. He took the time to clean his handgun and the grenade launcher. Then he checked the ammunition for any possible defects. The oil lamp in his room swung gently with the motion of the ship casting shadows that crept across the room.

Thomas sat with his head down, mindlessly cleaning his weapons while he thought about Cynthia and what had become of her. His mind went through every scenario. Maybe she was being treated well, maybe she was in the brig, maybe she was dead, or possibly she had escaped on her own. Thomas became dizzy thinking of the best and worst case scenarios. While extremely worried, his wandering thoughts strengthened his resolve to get to her before the Lemurians.

The next point of contention for Thomas was Captain Swan. Yes, the man was a pirate–and a captain at that–but this was betrayal in the extreme.

Thomas lay back against his flat pillow, still polishing the spotless handgun. A million scenes went through his head. What would he do? How would he handle tomorrow's meeting with The Pyre's Fortune? How would he deal with Captain Swan? Somehow the thoughts muddled together and blurred into one congealed vision in his head. Before he knew it, his eyes had closed and he fell asleep with his gun in his lap.

A loud knocking woke Thomas. The pounding was so strident he thought someone was trying to break the door down. He snapped upright in bed and the gun he'd fallen asleep with hit the floor.

"What?" he blurted. "Who is it?"

"Mister Riley," A hoarse voice said. "Lieutenant Burges wants to see you right away!"

Thomas reached down, picked up the gun and took a moment to load it in case of trouble. He opened his cabin door to find a pirate who'd been a regular in the crow's nest of The Pyre's Fortune. The man was gasping, desperately trying to catch his breath. Despite being one of the most weather-worn pirates aboard the ship, he looked like he was having an anxiety attack.

"What is it?" Thomas asked calmly.

"Lieutenant Burges wants to see you, sir."

"Is that all you can tell me?"

"It's of the utmost urgency and it has to do with The Pyre's Fortune. That's all I know."

Thomas looked at the leather-skinned pirate suspiciously and sighed. "All right, let's go."

They walked through the black halls of The Blood Countess but instead of going to the captain's cabin as Thomas expected, the pirate led the way to the bridge of the ship. The bridge was just as magnificent as The Pyre's Fortune, but with the daunting black and copper motif that colored the entire ship and a large, worn oriental rug in front of the captains' chair. Sam stood at the front of the bridge next to a man operating a communication device. He turned around as Thomas entered the bridge.

"Thomas! Good of you to come."

He appeared pale and sickly. Thomas wondered how Sam even managed to stand upright. With his arm in a homemade sling he winced in pain with every movement.

"What's going on?" Thomas asked as he approached.

"We got the tracking device and the telegraph working last night," Sam said, with a little cough. "We located The Pyre's Fortune and she seems to be just inside the border of Lemuria. The odd thing is that she is not heading toward Lemuria City. She is traveling along the border. I had a man contact her with my password. They responded at first, then when we asked what her destination was, we didn't get a response. It has been two hours now and we have repeated the message four times."

"Could The Pyre's telegraph have gone out?" Thomas asked.

Sam shrugged out of habit. His face wrinkled with pain. "Something isn't right."

"Five minutes until we get a visual with The Pyre," the Tracking Officer said.

"Well, I guess we're going to find out pretty quickly," Thomas said.

Sam hobbled back to the captain's chair, sat down and

picked up The Narro Phone attached to it. A crackle from the speakers rang through the ship. "All crew man your stations. All guns ready to fire on my signal only. Boarding party on the top deck in two minutes. Communication room, try to hail The Pyre again."

Thomas had no idea how long he'd been asleep, but it was light outside. Thin grey clouds swirled past the windows as The Blood Countess flew toward uncertainty. Other than the roar of the engines and the hum of the controls on the bridge, the room was silent. Every minute that ticked by seemed like ten as Thomas and Sam squinted through the morning sun looking for any sign of The Pyre's Fortune.

"Boarding party is on deck," a wind-whipped voice called over the bridge speakers.

Sam grabbed the Narro Phone again and flipped a specific switch. "Communication Room. Any word?"

The speaker crackled. "No, sir."

"We should have a visual," the Tracking Officer said.

Thomas' eyes narrowed to slits. "I see it."

Sam put his hand up to his brow like a bill of a cap and leaned forward to see a tiny dot in the sky ahead.

"Communication Room. Hail them again," Sam ordered. His voice was stressed and raspy.

The dot that was The Pyre's Fortune grew larger by the second.

"Transmission from The Pyre is coming in," an excited voice said over the speakers.

The man in the communication room left his speaker on. The ticking of the paper from the telegraph clicked through the metal cone like an irregular heartbeat.

He read aloud. "From ATHENA. LIEUTENANT BURGES. STAY AWAY. CHANGE COURSE FOR ABERNATHY BAY. FURTHER INSTRUCTIONS LATER. END."

"Who is that?" Thomas asked.

"It's Ann," Sam said angrily.

Sam picked up the Narro Phone and flipped another switch. "Engine room. Full stop. We will cruise at remaining velocity."

He reached down and flipped more switches. "Communication room. Send the following message to The Pyre: CODE HECATE. AS LIEUTENANT I HAVE THE AUTHORITY AND DEMAND TO KNOW SITUATION. END."

They could see The Pyre's Fortune in full view now. It appeared most of the major damage was repaired, proving a team of skilled people had worked on the ship. It had only been a few days since Sam and Thomas had been separated from The Pyre so it was plausible that Lemurian repairmen had done the work.

Several minutes went by as The Blood Countess drifted closer to The Pyre's Fortune, the tension building in every second without a response.

"Someone is dictating the response," Sam said to himself. "That must be why it's taking so long. They're choosing their words carefully."

The Speakers crackled again. "From ATHENA. ODIN'S ORDERS. STAY AWAY AND PROCEED TO ABERNATHY BAY IMMEDIATELY. CHANGE COURSE OF YOUR VESSEL UNDER PENALTY OF MUTINY.

Sam ran his good hand through his hair. "This is unbelievable."

"I assume Odin is Captain Swan?" Thomas asked.

Sam just nodded, his mind wandering, contemplating what to do. Deciding, Sam held the cone of the Narro Phone up to his mouth.

"Communication Room. Send the following message to The Pyre: HECATE. I WAS NOT INFORMED OF SITUATION AS IS MY RIGHT AS LEIUTENANT. I DEMAND TO KNOW THE SITUATION. IF PROCEDURE IS NOT FOLLOWED THEN ODIN IS BREAKING THE PYRE'S CODE AND SUBJECT TO CREW COURT. END."

The ships glided ever closer. Sam ordered the pilot to turn The Blood Countess and drift up broadside. Each ship was poised to strike.

Thomas strolled to the side window to take a closer look at The Pyre's Fortune. He could see the fresh patches of repairs in detail on the hull of the ship as well as new planking on the top deck. It was obvious more than the skeleton crew had made these repairs in such a short time frame. The most menacing sight was a sizeable gathering of crew members on the deck, armed with all manner of weaponry. Several of the smaller cannons were also manned and ready to fire. Thomas knew the feelings must be mutual aboard both ships. While no one wanted to fire on their crew mates and friends, they would if told to do so.

After several more minutes of no word from The Pyre's Fortune, Sam began to pace the bridge, hoping for a favorable response. He picked up the Narro Phone again.

"Nothing?" he asked impatiently.

"No, sir."

"I know they're receiving the transmissions. Send them this message: "HECATE. ANN I MUST BE ALLOWED TO BOARD THE PYRE. I NEED ANSWERS AND A SAY IN THIS MATTER. RESPOND IMMEDIATELY. END."

He switched the Narro Phone station again. "Boarding crew! On my order, fire grappling hooks and board the ship. All cannon prepare to fire!"

The speaker cone cracked again. "Sir we are receiving an answer." The communications man said. "'ATHENA. SAM WE ARE UNDER ODIN'S ORDERS. PLEASE DON'T MAKE US DO THIS. AT THE FIRST SIGN OF AGGRESSION WE WILL FIGHT BACK. END.'"

Sam cursed loudly. "What is she thinking? I know what it is, she's trying to protect a deal that was made without approval. I have every right to board that ship. If they deny me access, I have every right to blow them out of the sky."

With his head down, Sam paced angrily around the bridge

again. He looked so stressed; Thomas thought he might fall over from pain and frustration.

Sam snatched up the Narro Phone once more, flipped the switch that led directly to the communication room and held it up to his mouth. "Communications! Send message: HECATE. IF WE ARE NOT ALLOWED TO BOARD WE WILL BOARD AND DESTROY BY FORCE. END."

The skeleton crew in the bridge stirred in their seats. Thomas felt the tension rise. He closed his eyes wishing for a positive message from Sam's threat.

The speaker crackled again. It seemed like it took an entire minute before the communications man spoke.

"Sir! Message from The Pyre. 'ATHENA. NUTS. END.'"

Sam ignored the pain in his body and dashed back to his chair where he grabbed the Narro Phone.

Thomas waved his hands in the air. "Whoa, wait wait wait. What does that even mean?"

Sam's looked at Thomas with steely eyes. "It means they're going to fight."

"Boarding crew," he barked in the Narro Phone, "board The Pyre now! Small cannon crew fire at will!"

16
MAKING ENEMIES

Thomas heard popping noises and saw at least ten ropes with grappling hooks fly from The Blood Countess onto The Pyre's Fortune. Seconds later men were shimmying across the ropes with nothing but sky beneath them. The alarm blared and Thomas instinctively grabbed his pistol. He dashed out of the bridge to head back to his room. He needed his grenade launcher and the pepper bomb he had made the night before.

As Thomas ran through the corridors, men were frantically running through the ship. A loud, muffled blast shook the ship indicating The Blood Countess had let off a volley from the lower deck cannons. Thomas could only hope they were shooting to disable the guns on The Pyre's Fortune and not to kill personnel. This was a critical moment; everything could fail if Cynthia or Maier were killed in the ensuing battle.

Thomas rushed into his cabin, snatching up the backpack full of grenades, the launcher, and his cumbersome pepper bomb.

Without lingering, he ran out of his room and up to the deck. Just before he reached the daylight above, the crackle of small arms fire peppered the air. Keep your head down, Thomas thought, stepping onto the windy upper deck. Men hunkered down all around the railings of both ships, popping up to take an occasional shot at the other ship.

Several of The Blood Countess' crew had made it across on their crank powered zip lines and were fighting hand to hand aboard The Pyre's Fortune. Thomas ducked and ran in a crouch to the rail close to a zip line.

"If you go over there, you'll be outnumbered," a middle aged pirate yelled at Thomas.

Thomas looked at him disappointedly and poked his head over the rail to see what he faced. The pirate was correct. The few men who had made it over were desperately outnumbered. It wasn't going to be long before they were all cut down. Several more men hoisted themselves on the ropes and began to cross the precarious void between the ships. Thomas' heart sank as one of the ropes with a man hanging in the middle was cut. The rope went limp, dropping the man thousands of feet to his death. Thomas hunkered back down and looked at the pirate next to him.

"When I go across, can you give me covering fire? You can't let them cut this rope."

The pirate looked worried, but his face firmed into hard, angry lines. "Yes. Just move fast. I can't guarantee that they won't shoot you while you're on it."

"It's a risk I have to take. I'm going."

Thomas grabbed one of the loose zip cranks that were piled along the side of the ship. If Thomas let go with either hand he would fall to his death.

"Now," Thomas yelled as he stood up and placed the crank on the rope connecting the ships.

The pirate did as promised, standing tall and firing thunderous shots from his blunderbuss rifle. Thomas saw the men on The Pyre's Fortune duck, looking for cover behind anything.

Thomas raised the zip crank above his head, slipped it over the taught rope and leaped off of the side of the ship. The zip crank was faster than he imagined. For a brief second he looked down to see white clouds and a tiny toy-like landscape beneath him. The rest of the journey was a blur. In a moment his feet hit the battered rail of The Pyre's Fortune and his body fell forward onto the wooden deck.

A quick streak of pride and accomplishment ran through him upon landing but he had no time to enjoy his feelings. Thomas' pirate friend continued to fire, but now Thomas was in plain view of The Pyre's crew. He didn't want to kill anyone, but he was prepared to if the situation required. The men aboard The Pyre's Fortune poked their heads around their covered positions, firing at Thomas haphazardly.

Thomas looked around for a place to run, but thought a distraction might be helpful. Eyeing a large wooden box used to store chains and ropes just a few strides away, he turned and ran. Pointing the grenade launcher toward the mast he fired.

The little grenade blasted out of the launcher and impacted with the thick mast of The Pyre's Fortune, instantly raining chunks of splintered wood on the deck. The ear splitting sound made everyone on board duck to avoid the shrapnel. It bought Thomas just enough time to get behind the storage box. Before rounding the box, he randomly fired his pistol once, just to let them know he had other weapons at his disposal. Then he hunkered down behind the box while pings of small arms fire resonated around him.

"I don't want to hurt you," Thomas yelled, hoping to get some sympathy from his attackers. "I just want to get Cynthia off the ship!"

The response to Thomas' plea was answered by more gunfire. The shots were close, prompting him to squat into a ball behind the storage box. He only worried about having an explosive drop nearby or having someone sneak up on him due to his limited visibility.

"I'm not joking around here," Thomas yelled. "I don't want to hurt you!"

"Then surrender," someone yelled back.

The fighting sounded mild compared to Thomas' first experience boarding a ship. It seemed many of the men were shooting to wound or intimidate rather than to kill. Thomas laid the homemade pepper bomb on the deck and dared a quick peek over the storage box. He saw the men he was blindly yelling at in a hand to hand fight with some of the crew from The Blood Countess. His heartbeat rose as he watched members of the same crew clashing.

The scene momentarily distracted him. Through the noise of the fighting, he heard a soft thump behind him and felt the boards beneath his feet vibrate. It was so inconsequential that he didn't take the time to turn around. Something heavy and blunt rammed into his back throwing him face first into the storage box. He smacked hard against the wood and crumpled to the deck. Pain shot through his body and he flopped around to see Ann Read standing above him with a rifle in her hands.

Ann had taken care to look as intimidating as possible. Her trademark combat red bandanna covered her nose and mouth. With her shiny black goggles on her forehead, she wore thick red eyeliner making her dark eyes look even more savage than normal. She raised the butt of the rifle and swung it down like a club. Despite every aching muscle in Thomas' body, he rolled to avoid the strike. Just inches from making contact, the end of the gun slammed into the storage box, breaking a hole in the side. She abandoned the makeshift club, stepped back and slung her cutlass from its sheath.

Thomas painfully scrambled to his feet and reached for his hand gun, but it wasn't in the holster on his hip. He had no time to look for it and he couldn't fire the grenade launcher this closely without endangering himself, so he responded with pulling his own cutlass.

"You were told not to board," Ann screamed from behind her bandanna. "Where's Sam you scum?"

She took a brave step forward pointing the end of her cutlass at Thomas. With the grenade launcher in one hand and his cutlass in the other, he clashed swords with her to make sure she didn't have an offensive move.

"Where's Cynthia?" Thomas yelled.

Ann's eyes narrowed. She whipped Thomas' cutlass to the side and in a fluid motion, swung the blade. Maybe it was dumb luck, or maybe it was something unconscious, but Thomas' sword was in a defensive position at just the right second. The metal clanged together causing an agonizing vibration to shoot through his sword and into his arm. He almost dropped his weapon, only managing to hang on because losing it meant certain death. Backing up a few paces, two bullets impacted next to his feet, making his aching legs dance. Ann laughed and lunged.

Again, Thomas' vulnerable position left one foot in the air as Ann moved in to skewer him. She ran into his leg and he icked her in the stomach, sending her flailing back into the broken storage box. She quickly struggled upright.

"Stupid man," she yelled. "You don't know what you have gotten yourself into."

"Just let me have Cynthia and I'll happily leave," Thomas snapped back.

Ann lifted her cutlass above her head. "There's nothing happy about how you're leaving!"

She advanced on him and fiercely swung the curved sword downward. Thomas again blocked the initial swing above him, but she quickly raised the blade again and swung down and down again as if she was hammering nails into the deck.

"Die," she screamed on every swing.

After Thomas' fourth block, his hand gripping the handle gave way and the cutlass dropped to the ground. Falling over his own feet, he backed up to the open area of the deck. There were bodies and wounded men all around him. Anyone who wasn't occupied could have picked him off in a second, but his main worry was Ann moving confidently toward him. With his only weapon available, Thomas raised the grenade launcher and fired it intentionally behind Ann.

The little walnut shaped projectile jumped out of the barrel and zinged past Ann's arm. It hit the cabin wall behind her with a dull thud and bounced just behind the storage box that he'd previously hidden behind. He knew it was a bad decision, but it was the only option to keep Ann from slicing him to pieces. The grenade exploded, shattering the heavy storage box. Ann flew forward into Thomas. Thousands of pieces of wood and chunks of heavy rope sprayed in every direction. Thomas was pinned between the hard wood of the deck at his back and the infuriated Ann on top of him.

The explosion set off the pepper bomb he had left behind the storage box. A spray of misty water mixed with pepper covered half the deck, drenching Thomas and Ann from head to foot. The pepper burned his eyes and nose, stealing his breath. With her head lying on Thomas', Ann hissed in pain. Thomas threw her off of him and stood up on a panicked, adrenaline fueled rush. He tried to open his eyes but the pepper did its job making eyesight a painful blur. He staggered around the deck not caring if he would be an easy target in search of water to wash his face.

Thomas rubbed his eyes, knowing it was a mistake, but at least it would clear away the smaller granules of pepper. The pieces he did not clear only imbedded deeper causing more pain. He screamed and dropped to his knees. Each second felt like hours. Thomas knew that without water to rinse his eyes, he would have to painfully wait for his tear ducts to wash themselves clean. He sat, not knowing where he was and tried to wait out the suffering. He heard Ann screaming as well as several others who had been sprayed by the bomb. Thomas regretted making the thing.

On, his knees, breathing heavily, Thomas listened. He could hear the wind rolling over the ship. The yelps and anguished cries of injured people rang through his head like fire alarms. His only comfort was that the gunfire had slowed to sporadic, distant shots. If he had to guess, they were actually coming from the deck of The Blood Countess. He wondered if his freak explosion could have stopped most of the fighting on the ship. Someone grabbed Thomas' arms, lifted him, and dragged him backwards. He struggled, knowing he only had seconds to live.

"Calm down," huffed a gritty voice with a British accent.

Thomas was being hauled across the deck, the heels of his boots bumping over debris. He was soon propped against a wall and a heavy hand landed on his shoulder. "What can I do to help, sir?"

Despite the pain, Thomas wanted to smile. He couldn't believe the one person who'd found him was on his side.

"Water," he groaned. "I need water!"

The man who'd pulled him away from the open deck let go of his shoulder. "Water," he yelled. "Send water over immediately!"

Thomas' nose was completely clogged and he felt the uncontrollable drool dripping from his mouth. He breathed hard, trying to clear the wet mess from his face.

"Don't worry, sir," the man said. "It'll be just a minute."

Thomas aimed his face in the voice's direction. "Who are you?"

"Loyal Pyre deck gunner Reginald–I mean Reggie Wallingford."

"Thank you Reggie."

"I see 'em, sir. They're coming with water," Reggie said.

The gun fire dropped to a few shots every minute. The fight was over, or at least suspended for the moment.

"Reggie? What is going on? I can't see anything. How did you escape the blast?"

"Something nasty exploded, sir. I was zipping over when it happened."

"Almost everyone on the deck is wounded. I didn't know we had anything like that aboard The Pyre. It had to be a chemical."

"You didn't have anything like that on board," Thomas explained putting his hands over his face. "I made it. It was just steam pressured powdered pepper."

"It looks really bad, sir. At least it stopped everyone from killing each other."

Thomas took solace in Reggie's account. Even though everyone was in pain, he had possibly saved some lives. The squeaking sound of a zip crank whined close by and he heard a heavy thump as a man had come across and landed on the deck.

"Here," Reggie exclaimed.

He grabbed Thomas' hand and put a small hose in his palm.

"Wait, what's this?" Thomas asked.

"It's a water fire extinguisher, sir."

Thomas knew it would shoot water out with a lot of pressure. He squeezed the latch and aimed the hose at his chest to make sure he wouldn't put his eyes out with the stream of water. It blasted against him with great force, but not enough to really hurt him. A little pain would be nothing compared to the burning in his eyes and nose. Squinting his eyes hard, he aimed it at his face and sprayed.

While the cold water beat against his face, he felt the pepper washing away. He continued to rinse his face, ignoring the awkward feeling of water rushing up his nose and into his eyes. After a few minutes of clearing his face with the fire extinguisher, he tried to open his eyes.

The sight, while terrible, was a welcome relief that he could see anything at all. The deck of The Pyre's Fortune was littered with people writhing on the deck. All those who could move were cupping their faces. The unfortunate ones were clutching wounds that were now burning with pepper. Thomas tried to stand and Reggie grabbed him.

"Take it easy, sir. Give it a minute."

"I have to find Cynthia."

"All right," Reggie said. "Just don't go rushing out there. You need to recover."

Reggie had dragged Thomas to the side of The Pyre where he was relatively shielded from the open deck. Thomas blinked quickly trying to regain his sight. He needed to find Ann. If she was still alive, she would know exactly where they were holding Cynthia.

As his sight returned, Thomas tried to locate the storage box where he'd tangled with Ann. Replaced with a gaping hole, the box was gone and a few feet away, he saw Ann laying face down on the deck.

"Reggie, help me get over there. I need to get to Ann Read."

"Of course, sir. But don't you think you should give it a few moments?"

"No Reggie, I need your help now. Can you come with me and cover me if there's trouble?"

"Yes, sir," Reggie said hesitantly, looking around the deck for possible attackers.

Thomas tried to stand on his own and staggered.

"Wait. Sir. Please. Stay put, I will bring her here if she's alive."

Thomas breathed a sigh of relief. "Only if you're sure it's safe."

"It's safer than going to get you," Reggie said, already trotting off in Ann's direction.

Thomas gripped the rail of The Pyre's Fortune and tried to

appear unaffected. Reggie lingered over Ann's motionless body. He kneeled next to her and swiveled his head to make sure he was safe. After resting his hand on her back, he shifted her, slipping his hands under her arms and dragging her just as he had dragged Thomas earlier.

Within two steps, Ann let out a scream Thomas would never forget. She screeched like a large bird as Reggie brought her across the deck. At least she was alive. Waddling backwards like a duck, Reggie arrived with Ann and placed her at Thomas' feet.

"I'm sorry Miss Read," Reggie said.

She screamed again. Her pony tail drooped like a black wilted plant on her head and her bandana had fallen around her neck. With her cracked goggles and the water from the pepper bomb, her red makeup had melted and ran in rivulets all over her face.

"Reggie?" she moaned. "Is that you?"

"Yes...yes, ma'am."

"Get me help!"

Reggie turned to Thomas. "I think she has some shrapnel in her back."

"Who is that?" Ann asked. "Who are you talking to?"

"Me. Thomas Riley."

"Reggie," Ann shrieked. "You traitorous worm! You'll hang for this!"

"Ann, listen to me," Thomas said with all the calm confidence he could muster. "I have you. I won't help you until you tell me where Cynthia is."

"Probably dead," Ann snapped.

Even though she couldn't see him, she turned her puffy, swollen face in his direction. Strands of loose hair stuck to her face like they had been glued down. In obvious pain and clearly beaten, she still appeared determined.

"Where's Sam? You tell me about him and I'll tell you about Cynthia," Ann said in a childish tone.

"Sam is aboard The Blood Countess. He's injured. He gave the order to board. We came to get Cynthia. He came to get

211

Cynthia."

Ann gritted her teeth and her face scrunched up angrily. "Aaah! For Cynthia, eh? Sam is mine!"

Thomas was shocked by the revelation but decided to use the information against her. "Yes for Cynthia. Now where is she?"

"Give me water," Ann demanded.

"We had a deal! Now where is she?"

Ann tried to smile despite her pain. "You're too late. Captain Swan already sold her and the old man to the Lemurians. She's long dead by now Riley!"

Thomas bent down so he was face to face with Ann and he grabbed her wet throat.

"You don't have long to live unless you start talking. Where is Captain Swan? Where and when did you sell Cynthia?"

Ann's smile grew wider. "The good Captain went with the ship that we met up with on the Lemurian border. He wanted to make sure all of his precious cargo got where it was going safely."

Thomas wanted to choke the life out of her right there, but he hesitated.

"Where were they taking her?" Thomas snarled, increasing the pressure around her neck.

Ann coughed and sputtered. "You can kill me if you want Riley, but I'm not saying anything else until I speak to Sam."

Thomas released his hold, glancing up at Reggie who looked terrified by the entire exchange. "Can you get Sam over here?"

Reggie nodded and turned to another man who had brought the fire extinguisher from The Blood Countess. The other man hopped on the zip crank and within seconds he was hauling himself back to the deck of the black ship.

Thomas kept his word and began washing Ann's pepper covered face with the fire extinguisher. She looked like a miserable, wounded animal as he hosed her down. After a string of expletives and a lot of writhing on the deck, Ann opened her eyes.

Despite her refusal, Thomas made her turn around so he could inspect her wounds. The back of her leather vest was slashed in half and a large laceration angled like a crudely drawn check mark across her back. As far as he could tell, her wounds were not life threatening.

Thomas' inspection was interrupted by some yelling from the deck of The Blood Countess. He looked over to see a large man mounting the zip crank. Sam had one arm around the man's shoulder and appeared to be strapped to him with ropes. Sam's wounded arm and the mechanical splint hung helplessly to the side.

Reggie stepped on the grappling hook imbedded in The Pyre's deck to lend extra support. The big man, with an anguished look on his face, cranked his way across the space between the ships on the taught rope.

The two men arrived safely, and Reggie helped untie Sam from the big man. Sam walked over and stopped in front of Ann.

"You came back for her?" Ann asked, her eyes brimming with new tears as she looked up at him. "You did all of this because of her?"

Sam turned to Thomas and Reggie. "I'll need to speak to her alone."

Reggie assisted Thomas who was still uneasy on his feet and they walked away to another corner of the deck. The gunfire had ceased now that Ann and Sam were in view.

Thomas cleared his nose and watched Reggie move from one wounded person to the next, offering his assistance, no matter what side they'd been on just twenty minutes ago. All the pirates were essentially of the same crew and now that the fighting had stopped, there seemed to be no lingering grudges or hostility.

Thomas kept a blurry eye on Sam and Ann. He couldn't hear their conversation, but several times Ann raised her voice in anger. When the conversation ended, Ann hobbled away in one direction and Sam, with help from the big pirate, joined Thomas.

Sam's face was a mixture of anger and sadness. "We take the men loyal to me, and The Blood Countess. Ann stays with this ship and whoever chooses to remain loyal to Captain Swan."

"What's our destination?" Thomas asked.

"Lemuria of course. Things are about to get very bad Mister Riley. Now we'll have the Lemurians and Captain Swan to deal with."

"When do we go?" Thomas asked without hesitation.

"Immediately."

17
CONFESSIONS

Only seventeen men remained with The Pyre's Fortune, leaving Ann without enough hands to fly the ship effectively. She felt angry and betrayed by the amount of people who were loyal to Sam.

Sam took everyone who wanted to join his mission to penetrate Lemuria City and rescue Cynthia. The crew was motivated to find Captain Swan and make him pay for attempting to run off with the large sum of money the Lemurians had paid for Cynthia and Doctor Maier.

Additionally, Sam ordered anyone wounded beyond the ability to work to stay with The Pyre's Fortune, further hampering Ann and her crew.

After the boarding ropes were dislodged, The Blood Countess veered away from her wounded victim. With a mighty roar of the twin propellers, she rumbled away, leaving The Pyre's Fortune drifting in mid air.

Thomas stood on deck of The Blood Countess staring at the smoking ship as it hung in the sky like a lost balloon. The cold wind blew through his hair sending chills through his body.

"How are you holding up?" Sam asked, walking up behind him.

Thomas turned. "I'm fine. Just worried."

"Don't be. We'll find her. I have the communications room working on any leads as to where she might be. We have plenty of connections and if we have to bribe someone to give us information, so be it."

"Why are you doing this Sam? Do you really care for her?"

Sam paused and looked away from Thomas for a moment. "I do care for her. The life I live is a temporary one. Even the best pirate doesn't last long in the profession. Only the rare few get out of it before they are killed. I think our meeting wasn't a coincidence. I think my feelings for Cynthia are a sign that that there is a better life for me out in the world. I'm doing this for her you know. The other men are doing it out of loyalty to me and the hope that we find Captain Swan. They want their cut of that money from the Lemurians."

Thomas knew he was showing his discomfort by not looking Sam in the face. He forced himself to look the man in the eye.

He wanted to argue with Sam, to threaten him, anything to make him abandon his feelings, but he dared not say anything. Sam and the crew of The Blood Countess were his only method of reaching and hopefully rescuing Cynthia. He studied Sam intently, unhappy with what he was hearing, but understanding at the same time.

"As you can tell, we live a dangerous life as well," Thomas said. "West Canvia is constantly under attack and the guerrilla fighters have become a daily threat."

"That's what I am talking about. We can escape this madness. I know hundreds of places where Cynthia and I could live without fear in every day of our lives."

Thomas bit the inside of his lip to control the anger that was rushing through him. "That'll be an issue you will have to take up with Cynthia. She's quite dedicated to her work."

"I know," Sam said, looking down at the deck. "There are many things to consider. It will take some time. I just know I would regret it if I didn't try to rescue her. Maybe I blame myself for not knowing what Captain Swan was up to or maybe it's something else. Either way, I know this is something I have to do. Let's not forget that we'll be looking for our old beloved Captain as well."

A man emerged from one of the newly patched decks and waved his arms in the air to get Sam's attention.

"Lieutenant Burges," the man yelled, his voice barely audible over the engines and rushing wind around them. "A message in the communication room for you!"

Sam raised his good arm to signal his understanding. He

216

nodded at Thomas to join him so they could listen to the message together. Thomas followed Sam to the door and down the stairs to the communication room under the main deck. Two men were operating the various communication stations desperately searching for any word on Cynthia or Captain Swan.

"We received a message from The Pyre, Sir," a bearded pirate announced. He handed Sam a long slip of paper from the air telegraph. Sam held it out with one hand studying the communication.

"Perfect," Sam said, reading the paper.

"What is it?" Thomas asked impatiently.

"It's from Ann."

He read aloud. "This will be the last friendly communication that you will receive from me. From now on, consider our ships enemies. If we are to encounter each other again, you and your crew will be killed under the charge of mutiny. So that you can charge headlong into suicide, I have information on the people you are looking for. Your precious Cynthia is being held in the Lemurian Royal Palace where the soul of the Canvian Duchess is to be extracted. She is scheduled to be executed for war crimes and association with pirates when the process is done. I imagine they will make this a bloody and humiliating process. Captain Swan is at one of the Lemurian summer mansions in the South. We do not know which one yet, but we will find him soon enough. Good luck on your suicide mission. Forever Yours, Captain Ann Read."

Sam picked up a Narro Phone off the wall. "Bridge, this is Captain Burges. Change course for Lemuria City."

Thomas squeezed the bridge of his nose. "Executed? Sam, how soon before we arrive in Lemuria City? How fast can we go?"

"Thomas, calm down. The ship is on a direct course and there isn't anything you can do to make it go faster."

Thomas took a deep breath and adjusted his jacket. "Okay. I'm sorry."

"Don't worry. I'm sure Ann's just posturing. Even if what she says is true, we'll be there before they do anything."

217

Thomas hid his anxiety by changing the subject. "Ann seems quite angry with you."

Sam looked up from the paper. "Well, we were an item for a time before we joined with The Pyre."

Sam looked away and took a step as if he wanted to walk away. He obviously didn't want to give any details. Thomas thought it might be productive to probe this issue further. "So, what happened?"

Sam looked up at him, clearly annoyed. He stuffed the air telegraph paper in his jacket pocket and walked out of the room. Thomas followed closely and as they ascended the stairs Sam spoke without looking back. "Ann and I were in a relationship for a long time before we joined Captain Swan. I was an airman in the Coastal Frontier Militia and Ann was a nurse aboard our ship. As you can imagine, Ann isn't cut out to be a nurse. She's a brash woman. She's not afraid to speak her mind and she is not afraid of blood or fighting."

"I noticed," Thomas said coldly.

"When we joined Captain Swan, we both moved up in the ranks quickly. The opportunity came for us both for different reasons. Men were killed, some deserted, and Ann and I had certain traits Captain Swan found useful. He liked my ability to remain calm while under fire. He also liked that I always used extreme measures when things got hairy.

"He liked Ann's ability to intimidate and he loved the fact that Ann is an absolute viper in a fire fight. We were a good balance on the ship."

"And why does she hate you now?" Thomas pressed.

"She's been angry with me for quite some time. When we were promoted I was made Lieutenant and she Ensign. She had her way of doing things and I had mine. While she preferred to run someone through at the first opportunity, I preferred to take them hostage, get information from them or use them as ransom. If it were up to Ann, we would not have gotten a single piece of gold in our exploits because she would have obliterated every ship we encountered."

"It sounds like she has some anger issues."

Sam turned and glanced at Thomas. "She can be quite aggressive. When you get to know her, she is a good person on the inside. It's deceiving since she never shows that side of herself to strangers."

Thomas was quickly becoming uncomfortable as Sam poured his heart out to him, but he didn't want to seem insensitive since he'd provoked the conversation.

"So what happened between you two?" Thomas asked.

"We butted heads on almost every issue. If I wanted to do a night raid on an island weapon depot, she wanted to hammer it with cannon fire and see what was left. If I wanted to board a merchant ship she wanted to shoot it down. Some of the men began to respect her harshness while others sided with me because I could make them more money...and keep them safe. We basically disagreed on every action that Captain Swan ordered and it caused a rift between us.

"I will tell you this," Sam continued. "When she gets The Pyre's Fortune repaired and pulls enough of a crew together, I guarantee we will be her first target."

"Let's hope she doesn't get that far."

Sam shot Thomas a *you are so naïve* look. "Oh she will get it back running again. Like I said, she's brash and she carries grudges until she feels vindicated."

The wind was freezing as Thomas and Sam stepped out on the top deck of the ship. Dusk was falling and the sky was lit with an orange glow.

The two men went to the bridge and found it a hive of activity. Crewmen were scurrying from station to station, the lights on the controls blinked in their copper casings, and the sounds of machinery clicked and rumbled through the cabin walls. Sam took his place in the captain's chair and Thomas followed, standing next to him. Sam picked up the modified Narro Phone and clicked several buttons on the side of the brass box.

"Attention, crew. I want a direct course for the royal palace in Lemuria City. We will be cruising at twenty three thousand feet to avoid pressure problems and Lemurian interceptors and detection."

Thomas recognized the nerves of the bridge crew. Flying just under the ceiling that most frequently caused altitude sickness was dangerous for many reasons. If they were forced to go any higher the crew could pass out or suffer from fatigue. If a Lemurian fighter squad or a battleship found them, the only direction they could go was down which would put them in a compromising position in an air to air fight.

"When we reach our cruising altitude everyone is to be at their post and only essential personnel are to be on the top deck," Sam continued. "When we can make a straight descent into Lemuria City, we will land in the square in front of the palace where we will make a direct assault. This is probably the last thing the Lemurians expect anyone to do and it will give us an element of shock and surprise."

Sam pulled the cone of the Narro Phone away from his face as if he was thinking of what to say next. "If anyone does not want to continue on this mission, I am giving you the opportunity to disembark at the town of Kathain just before we cross into Lemurian airspace. It'll be a bloody fight. Those who do not want to continue will meet on the top deck in one hour. You will not be judged for your actions but you will no longer be considered a member of this crew."

Sam put the Narro Phone back on the receiver and sat back in his chair. He winced as he hefted his metal-braced arm onto the side of the chair.

Thomas' head cocked sideways. "That's it? You want to land directly in front of the Lemurian palace and storm in it?"

Sam looked him straight in the eyes. "Yes. That's exactly what I want to do. They won't expect a pirate ship to land in their most famous square and begin firing the cannons directly into their palace. The only thing we have to worry about initially is their anti-aircraft weapons. When we get into view, they'll surely fire on us."

"Well, it sounds like Ann was right. Maybe this is a suicide mission," Thomas said.

Sam looked at him crossly. "You can join those who want

220

to leave if you wish."

"No, you're not going to call me a coward," Thomas snapped back. "I'll be there for Cynthia."

"After the second volley I am going to take a small team of men to a side or back entrance where I hope to gain access to the palace while the guards deal with the ship. They can't just leave the thing out in front pounding them. We have the firepower to level the place. I'm not calling you a coward and I'd be honored if you were among that group." Sam explained.

"Of course I'll go. But if we're going to rush into this then I want you to be as equipped as possible." Thomas said. "I can modify that brace with a weapon in a few hours if you can stand being without it."

Sam looked at Thomas suspiciously, uncertain if Thomas had just insulted his pain threshold.

"Take it," Sam said, looking down at his arm. "I'll need all the firepower I can get."

Thomas knelt next to Sam and began to unscrew the fittings that held the brace together. The brace looked like an exoskeleton with copper tubes that connected to a swiveling rotation piece on the elbow. It could hold Sam's arm up and hold weight without causing too much pain.

Thomas took the brace below deck to a small room where firearms were stored along with ammunition and stacks of cannon shot. The room was small, the walls covered in a metal alloy that would shield its contents in case of a nearby explosion. Much of the best weaponry had been picked over and several men had supplemented their personal arsenals since Sam's announcement.

Thomas inspected the weapons, looking for what would be most useful. His plan was simple and he wanted a gun that could fire multiple shots and yet was small and light enough to be mounted on Sam's brace.

There was an array of small handguns that looked to be in bad shape and some long rifles that had seen better days, but the weapon that caught his attention was a slightly beat up personal Gatling gun sitting in the corner. He picked it up and inspected the cylindrical weapon.

The Gatling gun was as large as a man's arm with six brown colored metal barrels. It had a long wooden stock which Thomas knew he could saw off. It was heavier than he wanted, but with some slight modifications to the arm brace, he thought he could solidly affix the gun without much problem.

This particular weapon fired simple round shot that was purely an anti-personnel weapon. While it wasn't the most accurate form of ammunition, he thought the number of rounds it fired could make up for the lack of accuracy.

The hour that Sam gave the men had passed and his voice echoed over the metal speaker cones throughout the ship, "This is Captain Burges. I am happy to report that no one has decided to leave the ship in lieu of this dangerous mission. I am proud to have such a fine crew."

The Blood Countess had a large room on the lowest deck of the ship was used for making repairs on the fly. Connected to the cargo hold, the room was a disorganized mess of tools, wood beams and bolts of thick canvas used to make minor repairs on masts, deck flooring and sails.

Thomas found an old, rusty welding torch and handsaw missing half its teeth. He cut the stock off the Gatling gun, shortening it by two feet, and leaving only the magazine, the barrels and the small pressurized tank. Next, he removed the trigger guard and replaced it with a long piece of metal that could reach Sam's forefinger. Noticing how heavy this made the brace, Thomas extended the back of it with copper tubing so it would wrap over Sam's shoulder for extra support. The crude but imposing device would make anyone standing in front of it run in the other direction.

Thomas lifted the brace and tried it on. The support in the elbow was weak and it felt like it might break with any added stress, so Thomas removed the joint that held the forearm upright and replaced it with a spring loaded joint that would move up and down. This would give Sam more motion in his arm as well as bear the gun's additional weight. He slipped the brace on again. This time it was solid and the springy elbow was much more comfortable.

By the time he was done with his modifications, it was nearly morning and the sun had just begun to light the night sky. The black ship leveled off as they reached their cruising altitude. Despite the dangers of going out on the top deck, Thomas stepped into the powerful wind of the morning sky.

He put his goggles over his eyes and took one step out on the back part of the deck, bracing himself against the door frame. The wind was so strong no one could just go strolling on the deck without being blown off their feet.

He latched the round copper magazine full of shot onto the side of the gun and flipped the safety button next to the trigger. Aiming the brace and the gun into the sky behind the ship, Thomas tickled the extra long trigger with two fingers. He had set the trigger to respond to a firm pressure so that a slight touch wouldn't set it off. He curled his fingers tighter and squeezed. The gun fired three rounds a second, the barrel turning in a jerky motion as each bullet fired. Thomas held the trigger down and let the magazine run several revolutions before he let go.

The loud bangs gained the attention of the poor man in the strapped in the crows nest. This was surely the worst duty aboard any ship in flight. When he stopped test firing, Thomas looked up and waved to make sure he hadn't caused the man any undue alarm. The man waved back, understanding nothing hostile was going on beneath him.

Thomas removed the arm brace and leaned against the cabin wall letting the incredibly cold wind rush through his lungs while he watched the deep orange clouds roll by in the sky. In a short time, they would be over the heart of Lemuria looking death in the face once again.

After testing Sam's new gun on the deck of The Blood Countess, Thomas returned to the bridge to find Sam still sitting in the captain's chair with his injured arm in a white cloth sling. Only the soft *whirring* of instruments, broke the eerie quiet. Thomas walked up with the modified brace hanging from his hands.

"Are you going to turn me into a robot?" Sam joked.

Thomas smiled. "Why are you still awake?"

"I am making sure we don't get ambushed by Lemurian fighters."

"How long until we reach Lemuria City? You should get some shut eye if you are going to go with me on the ground."

"We are about four hours away." Sam looked worn out. His eyelids were puffy, reducing the bright blue gaze Thomas was familiar with to narrow slits. "By the way, you're the one who should get some shut eye if you're going to go with me on the ground," Sam said with a sly smile.

Ignoring the dig, Thomas presented him with the new brace. "Put this on. I want to make sure it fits."

Sam shot Thomas a sneaky, thankful look. "A Gatling gun? A bit extreme yet brilliant at the same time."

Thomas smiled as Sam took the clunky brace with his good arm and tried to maneuver his limp arm into the copper shoulder tubes that held his arm in place. Without saying a word, Thomas leaned close and helped him into the brace. Sam shot Thomas a nasty look, but he did not resist. There was something behind Sam's rough exterior that seemed to like and understand Thomas.

"Thanks," he said with a bit of respect.

"If it will help us, the work was more than worth it. It wasn't that difficult. I have done this before with wounded West

Canvian Soldiers that couldn't stand to be away from the action."

Sam admired his new bionic weapon. "I appreciate your work."

Thomas yawned. "Glad you like it. It will be quite nasty in battle."

"I thank you again," Sam said, as he tried the new easy mobility of the brace. "Do me a favor Thom, please get a few hours of sleep. There's no reason for you to stay awake. I'll wake you when we get close."

Thomas couldn't deny that he felt like he was going to pass out, but he didn't want to admit it. He looked at the floor. "I'll try."

"We're in luck," Sam said, looking up at Thomas. "The Canvians have mounted an attack on the Western border of Lemuria. It's the only reason I think we have not been pursued by fighters yet."

"I'll be amazed if we are still airborne within five miles of the palace." Thomas said.

"You have such little faith. We're above where the Lemurian fighters can reach us in altitude. Those little ships would get batted out of the air at this height. Get some sleep. I will make sure you are up an hour before we start our decent."

Thomas nodded. "I think that's a good idea."

"Thomas. Thank you again for making this."

Thomas gave Sam a half hearted smile, waved and left the bridge. When he arrived at his cabin he fell on his bunk and didn't bother to cover himself with the thin sheet. While he was nervous about the upcoming battle, Thomas' eyes shut quickly. As he succumbed to sleep, his brain played out scenarios of the upcoming incursion. Would they make it to the ground? Would they get shot out of the sky? Would they all be killed as they exited the ship? Was Cynthia even alive? He didn't know the answers, but he was too exhausted to think anymore.

The rapping on Thomas' cabin door sounded like a hammer pounding against his head. Whoever Sam sent to wake him was probably being gentle, but waking up was the last thing Thomas wanted to do. He groaned as he rolled over.

"Mister Riley," a voice called from the other side of the door. "Mister Riley, please wake up!"

Thomas sat up. His entire body ached. "Yeah," he said groggily. "I'm up. I'm up."

"We are starting our decent into Lemuria City. Captain Burges wants you ready right away. We have just over fifty minutes before we touch down."

The crew had provided him with a mish mash of used clothing. Thomas slipped on a heavy, high collared navy blue jacket with oversized cuffs and tarnished gold buttons, and black leather gloves. He adjusted his goggles on his head, picked up his hand gun, cutlass and hand held grenade launcher. On his way out, he grabbed the backpack of ammunition and slung it over his shoulder.

A short but rough looking pirate stood waiting in the hallway, a sly grin on his face.

"You look happy," Thomas said.

The pirate grinned. "Battle always winds me up Sir."

"That's good to know."

"Captain Burges wants you on the bridge, then you will assemble for your team to gain entrance to the fancy place."

"You mean the palace?" Thomas asked as they walked.

"Yep, the fancy place," the pirate said. "I expect it won't be too fancy for long, not after we're done with it that is."

"Probably not," Thomas agreed as they ascended the stairs to the bridge.

Thomas could feel The Blood Countess had pitched downward as it began its descent on the Lemurian capital. While he would never admit it, his nerves woke him from the dregs of sleep like a pot of strong coffee. On the bridge, it looked as though the crew had doubled from just a few hours ago. The room was busy with people bustling about checking all of the devices and gauges. Sam was still in the captain's chair, his oversized brace and Gatling gun in place.

"Have a good nap?" Sam asked cheerfully.

"Um, yeah. I imagine I did. How are you still awake?"

"I am used to this. I caught a few winks on our way in."

Sam picked up the Narro Phone and flipped a switch. "Are the ground baffles in place?"

"Yes sir," a tinny voice answered.

"Good. Ten minutes before visual, be ready for anti-air." He flipped two more switches on the Narro Phone. "Report on first assault team and cannons."

The replies came back rapidly. "Assault team is armed and ready."

"Cannons are loaded and manned."

"We're going to add a little insult to injury boys," Sam said with a smile. "We're landing in the middle of the square in front of the palace, directly on top of a bronze statue. When you feel us touch down, I want all port cannons to fire at will. After the volley, lower the ramp and the first assault team will disembark."

"Yes, sir," the voices replied simultaneously.

Sam flipped off the Narro Phone switches and looked up with an adrenaline-fueled smile.

"Ladies and Gentlemen," he announced. "Crash and bang! Land, destroy, and fend them off until we get back. They should be shocked out of their minds that we just landed a ship on their front lawn."

The crew stirred in their seats and some started whooping loudly with excitement. Thomas had never witnessed anything like the adrenaline of pirates before a plunder. He couldn't help getting wound up himself and his exhaustion washed away with the fresh jolt of excitement.

"Are you ready?" Sam asked as he popped up from his captain's chair.

"I am now," Thomas answered, holding his grenade launcher close to his chest.

Sam bolted ahead, making Thomas quicken his step to keep pace with him. They trotted down the stairs and down a few decks, passing a staging area where more than a dozen armed pirates were yelling and psyching themselves up for the oncoming battle. With cutlasses in the air, many were boasting about the horrible things they would do to the Lemurians when they got off the ship. Others would respond with a loud cheer,

228

joining their pirate brethren in a toast of raised swords. Thomas couldn't help noticing the heavy, choking body odor as he passed the staging room.

They walked on to another room where four huge pirates waited. The men were so tall and muscular; they made Thomas feel like a child standing next to his father. Two had shaved heads and wore dirty, red high-collared linen shirts. They looked like typical pirate thugs with unshaved faces full of scars, wild eyes, and a facial twitch most commonly associated with maniacs. The third had long, stringy black hair and wore a cavalier's hat tied at his chin. The last monstrous man had a trimmed beard and wore a tattered coat that looked like it once belonged to royalty.

They were all armed with enormous guns hoisted upon their shoulders. Two had bandoleers of extra bullets strapped across their chests and several glass bulbs filled with a menacing green liquid hanging from their belts.

Thomas had seen these guns like this before, but only in their original purpose as stationary guns mounted in foxholes or on ship decks. They used long, splintering lead bullets propelled by a small steam generator strapped to the pirate's backs. Two thick rubber tubes circled over their shoulders and into the rapid-fire rifles. In the hands of men like these, the massive guns resembled ornate hand cannons. All four pirates gave Sam a snarling smile as he entered.

"You ready boys?" Sam yelled.

"Yes, sir!"

Thomas had never seen such love of anarchy. Even Sam, reserved at first, was now aglow with the excitement of marauding. He'd suffered a major, debilitating injury and he'd not gotten as much sleep as Thomas. How could he even be awake, much less bursting with energy for a fight?

The small room had a vertical door that opened to drop a short staircase to the ground. Two portholes revealed treetops and the roofs of buildings. The Lemurians had to know they were coming by now. Thomas imagined hundreds of guards jumping up in surprise at the sight of the large black ship dropping out of the morning sky. He pictured them hastily grabbing weapons and trying to load the anti-aircraft cannons before the ship landed, or worse, crashed into something important.

One of the bald men pushed ahead and cupped his face against the porthole. "Not long now," he said like a kid waiting for Christmas. "I can see the palace." He broke out in hysterical laughter. "You should see the people running around below. They're like terrified ants!"

The other huge bald man began to hop in place, unable to contain his energy.

Thomas checked his grenade launcher, and clicked the safety off his hand gun. With a quick glance at his cutlass to make sure it was latched, he was ready to go. There was nothing he enjoyed about combat, but the excitement from the other men in the room bled into him. He felt his heartbeat rising and he caught himself cracking his knuckles–something he'd never done before.

The first bald man stepped to the side and cocked his huge rifle.

Thomas saw the ship had dropped between the buildings and was flying through the streets of downtown Lemuria City. He heard several pops in the distance and a second later, a thunderous explosion rocked The Blood Countess. All of the pirates, including Sam, burst out in hearty laughter. Thomas smiled nervously. He just wanted the ship to touch down so they could get out of this big black target floating through the city.

Another ripple of anti-aircraft shots went off in the distance. This time the shots rattled The Blood Countess with a direct hit somewhere on the top deck. The ship vibrated as if it would fall apart, but the battle worn pirates just steadied themselves on the walls.

The bald pirate looked at the door. "It's gonna take more than that!"

Sam peered through porthole. He looked back at his men. "We're close. Get ready!"

The Blood Countess' airspeed slowed dramatically as the

crew on the bridge threw the propellers into reverse. A few seconds passed before the whine of bending bronze screamed beneath the weight of the ship.

"Hear that?" Sam yelled over the noise. "That's the Duke's statue!"

The pirates looked at each other with wide eyes and laughed like madmen, though the sound reminded Thomas more of barking. It was as if he had been swallowed a surreal dream. He thought he had gotten to know these people, especially Sam, but they were acting more like hungry animals. While his scientific curiosity wanted to analyze the behavior, Thomas didn't have time. They were seconds away from actual combat. It was time to shoot first and think later.

Thomas pushed his way forward and peered through the porthole. The palace was a grand place, tall, with at least ten spires pointing up from the multi-storied building. The entire façade was dirty, as if no one had ever thought to clean it and innumerable gargoyles guarded every window and corner.

The Blood Countess rumbled as all of its weight pressed against the squashed statue and the cobblestone square beneath them. When the ship came to a halt, the port side cannons fired in near unison. The din was reminiscent of a fireworks grand finale and the vibration of the massive guns rattled the grounded ship like an earthquake. The front of the palace was punctured with twenty explosive shots, powdering the front of the grand structure and sending huge columns of smoke stretching into the air.

A moment later the main ramp of the Blood Countess fell open with a giant thud, and though he was still inside the ship, Thomas heard the first assault group rushing out screaming like madmen. Shortly after gunfire erupted. From Thomas' limited view, the assault group was targeting anyone left alive after the cannon volley.

"Sixty seconds," Sam yelled, craning his neck to see the action outside.

Thomas watched as the first group sprinted forward eliminating every living person in their way. While Thomas had

231

seen his share of fighting in the last week, nothing could have prepared him for the brutality he was witnessing now.

Sam put his hand his hand on the door. "Ready?"

The other pirates barked with enthusiasm and Thomas felt the extra surge of adrenaline rush through him. Sam yanked the door latch and it fell open, quickly slamming on the ground.

"Let's go," Sam roared, charging out first.

The moment he was down the stairs he fired off a few random rounds from his arm brace Gatling gun. Thomas didn't take time to look at what or who Sam was shooting at, finding himself behind the other pirates. Outside, he saw the first assault group had already made it to the two story palace doors and were shooting off handles and the hinges to gain access. Several of them were throwing glass grenades at the doors as well.

Thomas and his pirate team dashed around the side of the palace unseen, as the few guards who were left were completely occupied by the pirate force at the front door. The small team ended up in a high hedgerow garden.

Thomas had never seen such a garden. Tall flowers spanning the entire color wheel grew everywhere. Paths were neatly cut into the garden to make an enjoyable walking experience for the royal family.

Curiously, a young man with an out of date rifle stood next to an ivy covered section of the palace wall. Sam's group rushed him. The younger man fumbled with the rifle, took one shot but he missed and the biggest pirates were on him, tackling him to the ground. Two of them withdrew their cutlasses and angled them at the kid's face.

"What are you doing boy?" one of the bald pirates screamed. "Think you can kill us with that old piece of junk?"

"No. No, sir," the young soldier said.

The kid couldn't be older than sixteen. He wore a fancy red and grey uniform with a feathered hat.

"Well you're a bad shot," one of the pirates with the grenades said. "Are you actually guarding the garden?"

"No. I am a cadet. I am watching…"

"Watching what?" Sam yelled in his face.

The boy hesitated. "The garden... I mean. Please don't kill me, there is an entrance here."

"What entrance?" Thomas asked.

The boy pointed behind him to a patch of misplaced ivy on the wall behind him.

"That's a good man," Sam said. "Run home and be thankful we didn't run you through!"

The boy needed no further instruction. He jumped up and sprinted through the garden.

"Should I hit him?" The long haired man asked, holding up his rifle.

"Nah," Sam said. "I think he learned his lesson. Besides, we got what we wanted from him."

The pirate looked disappointed, but lowered his rifle.

"Let him tell his cowardly story," Sam said, pressing his hand into the ivy. "It's a door. The kid wasn't lying." He tore away some of the ivy and frantically searched for the handle or release.

"I can blow this thing down," the second bald pirate said, withdrawing a glass grenade.

"If need be," Sam said. "Just hold on."

Massive gun fire and grenade explosions echoed from the front of the palace, keeping the pirates' heads swiveling in case a soldier spotted them.

"Hurry Captain," the long haired man said. "They'll surely find us soon."

"Hang on," Sam yelled. "I am looking as quickly as possible! Ha! I found it!"

He shifted his weight and pushed on a large lever at the bottom of the hidden door. The secret entrance gave a sucking sound indicating it had been sealed for quite some time. As Sam turned to wave his men inside, a single shot rang out from a window above. It struck one of the bald pirates in the chest, sending him hard to the ground. The pirate was dead within a second of hitting the ground.

The other bald pirate, the angrier of the two, aimed his cannon and began firing at every window in view. Huge chunks of black mortar and stone exploded with every shot.

"Inside," Sam ordered. "Get inside now!"

Sam was the first one in, followed by Thomas, then the others, but it took no little encouragement from Sam before the bald pirate stopped firing and joined them inside.

The five of them stood in an arch shaped stone tunnel with a damp dirt floor. The dark corridor was lit by gas lamps so weak the men could barely see each other.

"This is it?" Thomas asked, his grenade launcher raised and ready.

"Yes," Sam answered. "We made it. Now it is time to wreck this place and find Cynthia, and Maier."

19
THE ALCHEMY ROOM

As the men moved into the tunnel, they were all shaken by their comrade's sudden death. While pure survival instinct pumped through Thomas, it appeared the four pirates were so angry they intended to kill every living creature in the palace. They cursed and grumbled with their guns at the ready and Thomas was afraid their noise would give away their position.

They walked on until they arrived at a thick wood-paneled door with iron slats running across it. Surprisingly, it was unlocked. Just beyond the door was a steep, narrow staircase leading up. Sam stopped his team.

"I'm going to take a look. If something happens to me, Thomas here is in charge."

Sam ascended the stairs with his gun forward. Thomas leaned against the wall. The pirates didn't say a word, only their huffing, animalistic breath echoed off the walls. Barely a minute went by when Sam's soft footfalls came back down the stairs.

"Alright, come on. You're not going to believe this," he said with a smile.

Upon reaching the top, they were met with the epitome of magnificence. A huge, high ceilinged banquet hall was in front of them with a series of fine dining tables stretching the length of the room. Oil paintings of scenes from the various Lemurian territories covered the walls and statuary from every culture imaginable outlined the room.

Thomas and the pirates ambled through the room with their weapons fixed on the two exits on the far side. Thomas forced himself to focus on the mission instead of indulging in a study of the museum-like palace. They checked the exits but they were alone. Apparently the battle outside had garnered every guard's attention just as Sam planned.

The next room trumped the dining hall with an unimaginable show of wealth and beauty. Everything was crafted of fine marble. A green marble floor and columns outlined a huge, circular lobby with giant murals painted on the vaulted ceiling. There were many exits surrounding the space, leaving the men exposed again. With no way to cover all of the doors, they wheeled around with guns raised like paranoid hunters, moving from column to column for cover.

Loud, quick footsteps echoed through the room. Someone was coming, but they were not sure from which direction. Sam waved his good hand in the air to signal his men to stop, making sure they were as hidden as possible. The footsteps grew closer until four Lemurian guards in ceremonial dress came into view. They escorted a young woman in a formal, pale blue dress and a gaudy white hat with the brim curled upwards.

Thomas could just see Sam's back hunkered down behind a column, but he saw Sam fishing for something in his coat pocket. Then Thomas caught a flash of movement as Sam threw something small. It clicked loudly as it bounced once and then rolled toward the group.

Two of the guards spun, firing blindly with their fancy rifles, but they were only able to get off a few rounds before the small grenade exploded. While this grenade was the same size as the one Sam had revealed at The Seychelles Islands bar, Thomas could tell by the sound that this one was a hybrid concussion and fragmentation grenade.

The entire group was blown off their feet by the explosion. The woman's hat flew high in the air as she was thrown back. Sam jumped out from behind the column with Thomas and the pirates on his heels. He went straight for the reeling guards who were bleeding profusely from the explosive's fragments.

The pirates shoved their guns into the chests of the conscious guards and everyone started screaming. There was no way anyone could discern who said what because everyone's ears were ringing from the grenade.

Thomas turned to the woman. She was awake, lying on her side with a bloody hand at her head. Thomas ran, sliding to a stop at her side.

"Can you hear me?"

The woman's eyes rolled wildly. Her dress was torn, exposing one pale white leg. Her long, curly blonde hair was splayed across the marble floor. Obviously the blast had rung her bell, but her only other injury appeared to be a laceration on her forearm from a piece of shrapnel. He cradled her face gently and swiveled her head so she was looking at him.

"Can you hear me?" Thomas asked again.

She blinked rapidly, trying to focus. "Who are you?"

"It doesn't matter. We're not here to hurt you."

The bald pirate chuckled as he pressed the barrel of his enormous rifle into a guard's chest. "He might not be, but I'm here to hurt you. You're going to look like spaghetti when I am done with you!"

"Shut up," Thomas shouted.

The bald pirate shot Thomas an angry look, but was quelled by a stern look from Sam who was inspecting the wounded guards.

"Listen," Thomas said stroking the young woman's face. "No one is going to hurt you, but you have to tell me about a woman that was brought here recently. She has chin length curly blonde hair. Do you know who I'm talking about?"

"A woman?" she said, eyes flickering.

"Yes," Thomas said. "Stay with me. Do you know who I am talking about? She was brought here as a prisoner."

"The Canvian?" the woman said drearily. Her eyes rolled again as she threatened to pass out.

"No! Don't faint. You're fine. You just have a little cut on your arm. You'll be fine, just pay attention okay?"

Thomas' quick and inaccurate medical explanation seemed to comfort the woman. She blinked again and looked at him with slightly clearer eyes.

"Yes the Canvian woman," Thomas said. "Have you seen her? Do you know where she is?"

The woman mumbled something incoherent.

"What? You have to tell me or these men might do

something drastic."

The gunfire and cannon shots outside continued, making the palace rumble. The woman turned her head to look at the pirates who held her guards at gunpoint. "I haven't seen her. I think she is in one of the towers."

Thomas leaned closer to her. "Which tower?"

"They always put important prisoners in the tallest one. That way."

She scooted her bleeding arm above her head on the floor, pointing to an arched exit to Thomas' right side. "Please don't kill me."

Thomas smiled. "No one is going to hurt you, just stay here."

"No happy promises for you," the bald pirate barked at the guard.

"What are we supposed to do, Riley?" The long haired pirate asked angrily. "You just want to leave them here so they can tell everyone that comes by where we're going?"

Thomas did not have an answer. He didn't want to hurt the woman. She reminded him of the entire reason that he and Cynthia were in this mess. By her clothes alone he could tell she was a member of the royal court and probable prejudices aside, she seemed innocent.

"Don't kill anyone," Sam said. "These two are already dying and I am sure the others would stop at nothing to find us if we kill the woman. I have a solution."

Sam rose to his feet, sheathed his cutlass and gently reached inside his jacket where he withdrew a thin glass syringe with copper finger holders. The liquid inside was a milky white and the needle was easily four inches long. "This was supposed to be for Maier if we found him. But now it looks like everyone gets to share."

The pirates chuckled at Sam's candidness. He walked over to the woman and knelt next to her. "Don't be scared. This will just put you to sleep for a while."

He grabbed the woman's uninjured arm and jabbed her without much study. She made a pathetic yelp at the prick of the needle. He pushed about a third of the liquid in to her and withdrew the syringe.

"Who's next?" he asked as if making a joke. "Don't worry. You are all going to take a little nap. Before you go to sleep, I hope you have good doctors, because I surely wouldn't want them to bury you alive."

The pirates chuckled again. Thomas just watched in awe as Sam performed like he was on stage. He was actually enjoying this. He went to each conscious guard and cracked another joke as he injected the last man. "For your sake, I hope the others don't have any blood diseases." He leaned in closer to the last guard, "I wouldn't be too sure about the lady, though."

The pirates waited for their captives to fade into a drug induced sleep before they took off up the wide green marble stairs the woman had pointed out. Tall windows adorned the length of the stairwell and the clear morning sky outside was hazy with black smoke from the ongoing fight in the square.

They climbed up and around repeatedly on their way to the tower, but the stairs ended in a room that was more showcase than prison. Thomas stopped in his tracks, amazed at the marvels neatly displayed all around him.

The room served as a safe for highly sophisticated pieces of technology. Each item was protected from the elements in sealed, custom-built glass cases. Thomas couldn't understand why the inventions were displayed like this unless the Duke was some kind of collector. Taking a moment to catch his breath, Thomas walked up to a steam powered jetpack gleaming under a glass dome. Large tubes protruded from two stretched tanks with long cone shaped riveted rockets on the sides. There was another case with mounted firearms, all custom-made prototypes Thomas had never seen before. They were shaped like hammers had been mixed with hand guns. Thomas could have spent days looking at the machines but there were more pressing matters at the moment.

He headed back to the stairs when he caught a glimpse of his own T-7 rifle mounted in a case by the door. Apparently the Duke of Lemuria admired his work. He couldn't help feeling a bit flattered, but more, he wished it had ammunition and fuel.

Behind him, the pirates lingered, tempted by the more exotic weapons. When Sam saw Thomas start up the stairs, he called his men and they quickly followed. Thomas had his head down as he trudged upward and suddenly he collided with someone coming down.

Thomas wobbled, catching himself on the smooth, cool walls of the tower's interior, but the other person–a woman–let out a terrible screech as she fell backward. She looked a bit older than Thomas and she wore a white bonnet and a modest white dress with an apron tied at her waist.

Thomas yanked his hand gun from his holster and pointed it at her. She quickly raised her hands in front of her face as if she could shield herself from a bullet.

"Who are you?" Thomas demanded.

"Catch you a maid did ya?" the long haired pirate said when he reached them.

"Please sir," the woman said. "He's right. He's right. I'm just a maid."

Thomas kept the gun trained on her. "Where are you coming from? What's up there?"

"The alchemy room. Then the solitary room," the maid said quickly.

"Who's up there?"

"The Canvian woman. She's up there she is. In the solitary room."

"And what are we going to do with this one?" Sam asked. "I can't knock her out too."

"She goes with us." Thomas said.

The maid looked horrified. She clasped her face and stared at Thomas as if she'd been sentenced to death.

"Get up," Thomas barked. He heard the agitation in his voice, but it was uncontrollable. The adrenaline that had been pumping through him since they'd left The Blood Countess had turned into a deep paranoia. He could be killed any second and he feared every minute they wasted meant Cynthia would be dead or moved.

The maid cautiously got to her feet so she wouldn't alarm the intimidating men taking her hostage.

"Ladies first," Thomas snapped, holding his hand gun to her back. His other hand flexed around the small grenade launcher at his side.

"So what is this alchemy room?" Thomas asked the maid as they walked.

"It's where the Duke keeps treasures and gifts."

Thomas heard the pirates behind him mutter excitedly at the word treasure. The group trudged on, up the endless stairs, until they reached the alchemy room.

Round, with barred windows set into the walls, this room was more impressive than the weapons room. Though filled with dozens of different sized glass cases like the weapons collection, the items ranged from odd to bizarre and most Thomas couldn't identify. There were gory relics like withered hands of long dead martyrs, several large crystals the size of a man's head, glistening swords and vials, and corked carafes filled with unnaturally colored liquids. Thomas' attention was inexorably drawn to a collection of crystals that gave off odd colors of light as if they carried some kind of mystical energy. He was frustrated to see no labels or descriptions or explanations on any of the cases.

"Some of these things could answer some of the world's mysteries." Thomas said to himself.

"Take what you want," Sam replied.

"There's no time for that," Thomas rebutted. "I'm here for Cynthia. Aren't you?"

"Of course," Sam snapped. "But it wouldn't hurt to get a little extra in the endeavor."

Thomas found himself staring at a specific fist sized rock resting on a velvet pedestal. It seemed to glow with a dull red color.

"You want that?" Sam asked.

"There's no time." Thomas replied.

Sam shot him a disappointed look and walked over to the case. With his substantial arm brace he jerked forward, smashing the case. He reached into the mess with his good hand and plucked out the glowing rock.

"Odd, It's warm," he said, holding it out for Thomas. "Take it. Now you're a pirate."

Thomas reluctantly took the rock and slipped it in his side coat pocket.

"What? I told you it would be quick and easy."

"Begging your pardon," the maid said. "You shouldn't take that. The Duke is quite obsessive about his treasures."

"Shut up, wench," the bald pirate grumbled.

Like an unannounced thunder storm a rapid succession of booms exploded from the far side of the room. The crystal cases shattered as chunks of what had been the tower wall flew in every direction. Thomas saw the maid spin around and slam to the ground. Sam fell straight backward as a healthy portion of glass struck him in the face. Thomas ducked, slamming himself belly first on the floor.

"Is that you Riley?" a familiar voice asked. "You are so much dumber than I thought!"

Isaac Maier. Annoyed, Thomas scrabbled across the floor looking for the other pirates. Sam slipped behind a marble pedestal and was pulling sizeable pieces of glass out of his face. As the dust cleared, Thomas saw the other pirates were lying bloody and motionless where they'd fallen, as was the maid.

Thomas dared a peek around a crystal case. Maier stood at the far end of the room next to a series of stairs that had been cloaked in the natural shadow of the exit.

Without warning, Sam flung his braced arm around his cover and fired off five shots from his Gatling gun. The heavy round shout slammed into the wall behind Maier making sizeable holes and a small cloud of marble dust.

"Is that how you want it Burges? You worthless gimp! I thought I recognized your foul pirate stench." Maier said hatefully, punctuating the reply with another barrage of cannon-like gunfire.

More glass broke and flew all around the group. Almost every display had been hit and shattered to bits. Thomas popped out and let two quick rounds go from his hand gun. Again, nothing seemed to hit Maier.

"Who was that?" Maier demanded. "Riley? It has to be you. It's your normal lousy marksmanship. It doesn't matter. You all only have a few moments to live so pray to whoever you Canvian scumbags pray to. Maybe they'll let you die fast."

Maier let off another volley. Thomas knew he'd never encountered this weapon before. It was rapid firing, with large bullets, and a devastating impact on both stone and flesh.

"You wanted my help and you got it, Riley," Maier yelled. "Just not the way you wanted."

"If you have hurt Cynthia…" Thomas started.

"Yeah, yeah." Maier interrupted. "You will kill me and all of that. I've read it before all the heroic books. The problem is that you're the one pinned down. Either you will make a run for something or I'll sit here until you get up and then I'll cut you in half!"

Thomas knew he was right. He wanted to launch a grenade, but he knew Maier was poised to shoot anything that moved.

"This is it Riley! It is time to die!"

20
Phantoms

The remainder of the glass case Thomas was hiding behind exploded over his head sending razor sharp shards crashing over him. Maier cackled with laughter as he demolished the alchemy room with his unusually powerful rifle. The weapon fired with such speed, Thomas was afraid to peek around his cover or even make a blind shot in fear of giving his exact position away. Sam mumbled curses as he pulled more broken pieces of glass from his body. Thomas was afraid to fire the grenade launcher as the room was just small enough that he might blow himself to bits if the explosives bounced or ricocheted the wrong way.

"See, Riley," Maier yelled between shots. "I'm going to end this! You're the one that invaded my home, drugged and kidnapped me! You are the criminal and now I will get justice!"

He fired three more shots in Thomas' direction, blasting apart large chunks of the wall.

"I hope you aren't dead when I get my hands on you! I want to stick you in a box like you did me! Maybe I'll bury you alive!"

Thomas had known Isaac Maier was unstable to begin with, but now the man was in a rage. Two more shots blasted out, this time striking the base of the case Thomas was using for shelter. The case split apart revealing the upper half of Thomas' balled up body. It was now or never, Thomas couldn't wait for the dust to settle, he had to move or Maier would surely and cut him in half as promised.

Thomas jumped up, firing two quick shots with his hand gun in Maier's direction as he ran for another semi-intact base to hide behind. His bullets didn't their mark but the shots made Maier pause for a fraction of a second. Four, five, six steps in the open were all he needed before he could duck down and grant himself another moment of life.

On his last step he didn't hear Maier's shot but he felt an impact on his hip that took his legs out from under him. Thomas was airborne for a surreal amount of time. He had actually had a moment to realize he was airborne before he landed, skidding through broken crystal, to rest behind a more substantial case.

His first instinct was to not look at his hip. He was afraid his leg would be gone or there would be a gaping hole that would leave him at Maier's twisted mercy. But Thomas' hip and left leg were completely numb so despite his fears, he looked down. The bottom of his long jacket was shredded and blackened as if it had been on fire. The entire pocket was gone and he touched his leg which thankfully was still intact. As he touched his hip, Thomas realized that there was no blood or even a hole in his flesh, just a tingling numbness. Thomas was confused. What had Maier shot him with? He had never heard of a projectile that made its victim numb upon impact.

He had to get into a defensive position fast. Maier would surely be coming at him with a fresh barrage of bullets and insults. But he had to know. Grabbing his tingling leg with both hands, he lugged it in front of him for a quick inspection and slowly realized what had happened.

Sitting in the rubble strewn pathway he'd just darted through, was the fist-sized rock he'd put in his pocket. It was split in half and glowing with a red color. Maier's bullet had miraculously struck Thomas in the pocket with the stolen rock and it had exploded out from the cloth.

Why had Maier not fired again? It had been too long. Thomas knew the crazy old man wouldn't have given up. He wasn't sure if it was the shock of getting shot, the adrenaline blasting through his body, or sheer exhaustion, but Thomas suddenly felt cold and nauseated. He dragged his leg close to his body and inexplicably began to shiver.

"Riley," Maier yelled. "What have you done?"

Thomas didn't want to say anything. It felt like he was going to throw up any second now.

"Thomas," Sam said from behind him. "What the hell is going on?"

246

Thomas didn't understand why everyone was asking him questions. He shut his eyes tightly against the pain as his stomach threatened to implode. Something was violently wrong. He shivered as his body temperature dropped radically.

"What is this Thomas?" Sam asked again.

Thomas, annoyed with everyone yelling at him, opened his mouth to tell them both to shut up, but as he did a rush of unnaturally cold air chilled his tongue. It wasn't his body getting colder–it was the temperature in the room that had dropped. Despite his pain, Thomas opened his watery eyes.

Thomas immediately noticed he could see his breath in the air. Next, and more startling, was the crowd of people surrounding him. He looked around the room, thinking he was hallucinating, but the entire room was packed with people. Men, women, and children of all sizes were jammed shoulder to shoulder in the room, all with expressionless faces.

"You've done something very bad, Riley," Maier said with fear in his voice. "It takes a quack like you to make something like this happen!"

Maier pushed his way through the mass of people filling the decimated alchemy room. They didn't resist him, nor did they protest, as he angrily shoved them out of his way. He crunched over broken glass and through the crowd, passing Thomas and Sam in a quick trot.

"This is your can of worms, Riley," Maier yelled as he descended the stairs.

Thomas' stomach gurgled in pain, but he did his best to ignore it now in light of this miracle. None of the crowd was dressed in the current fashion. All of them wore simple clothes of an earlier era. Thomas looked up at the woman nearest to him. She was thin with unkempt shoulder length blond hair.

"Who are you?" Thomas asked.

The woman slowly looked down at him. Her face was sallow and her eyes were shadowed by dark circles. Her big pale blue eyes seemed to look right through him.

"It's so hot," she said in a monotone. "Who are you?"

Thomas noticed the woman's lips were severely cracked.

"My name is Thomas. How did you get here?"

The woman's head turned to the side. "I think I am dreaming."

Thomas noticed there was no cloud of heat and moisture from her mouth as she spoke. That could only mean she wasn't breathing.

"Thomas," Sam called out. "Who are you talking to? What's going on?"

"I have no idea," Thomas replied, frustrated.

He focused on his tingling leg, gently putting weight on it. Thankfully some of the feeling had returned. Grunting with the effort, Thomas used his hands and the ledge of the case, hoisting himself to his feet. He was now face to face with the woman and the entire crowd around him. They all continued standing there, some wobbling a bit, but no one was speaking or walking. This entire crowd of drugged zombies had appeared out of thin air.

"Where do you live?" Thomas asked the woman in a strained voice.

The woman took several seconds to answer. "I live in Lemuria City. I don't want to die."

"What?"

He hunched over, feeling ridiculous and clutching his stomach as it turned cartwheels inside of him.

"There were bombs when I fell asleep," the woman said.

"There are no bombs." Thomas assured her.

"Well there were."

"I am sorry. I would love to stay and chat and find out how you got here, but I have a friend in need and I need to tend to her."

Thomas took a cautious step forward, brushing against the woman's thin arm as he moved. Her ice cold skin stopped him.

"Sam? Can you walk?"

"Yeah. My face is just messed up."

"We are going to get Cynthia. Don't pay attention to these…people. Maier was right, something is very wrong."

Thomas heard Sam stand up, his feet crunching in the broken glass.

"Thom? Where did these people come from?"

"I have no idea."

"Thom?" Sam asked again. "There is a guy back here with no eyes."

"Just ignore them and keep walking."

"That's easier said than done," Sam argued.

Thomas made it through the crowd and stood on the stairs surveying the odd situation. They remained still, staring at each other or off into space. Sam pushed the cold people out of the way as he moved to join Thomas on the stairs. His wide eyes nervously darted around the room.

"I've seen a lot of things, Thom. But I've never seen anything like this. How did this happen? Who are these people and how did they appear out of nowhere?"

"I have a vague idea. I truly wish I could tell you, but we don't have time to find out for sure."

"The others are dead? You're sure?" Thomas asked.

"The ones that came with us... yes. But I can't tell you about the maid."

"If she isn't dead, she will be," Thomas answered. "I think she might have been bait anyway."

Sam nodded and was obviously trying to shake off the strange events that had just happened. Thomas took the initiative, starting up the next flight of wide marble stairs. Sam looked bad. His face was sliced in at least a dozen places making him look more like a botched paper doll than a human. Fearful of what they had just witnessed and nervous about what strange occurrence might come next, Thomas and Sam walked up the stairs as quickly as they could without falling over from fatigue.

"Thom? Were those people dead?"

"I don't know. One woman told me she was dreaming, but that means nothing."

"Yeah," Sam said hesitantly. "That was frightening."

Thomas agreed but he didn't want to talk about the weird crowd packed into the room below. After climbing another circular flight of pristine green marble stairs, they arrived at a thick, heavy wooden door covered with extra iron supports from top to bottom. A large plank of wood was lowered into brass fittings, locking it from the outside.

Thomas pressed his face to the door. "Cynthia? It's Thomas! Can you hear me? Are you in there?"

There were soft footsteps on the other side of the door. "What is your middle name?" Cynthia's voice asked.

"Grahame," Thomas replied.

"Get me out of here," Cynthia yelled.

Thomas lifted the wooden crossbar that locked the door and pulled on the handle. Cynthia was barely a foot away from the door. Without hesitation, she rushed forward and threw her arms around Thomas.

"Oh my god, Thom! They did it! They extracted Lillian from me. Maier was successful."

"Are you alright?" Thomas asked.

"Of course. A little tired, but nothing a little revenge can't fix. Somehow, Maier knows exactly how to use the Lifeblood!"

Cynthia was wearing a bland tunic that resembled a potato sack more than an actual prison uniform. Either way she looked awful. Her hair was a mess and her lack of make up made her look much older.

"I knew it was you when I heard the cannons firing. Are you still on The Blood Countess?"

Thomas nodded, taking a few steps into Cynthia's cell.

"The main thing is that you are alright," Thomas said.

"Oh my! Sam?" She said craning her neck around Thomas. "What has happened to you?"

Sam hobbled in with his bloody face and his large arm brace that Cynthia had never seen. She ran to him, but only gave him a light hug, as if she feared too much pressure would injure him further.

"I'll be fine," Sam coughed. "We ran into Maier downstairs. He escaped."

"I heard the gun shots."

She looked at Thomas and Sam who both appeared to be seconds away from passing out of exhaustion. "Can we get out of here or what? Can you guys make it?"

Thomas and Sam just looked at her strangely for a second.

"What?" Cynthia asked.

"There is something weird going on below us," Thomas said.

"It is kind of hard to explain," Sam chimed in.

"We'll try."

Thomas sighed and looked at the floor. "In the firefight something odd happened. We opened something, a door perhaps, something beyond my comprehension."

"Look," Sam interrupted. "Somehow about fifty people that look like corpses magically appeared out of thin air and we don't know any more. Good enough?"

Cynthia cracked a smile as if she thought he was joking.

"He's serious," Thomas said solemnly.

Cynthia's smile quickly faded. "Are they dangerous?"

"I don't think so," Thomas answered. "They just look weird and they have packed the room below like cattle."

Sam sighed. "We have to go. The shots from outside are getting further apart. That's a bad sign."

"Wait," Cynthia exclaimed. "Lillian! Maier took Lillian from me. He extracted her and he claims to have caught her in a vial that he is giving to the Duke. I'm sorry, since he performed the lifeblood, I have been feeling foggy."

"When did he do it?" Thomas asked.

"Yesterday."

Thomas flipped his handgun around and handed it to Cynthia. "Take this; I'm sure you will need it."

Cynthia gripped the gun and her smile returned to her face. Despite what she had been through since the original battle with the Blood Countess, she seemed her usually chipper self. She was the unsinkable Cynthia Basset and she was living up to the moniker.

"We have to get her back or all of this was for nothing," Cynthia said.

"We came here for you," Sam said.

"I won't leave without her," Cynthia said sternly.

The men looked at each other grimly.

"I'll go with you," Thomas said.

"Don't think I am going to let you go get killed alone," Sam added.

Cynthia was the first one out of the door. Since she'd been a prisoner, she had more energy than Thomas and Sam put together. They had all been through a lot, but Cynthia's determination to retrieve Lillian's soul fueled the men's beaten bodies. She hurried down the marble stairs with Thomas and Sam in tow.

"So what exactly am I going to see?" Cynthia asked, stopping in her tracks, her mouth dropping open. "How did this happen? Who are these people? They look horrible!"

"I don't know. I'll try to explain later," Thomas answered. "Just push your way through them, they'll just stand there."

Cynthia stood in shock staring at the crowd of people in the demolished room.

"Fine," Thomas said. "Follow me."

Thomas stepped in front of her and as gently as he could, he walked through the mass. Cynthia was obviously taken aback by the sight. "Are they dead? It's so cold. I don't understand."

"Try to ignore them," Sam said from behind.

"Oh," Cynthia cried out in horror. "There's blood on the floor." She paused. "Thomas! There is a woman with half a head on the floor! Oh God, I think I know her!"

"Cyn, just keep it together. Maier shot her trying to shoot me."

After squeezing through the crowd and listening to Cynthia's squeamish noises, they descended the stairs at the other end of the room. Once the trio got away, the temperature became normal.

Cynthia grabbed Thomas' shoulder. "Thomas that was awful. I've never seen anything like that before."

"Me neither."

A large blast rocked the palace. The stairs shook and they paused for a moment to make sure the tower was not about to crumble around them.

Sam looked at the ceiling. "That's a good sign. It means

252

someone is still fighting."

When they reached the bottom of the stairs, they entered green marble lobby where Thomas and his pirate team had ambushed the guards and the noble woman. A group of five soldiers with Mohawk centurion helmets was inspecting the fallen guards. They must have heard Thomas, Sam, and Cynthia, because three of them were already pointing their weapons in their direction.

Quickly, Thomas body checked Cynthia, pressing her into the wall and away from the soldiers' view. The soldiers fired immediately. Loud bursts blasted from their weapons, the impact sent chunks of marble flying in all directions. Sam slid to the side and squeezed the trigger on his Gatling gun. It clattered away like a mini cannon, blasting shot after shot, pounding the floor near the soldiers and kicking up massive amounts of debris. He knew he had two direct hits because he saw the men fly back off of their feet.

Sam continued to fire, until the cloud of powdered marble completely obscured that portion of the room. No one fired back from the cloud. The only sign of life was the groans of two different voices. Sam trotted toward the cloud with his finger tickling the trigger of his gun.

Thomas peered out, releasing Cynthia from the wall.

"Thanks," she said with a touch of sarcasm.

Sam chuckled arrogantly. "I got 'em all. A few poor souls are still alive, but they don't look so good."

He kicked the guns out of reach just to be safe. With Cynthia behind him, Thomas approached with his grenade launcher at the ready.

"This is a nasty mess," Cynthia said with a sour face.

Sam held his brace mounted gun in the air. "Yeah, I like this gun. It does hurt when it fires though."

"You'll heal," Thomas quipped.

"They've removed the royal woman and the two guards we drugged earlier," Sam informed them.

"What woman were you talking about?" Cynthia asked.

Sam looked back at Thomas and Cynthia. "On our way up

253

we came across a woman who was obviously part of the royal court. Sam hit her group with a concussion grenade. We had to drug her and the survivors. I'm not sure who she was but–"

"AN EVEN TRADE," a robust voice echoed through marble lobby.

The three of them spun in all directions with their guns pointed forward looking for the source of the voice. Another series of cannon fire erupted from outside the palace.

"Mister Riley, you have caused quite enough problems," the voice said. "It's time for this to end."

Dozens of centurion dressed soldiers poured into the lobby from every arched entrance. Thomas immediately fired his grenade launcher into the first batch of men blasting several of them across the floor. Cynthia and Sam also responded by firing, but more centurions continued to rush in, stepping over their comrade's bodies to get a better position inside. Thomas fired again missing the center of the group he was aiming for. The grenade impacted with the wall above them blowing a large chuck out of the pristine marble and sending a sizeable piece crashing on the floor.

The centurions were the Duke's elite guards. They were the highest trained soldiers in the Lemurian Army and the most merciless as well. Soon Thomas' group would be overwhelmed, there were simply too many of them.

A hissing pressurized blast came from Thomas's left side. A large black object came hurling through the air. A thick net slammed into Cynthia, taking her off of her feet and sending her sliding across the smooth floor. She struggled against it but the more she moved, the more she became entangled.

"Cease fire," the booming voice yelled.

A group of centurions standing in a circular formation next to a far entrance separated, revealing Isaac Maier, still holding his large rifle. A tall, impeccably dressed man with long hair was with him.

The tall man stepped forward. He wore a starched black uniform with a heavy jacket trimmed with a high collar that rose to his jaw line. A top hat emphasized his height and his black knee boots were polished to a mirror gloss.

"Allow me to introduce myself," he said in regal tones. "I am Duke Ferdinand, ruler of the Lemurian Territories. It's a great honor to meet you Mister Riley, the tied up Miss Basset and…the vagabond criminal that you brought along, but I am afraid this is where your little party ends."

21
THE RUSE

The centurion soldiers quickly surrounded Thomas, Sam and Cynthia. The intimidating group dressed in red and black armor and ornate helmets with black horse hair fashioned in a Mohawk sprouting from the top.

Cynthia struggled against the black rope net they fired on her and she appeared to be unharmed for the moment. Thomas still had his grenade launcher at his side and Sam pointed his Gatling gun arm forward. There were simply too many enemy soldiers to win the battle. Obviously Duke Ferdinand had ordered them not to kill them or none of them would have had a chance.

"You two have been a thorn in my side for a long time," Duke Ferdinand said. "Honestly, I've tried to get my hands on one or both of you for years. Finally, you decide to come to me. The best part is that you simply walked into my palace. Did you really think you could make such a daring attack and actually get away with it?"

Thomas looked the Duke in the eyes. He looked younger than Thomas remembered from the pictures published by the West Canvian newspapers. Duke Ferdinand was a man of arrogance who must have spent an ungodly amount of time on grooming himself. He held himself pristine and proper in every way, even as his palace was being attacked by a rogue pirate ship.

"That's fine, stay silent. It doesn't matter," Duke Ferdinand said. "The war that started with my father will end as of today. There will be no bargaining this time. No exchange of prisoners. I have a wonderful deal to offer you.

"Miss Basset will be the one getting tortured and Mister Riley will provide the information. The less you tell me, the more she will have to go through. So you can spare her of any pain by your full cooperation. Of course we will keep her here to discourage any further bombings, but she will at least get to live."

Still tangled in the net, two centurions grabbed Cynthia by her arms and lifted her to her feet. Thomas and Sam both turned toward them, each contemplating blowing them away.

"Don't be hasty," Duke Ferdinand said in an admonishing tone. "You surely don't want everyone to die do you?"

"By the way, what is your name sewer rat?" Duke Ferdinand asked Sam.

Sam shot the Duke a nasty look. "Sam Burges," he said angrily.

Duke Ferdinand smiled widely. "Oh, you were part of Captain Swan's lot then. That makes perfect sense. The good Captain's living the good life now. Had you been more loyal, perhaps you would be in the same position."

Duke Ferdinand took a step forward and looked up at a painting on the vaulted ceiling. "Oh, wait a minute. Did you only come for Miss Basset? Now that's the funniest thing I've heard all day."

The Duke let loose a horrendous, thoroughly un-royal cackle. "I'll make something especially painful for you, pirate. You're the one who tried to blow my youngest daughter up earlier aren't you? She told me a man with a metal arm is the one who tried to kill her."

"Duke Ferdinand," Cynthia said from beneath the net. "We just came here to get Lillian Beaufort's soul out of me. I have already told you this. We just came to extract her and we simply were caught up in all of this. We didn't mean to cause any harm."

Duke Ferdinand walked out in the center of the lobby stepping over bodies of his fallen soldiers. "You make weapons that kill my people Miss Basset. There's nothing innocent about anything you do! You came here to kidnap Doctor Maier. Oh that sounds not at all innocent to me! You're a war criminal Miss Basset! The more my people suffer, the more money you make! Keep talking! I may just change my mind about letting you live."

Cynthia's plea did nothing but make him angrier, though she'd hoped since Duke Ferdinand's daughter lived, he might have some sympathy if she reiterated their original goal.

The Duke paced around the grand lobby, his shoulder length brown hair flopping against his high jacket collar as he walked. Suddenly he stopped in his tracks and glared at Cynthia. "I'm getting all worked up over nothing."

He slipped his thumb through a thin gold chain around his neck and pulled a small crystal vial out from under his shirt. He twisted the vial between his thumb and forefinger.

"See, I have Miss Beaufort right here." Duke Ferdinand held the vial out, taunting Cynthia with it. "I can crush Duke William with this. I will control West Canvia by Duke William's heartstrings. And any of you who escape my armies will be living in the caves and eating each other to survive."

The palace rumbled again, but this time it was wasn't cannon fire that rocked the building. A warmer tone accompanied by the buzz of propellers vibrated the hall and its large windows. Sam's eyes darted around the room, full of concern. A few seconds later, they saw The Blood Countess rising into the air. The dirigible was intact but the entire top deck was billowing heavy black smoke.

Duke Ferdinand glanced over his shoulder. "So much for 'all for one, one for all', eh? It seems your pirate family has left you for dead my good man."

Sam's eyes closed as if he knew he was doomed. He'd taken too long and the ship had obviously been battered. They made the choice to escape with their lives while they could. Sam sighed, knowing he would have made the same decision.

"When they get past the city limits, I have two squads of fighters poised to take that piece of junk you call a ship to the ground," Duke Ferdinand said smugly.

Sam turned to Thomas. "Sorry, mate."

Thomas frowned, confused. "What?"

Without answering, Sam turned to Duke Ferdinand. "Fine, I surrender myself to your mercy and your service. As an experienced shipman."

Cynthia's head turned. "Sam?"

"What are you doing?" Thomas added.

"I'm going to live," Sam said angrily "Which is more than I can say for you."

"After all of this, you're going to trade everything you and your men have fought for?" Thomas asked, amazed and shocked.

"Yes. I'm a pirate. This is how you survive in this wicked world. You should have learned that after two days of being on my ship, Thomas."

"I can't believe this," Thomas said. "You really are nothing but a lowlife. You have no morals, no beliefs, no heart whatsoever. What about the things you said about Cynthia. Why did you even begin this mission?"

Sam looked at Thomas, his eyes sparking with anger. "It was easy. If things didn't work out, I was sure that I could help Duke Ferdinand here with a number of things. Who doesn't need an experienced shipman with knowledge of Canvian airspace, secret bases and ammunition depots?

"So I didn't get the girl, there are plenty of other girls. Life has to go on for those smart enough to survive."

Thomas' head was spinning. He could feel the veins in his neck bulging. He blinked repeatedly, hoping the next time he opened his eyes everything would be different. Nothing changed and he instantly hated Sam more than Duke Ferdinand and Isaac Maier combined.

Duke Ferdinand smiled, clapping his hands slowly. He loved nothing more than watching his enemies bicker with each other. "You may get some leniency after all, pirate. Disarm immediately and I will consider letting you live."

Sam's head sunk and he looked at his arm brace. With his good arm, he began unscrewing the flat bolts that held it together.

"I will kill you," Thomas snarled. "No matter what, I will find a way to kill you."

Sam looked up at Thomas. "But you will be dead."

Cynthia was still standing under the net, her mouth open and her face wet with tears. She didn't know what to say. She'd never been completely sure of her feelings for Sam, but she'd wanted her attraction to him to be real. This betrayal was unfathomable.

Sam continued to unbolt the brace from his limp arm. He pointed it upward to get the strap off of his shoulder. Thomas saw red, not just at the edges, but coloring his entire field of vision. He was so livid he didn't care about consequence. Just as he was going to pounce on Sam, the man's brace jolted with a loud pop that echoed through the marble lobby.

A bright, magnesium-red trail snaked in the wake of a projectile flying from a tube on the bottom of Sam's brace. The thing produced an extraordinary amount of smoke as it smashed through a large window and toward The Blood Countess which was nearly out of sight. The odd shell exploded at a low altitude making a huge red ring of smoke that decorated the sky as a perfectly round circle.

Thomas was stunned. He'd been half a second away from tackling and killing Sam with his bare hands. But now…Sam had fired something from the brace Thomas had never installed.

"Sorry," Sam yelled desperately. "Sorry! It just went off. Typical Canvian technology. I'm taking it off."

The centurions had stepped away from Sam, knowing they could apprehend him without incident if the Duke so ordered.

In an instant, Sam lowered his arm brace and pulled the trigger. The two centurions attending Cynthia were struck in the chest and flung backwards.

Thomas didn't think about what had just happened or why. He simply recognized the trickery and the opportunity. He sprinted toward Cynthia who was temporarily unguarded and grabbed the net. With all his strength, he dragged her back toward the stairs. He didn't know what he was doing, but it was the only spot in the entire room not covered by centurions. Within a few strides, she'd slipped out of the net.

Sam continued to fire at the centurions. His bullets did not do much damage to their heavy armor but he was able to knock them down with a successful shot. Thomas and Cynthia dashed up the stairs but Thomas took a second to spin around and fire off a grenade toward the room. It caused precisely the effect that he wanted, blowing a hole in the side wall, causing more confusion and panic. Sam walked backwards using his gun to keep the nearest soldiers away from him as he moved.

The centurions were not firing their canister rifles, but approaching him with their long swords. Duke Ferdinand must have told them that under no circumstances was anyone to be killed without his permission.

"Cyn," Thomas yelled up the stairs. "Run back up to the prison room where you were! Hurry!"

He slapped a copper grenade into the launcher and fired another round directly at Duke Ferdinand. In a scene of loyalty Thomas would never forget, no less than five centurions threw themselves in front of the duke. The grenade's impact scattered parts of them all around their leader but Duke Ferdinand was only pushed to the ground by the blast. By the time Thomas was ready to fire again, Duke Ferdinand was screaming, "Kill them all! At all costs kill them all."

Cynthia appeared at Thomas' side. He didn't have time to say anything, but he tried to shoot her a disapproving look before launching his next grenade.

"If I'm dying, I'm dying here with you," she stated.

Without another word, she dashed down a few stairs until she reached one of the fallen centurion's canister rifles. She slid belly first to avoid any centurion fire and snatched up the gun in one fluid motion.

The entire group of fifty centurions rushed Sam like an angry mob. He squeezed the trigger of his Gatling gun and after five quick rounds the gun stopped firing but the barrel continued to spin. Out of ammunition, he reached into his boot and withdrew a dagger, the only weapon he had left.

Cynthia squeezed off three rounds with the canister rifle downing one man with a shot to the neck. The mob of centurions was ten feet from trampling Sam when the entire palace shook and rumbled with alarming force. Something blotted out the sunlight and the far side of the lobby went as dark as if someone had covered the tall windows with black cloth. Pieces of the walls and glass from the windows imploded inside the room as if a divine fist had smashed through the roof of the palace.

Thomas hid his face inside his elbow, but kept peeking out. Even if he lost his eyes, he had to know what was happening. The blackness seemed to grow, disintegrating more of the palace with each millisecond. It wasn't until Thomas fell back on the marble stairs that he realized the truth. It wasn't some new explosive weapon or cannon fire from above. The Blood Countess had actually rammed the palace. Sam's faked misfire was in fact a desperate signal to the men in his ship that he was alive and in danger.

The black ship barreled through the structure sending huge pieces of the beautifully painted roof crashing in on everyone. The Blood Countess spent only a few seconds cutting through the palace, but the destruction was so massive and the tactic so unexpected it had the effect of a giant bomb strike.

The centurions scattered, all of them trying to find some refuge amongst the chaos. Thomas took a few steps down the stairs, but the dust, debris, and the black smoke from The Blood Countess filled the entire room, making visibility zero. Then The Blood Countess was gone, exiting out of the other side of the palace and dim sunlight pierced the black fog surrounding him.

"Cyn," Thomas yelled. "Cynthia!"

The walls were still cracking and the colossal noise from the ship's hull smashing through marble had deafened everyone. Thomas pointed the grenade launcher forward, though it was unlikely he'd see anything to fire upon.

Frustrated and desperate, Thomas called out again, "Cynthia! Sam! I'm by the stairs."

No answer came, so Thomas ventured into the rubble of the low roofless lobby. He withdrew his cutlass, knowing the grenade launcher would do him no good at close range. Coughing and gagging as he went, Thomas tripped over huge planks of sharp wood beams, plaster chucks twice his size, and the wet, fleshy bodies of the unfortunate men who had been snuffed out by the falling palace ceiling.

"Cynthia," Thomas choked. "Wh-where are you?"

He didn't know why, but Thomas was sure Cynthia was had survived the collapsing ceiling. At least he refused to accept that she might be dead.

With his arms stretched forward, he lifted his knees high to avoid tripping over the wreckage. Thomas held his cutlass forward walking on with no clear vision of where he was actually going. A wet hand grabbed Thomas' leg as he walked by and without hesitation he spun in the fog of the debris, leveling his cutlass at the groper.

"Cyn? Sam? Who is that? State your name," Thomas ordered.

"Your humbled enemy," The feeble voice replied.

Thomas lowered the point of the cutlass closer to the man lying on the floor. "Who are you?"

"It's Duke Ferdinand," the duke groaned.

"What can you say in the next ten seconds that will prevent me from slicing you into a hundred pieces?"

"The vial. I have it and it's intact. I will bargain with you. I give you your Duke's daughter's soul and you leave me without harm."

Thomas paused, running the scenarios in his mind.

"Why wouldn't I just kill you and take the vial?"

"Because you are a man of honor."

Thomas decided to scare Duke Ferdinand. He gently pressed the end of his cutlass against what he thought was the man's chest.

"Give me the vial now," Thomas said, pressing the point of the cutlass harder against the duke.

Duke Ferdinand reached around his neck and pulled snapping the thin gold chain. Thomas waved his free hand in an attempt to clear the dust-filled air, but it did little good. He could tell the man was pinned down by a piece of his own palace, but Thomas wanted to know how severely Duke Ferdinand was injured.

Moans of pain from the wounded and dying centurions rang out randomly all around Thomas. He was shocked to be the only man that was not injured from the collapse, but he attributed it to the fact that The Blood Countess had not flown over the stairwell.

With the point of his cutlass firmly against Duke Ferdinand's body, Thomas bent down and snatched the vial and gold chain from the Duke's clammy hand. He stuffed it into the inside pocket of his tattered coat and buttoned it making sure it would only escape him if he was killed.

Duke Ferdinand sighed. "You're going to kill me now aren't you?"

"For some reason I'm not. I could end the war with your death. I could also make you a martyr. I am not going to take that risk. Maybe one day you will consider having the same mercy as I am showing you."

A gentle wind blowing in from the gaping hole in the roof began to clear away the thick dust, sweeping it out and giving Thomas a much clearer view of the carnage surrounding him. Massive beams and stones lay in haphazard piles. All but two of the columns had collapsed, taking nearby walls down with them. Two walls of the palace were so completely leveled Thomas could see the green courtyards on either side of the room. One was devoid of people, but the side that led to the front of the palace was full of bodies and people staggering about.

The centerpiece of the Duke's country had been reduced to ruins in a matter of seconds, but somehow The Blood Countess was still airborne. Thomas could hear the massive propellers in the distance accompanied by small arms fire as soldiers on the ground continued shooting, hoping for a lucky hit.

As the air continued to clear, Thomas got a better look at Duke Ferdinand. His legs had been gruesomely broken by a roof beam, he was sweating and pasty, and there was little hope of survival. Thomas wouldn't deliver the final blow, but if the Duke died because of the wreckage, Thomas would not lament leaving him trapped.

Without another word, Thomas turned away, carefully stepping onto one of the fallen columns to get a better vantage of the wreckage. He hoped for a glimpse of Cynthia or Sam.

"Cynthia! Cynthia Basset! Sam!"

He was only answered by wounded centurions calling for help. Thomas' head swiveled around looking for any sign of his friends, but still he saw nothing but red centurion armor protruding from the rubble. Soon a fresh group of Lemurian soldiers would be upon him and all would be lost. They would take him prisoner, Lillian's soul would be seized and Cynthia and Sam would be prisoners if they were not already dead.

"Riley," a strained, angry old voice yelled.

Thomas spun around one hundred eighty degrees.

"Is this what you're looking for?" The crusty voice asked.

Beyond the rubble, Isaac Maier stood in the small patch of grass that outlined the cobblestone square where The Blood Countess had originally landed. He had his large rifle connected pointed at Cynthia, who seemed to need the support of his free arm. She wobbled on her feet and she was covered in large patches of blood, turning her blonde hair a matted, crusty brown.

Thomas rushed forward, clumsily tripping over the remains of the palace lobby. He leaped over the two feet of rubble that was once the outer wall and held his cutlass forward.

22
THE SPOILS OF WAR

"You've escaped death too many times Maier," Thomas roared. "This time I swear you won't escape."

Somehow Maier had gotten out of the destruction with only a sizable gash on his semi-bald head and even his large steam-powered gun seemed to be intact and functioning. He looked up at Thomas, his thin lips stretched in a grin.

"I think I have the better hand this time, Riley."

Thomas took a step closer and Cynthia reacted, going into a fit of rage, summoning some adrenaline-fueled strength from her beaten body. She punched Maier in the face and grabbed one of the tubes that ran from the rifle to his steam generator. Maier swung the rifle and struck her in the head, dropping her to the ground in one blow. Thomas took a few more steps forward.

"Stop there, Riley. I'm going to enjoy this!"

"You can shoot me, just let her run. Just let her go and you can use me as target practice."

Maier cackled. "She can't even stand, Riley! Besides, why would I let anyone go? You're both going to die. I'm just going to make sure that you both are humiliated before you go."

Cynthia scrambled to her knees with another rush of survival instinct induced fury. She gripped Maier's steam generating backpack and pulled him to the ground. The old man collapsed, landing hard on his backpack. He rolled around on his stomach and Cynthia pounced, clawing at Maier's face. She went for his eyes, but she wasn't able to accomplish her goal before Maier speared Cynthia in the stomach with the barrel of the rifle. Her mouth opened wide and her eyes seemed to bulge in pain as she doubled over face first into the grass.

"What do you think you are going to do, woman?" Maier yelled as he clumsily regained his feet. "You have no chance!

The centurions will surely kill you anyway. There is no hope!"

Maier's head snapped up, a wisp of stringy white hair sticking to his bloody forehead. Thomas' hands were bone white on the grip of his cutlass. Cynthia rolled on the ground coughing and sputtering, trying to catch the breath Maier had knocked out of her.

"I'll offer you a bit of mercy," Maier said smugly. "You can watch me shoot Miss Basset here or you can spare yourself that sight and fall on your own sword right now. The choice is yours. She dies first unless you take the situation in your hands."

Thomas took three quick steps forward and Maier reached down, grabbing a fist full of Cynthia's hair and pulling her to her feet. Jamming the end of the rifle against her temple, he smiled angrily.

"Yes! Yes, Riley! One more step and you can watch her head disappear!"

Thomas could see The Blood Countess circling around in the sky behind Maier, the black smoke still pouring off its deck and filling the sky like a burning paper airplane. There would be no surprise rescue this time. The ship was too far away and they had no idea who was or wasn't on the ground beneath them.

"Come to me, Thomas," Cynthia gasped. "Just come here and hold me before we die."

Maier sneered down at Cynthia, his small rodent-like teeth showing. "He isn't going to get that chance my dear. Fall on your sword, Riley!"

Thomas was baffled. Cynthia had never asked him to hold her for any reason before. She'd never expressed any soft feelings for him in the past. Now, suddenly, at the moment of deaths, she wanted him to hold her? Nothing seemed more opposite of Cynthia's nature.

"Please Thomas," Cynthia yelled. "Please come hold me before we die!"

Through her pain she gave Thomas a look he'd seen thousands of times before when she wanted to show she was disappointed in him. He wasn't sure what the look meant, but Thomas knew one thing, he could always trust Cynthia.

268

Maier huffed impatiently. "I don't care how you want to do it! Make your choice!"

Cynthia's bloody face was still looking at Thomas in the same disappointed fashion, her eyes shifting from Thomas to Maier in a deliberate manner. Then it hit him. If there was ever a moment of eureka, this was Thomas'. It was a gamble but he understood what her look meant.

Thomas darted forward, running all out toward Maier with his cutlass raised high. Maier's face wrinkled, a sneer twisting his mouth. He pulled the trigger on the rifle and let go of Cynthia's hair. The gun only clicked.

Thomas sprinted as fast as he could toward Maier. In the moment Maier needed to realize the gun had not fired he backed up two paces and squeezed the trigger six more times. Each time he pulled the trigger the gun merely clicked and the tubes that connected the gun to the generator screamed like a boiling tea kettle.

Thomas was on him, cutlass poised to slice the old man in half, and then he tossed the cutlass aside and dove forward, tackling Cynthia. The impact lifted her briefly into the air as. With Cynthia under Thomas, she took the brunt of the tackle as both of them slid several feet away on the grass.

The noise from Maier's backpack generator rose higher and higher in pitch as he continued to squeeze the trigger. By the time Thomas and Cynthia had stopped sliding through the grass Maier understood the problem and panicked. He dropped the rifle and frantically tried to slip free of the generator strapped to his back. He got one side off, as the pitch rose so high it exceeded the range of human hearing. A millisecond later, the tanks on Maier's backpack exploded. The blast squashed the top half of Doctor Isaac Maier like a grape between two fingers and the lower half of his body dropped to the ground like a discarded doll.

Thomas and Cynthia covered their heads to protect themselves from any shrapnel but Maier's body had absorbed most of the harmful fragments. Spattered with pieces of their enemy, Thomas rolled off of Cynthia.

"Are you alright?" he asked anxiously.

Her eyes rolled for a moment, but she quickly shook off the shock. "I think I'm okay. It took you long enough to get the hint."

Thomas smiled at Cynthia's old, brisk attitude. "I had no idea at first."

"I didn't know at first either, but when he fell on the backpack, it made a tiny high pitched sound. I saw that his pressure regulator was smashed and the pressure feeder to his gun had been pulled out," she explained.

"So every time he pulled the trigger, more pressure built up, but it had nowhere to go."

"Exactly. I am just glad you finally got the hint."

"You can admonish me later. We need to get out of here," Thomas said standing and pulling Cynthia up by her battered, bloodied arms.

Thomas surveyed the grim courtyard for a way out. Small groups of centurions were running at the far ends of the square in front of the palace attempting to make a perimeter. Soon, no one would be able to escape on foot. The Blood Countess had made another turn and was heading back toward its impact point. Thomas could only assume they were coming back for Sam.

"Sam is dead isn't he?" Cynthia asked.

"I don't know. I couldn't find him in the wreckage."

"If Duke Ferdinand is dead, then Lillian is probably gone as well."

Thomas patted his jacket. "I have the vial in my pocket. Lillian is fine. I left the duke trapped under some rubble."

Thomas helped Cynthia to the ruined wall where at least they would not be in the open if someone recognized them. The sheer chaos of the situation worked in their favor. None of the able bodied men were trying to discern friend from foe, they were simply looking to reestablish order.

The only clear enemy to the centurions was the ominous Blood Countess still rumbling through the sky. The black ship circled and as it swooped back into the square the centurions fired their rifles again. This time, The Blood Countess returned fire with her heavy cannons. The shots crumbled the remaining outer walls where many of the centurions had taken cover sending dangerous pieces of cobble stone flying through the air. The ship slowed as it approached the hole in the palace where it had previously rammed.

"They're coming back for us," Cynthia said.

"I don't think they know we're here. I bet they're looking for Sam."

The wounded ship finally stopped, hovering right above Thomas and Cynthia. Most of the centurion's gun shots were random and infrequent. No one wanted to give away their position and be exposed to a cannon shot at this close range. Thomas tried to get in view of anyone on the deck, waving his hands like a lunatic to get someone's attention.

Whether they saw him or not, five thick ropes were tossed over the ship's side and seconds later, pirates were rappelling down like professional mountain climbers. Thomas had to move out of the way as one of the men almost landed directly on him. To show that he was a friend, Thomas grabbed the rope to steady it, making the gesture of assistance obvious. The pirate seemed startled, glaring angrily for a moment until he recognized Thomas.

"Mister Riley," he said, with a snarling sort of smile. "Where's Captain Burges?"

The other four men had reached the ground and were converging on Thomas and Cynthia for any news.

"He's in there," Thomas said, pointing to the collapsed part of the palace. "I'm not sure if he's alive, I looked but I couldn't find him. It's a mess in there."

"We saw his death signal," said another pirate with a large mustache and black goggles said.

"The flare you mean?" Thomas asked.

"The death signal. It means he is going to die and to take drastic action," the mustached pirate explained. "The Ensign decided smashing the ole duke's roof was pretty drastic."

"We have to get out of here," Thomas said. "They will bring heavier weapons any moment. And you need to know that the Duke said he had squadrons of fighters waiting for you outside

271

of the city."

The first pirate Thomas had spoken to smiled again. "I think we have that taken care of."

He quickly turned and yelled at the other men. "Search the palace for Captain Burges!"

Without hesitation, they ran over the rubble of the palace walls and into the ill-fated lobby where Sam was last seen.

The pirate turned back to Thomas. "Captain Burges contacted your government before the assault and told them what we were doing. They told us that they were sending quite a massive group to assist us. We were a bit dubious when they didn't show up by the time we landed, but we just got word that the two squads of Lemurian fighters on the outskirts have been destroyed. When we rammed the palace they told us that they were going to remain in place to ensure our safe passage and that they were sending two of their fastest scout ships to rendezvous with us here."

Cynthia looked up to the sky, which was clouded by the smoke still rising off the deck of The Blood Countess. The underbelly of the ship was full of gaping holes from the impact with the palace. "I hope they hurry."

"I wouldn't worry yourself, Miss Basset," the pirate said. "As long as we don't make ourselves an obvious target, we're pretty safe with The Countess here."

Cynthia's bloody face showed no sign of comfort. She had been through so much. Nothing had gone as planned from the moment Thomas was forced to perform the Lifeblood Alchemy on Lillian Beaufort.

A voice called from the deck of The Blood Countess hovering above. The pirate looked up to see a crew member trying to yell above the din of the engines that kept the ship stationary. He finally understood the message, through hand motions pointing first to the horizon followed by thumbs up.

"It seems your wish has been granted," the pirate said to Cynthia.

High pitched buzzing cut through the sound of The Blood Countess engines as two small and sleek West Canvian ships appeared over the tops of the buildings around the palace. The Blood Countess responded by firing three simultaneous green flares into the sky to mark where the ships should land.

As they came into view, Thomas felt more than a little relief, recognizing the ships as friendly vessels. One of the scout ships flew over the Blood Countess and circled around the palace to ascertain the situation. The other lowered its airspeed and quickly landed underneath the giant pirate ship.

The scout ships were shaped like a pyramid with a perforated tube on the back that housed a large single propeller and a small armored dirigible mounted on top. The side door flew open and Karlis Volmer's large frame lumbered out of the ship.

"Riley," he yelled over the propeller noise. "You are the most reckless man I have ever met!"

Volmer walked toward him and without stopping the huge marine flung his arms around Thomas, laughing gustily. Thomas blew out a sigh of relief. He thought after all of his troubles Volmer was going to reprimand him. For a brief moment, he even thought the man might assault him.

"Is Miss Beaumont still inside Miss Basset?" he asked, holding Thomas' shoulders with his meaty hands.

"No. Lillian was successfully extracted, and I have her soul in a vial."

Volmer grinned. "Brilliant! Then we have to get out of here immediately."

"But Sam. The crew," Cynthia interjected.

"They will have to fend for themselves," Volmer said. "We have a huge group waiting to escort them to West Canvia, but they'll have to get themselves out of here on their own. I am under orders to take you with me, by force if I have to, so make it easy on me, huh?"

"It's fine, Miss Basset," one of the pirates said. "We are going to find Captain Burges and we will be out soon."

Cynthia hung her head and looked at Karlis Volmer. "We will go. But you have to keep in contact about Sam!"

"Don't worry, Miss," the pirate replied with his crooked

smile.

Volmer hurried Thomas forward toward the small scout ship, making sure Cynthia was walking alongside. Before they knew it, all three of them were jammed in the ship, Thomas and Cynthia sharing the single passenger seat behind the pilot's seat. With only a few seconds needed to rev the engine back up to full power, the scout ship was in the air and buzzing quickly above the rooftops of downtown Lemuria City.

The scout ship moved blindingly fast. Within ten minutes Thomas and Cynthia could see dozens of ships waiting for them just as Volmer had said. They landed on the deck of a Sherman Class West Canvian battle ship which was the second largest type of ship in the air force. They were hurried off to a secure debriefing room in the middle of the vessel and the battle ship turned, heading back to West Canvia.

On the four hour journey back, Thomas and Cynthia were given time to clean up and provided with fresh air force uniforms. After a meal they were examined by a doctor and Captain Volmer sat with them, asking questions about their entire adventure.

In addition to her multiple cuts and bruises, Cynthia had a broken wrist and a concussion. Thomas, on the other hand, was only suffering multiple small lacerations, most of them from flying glass during the fight in Duke Ferdinand's Alchemy Room.

While they were treated well, the ship's doctor and Captain Volmer would not let Cynthia sleep. It was medically sound to keep someone with a concussion awake, but in reality Duke William was waiting for them at the rendezvous point and eager to speak with them. Thomas fought the urge to doze off and stay awake with Cynthia. When they landed, both Thomas and Cynthia were delirious with exhaustion. Being home again was indescribable after facing death more times than they wanted to remember. Captain Volmer escorted them through the ship and to the ramp that was being lowered.

"Has there been any word from The Blood Countess?" Cynthia asked Volmer.

He looked down at her somberly. "I will let the Duke talk to you about that."

Cynthia wanted to grab Volmer and question him more, but as the ramp lowered, she saw the giant crowd of people waiting for them on the airstrip. There was a guard detail finely dressed in heavy grey coats with half length capes forming a perimeter so the public couldn't get too close as they exited the ship.

It was early evening and as Thomas took his first step on the ramp, a deafening cheer erupted from the crowd. Thomas was shocked that anyone had come out to greet them, let alone cheer as if they were heroes.

Volmer leaned close to Thomas' ear. "We might have let it slip that you destroyed part of Duke Ferdinand's palace."

Four guards escorted them to a waiting room under the landing pad. The people were yelling, gleefully shouting Thomas and Cynthia's praises, while whistling and singing West Canvian fight songs. There were so many people that the perimeter guards had to hold their rifles flat against the crowd to keep the spectators from breaking through.

While it made them happy, neither Thomas nor Cynthia felt like celebrating. They were rushed down a ramp and into a chilly waiting room with a small stage, a blackboard and seats lined in a circular pattern around the room. Another group of the grey jacketed guards stood in rows of threes in front of the stage and Duke William popped up from a seat as they entered the room. He walked briskly toward Thomas and Cynthia with a huge smile on his face. He threw his arms around both of them, intentionally trying to be gentle because of their wounds.

"You've done the impossible! You are true heroes of this country!"

Thomas tried to smile.

"I know you must be exhausted, but I had to see you. I had to thank you in person. We thought you died when the Jupiter crashed."

"Begging your pardon, I feel like we didn't do what everyone thinks we did," Thomas said.

"You have done much more than you ever thought," Duke

William said. "Besides destroying Duke Ferdinand's palace, killing Isaac Maier and extracting my daughter safely, you have done the one thing that makes this the greatest victory of all. You have given the people of West Canvia hope."

"What's the word of the Blood Countess and her crew?" Cynthia boldly asked.

Duke William's eyes looked at the floor for a brief second. "The pirate ship was downed near the palace by a Lemurian battle ship. The remaining crew was taken prisoner."

"And what of their captain, Sam Burges?" Cynthia asked.

"He's alive. For now. We intercepted a telegraph that they have taken him captive as well."

Cynthia wanted to burst into tears. They were right there. The crew could have been saved; no one else had to die if they'd had just a little more time.

A pang of guilt jolted Thomas. Even though Sam had fooled everyone, he turned out to be a noble man. Changing the subject to get them some needed peace, Thomas held out the blood speckled crystal vial that still had Duke Ferdinand's gold chain attached to it. "This is her, Sir."

Duke William just stared at the vial for a moment, thick tears rolling down his face and into his mustache. He gingerly took the vial from Thomas and hugged him again.

"I will never be able to thank you enough."

"Your happiness is thanks enough," Thomas said. "I think Miss Basset and I would like to get some rest if possible."

"Yes! Yes, absolutely. I am sorry for making you linger," Duke William said. "Guards, show them to the infirmary. We have to make sure these heroes are in top shape soon. Thanks to them the people of West Canvia now have hope and soon this war will end."

Thomas and Cynthia were able to sleep in hospital beds parallel to each other; a white curtain separating them for privacy. A nurse checked Cynthia every hour for her concussion. Thomas and Cynthia didn't speak. They did not need to, because they both understood how the other was feeling.

"Good night Cyn," Thomas said, pulling the thin hospital

blanket over him.

"Good night Thom," Cynthia replied, her voice scratchy.

"You know we will get him back right? I swear it."

"Thank you, Thom."

Sleep came quickly as their heads swirled with the chaotic chain of events which finally brought them to this military hospital. They made so many friends, enemies, met people just like them, and people who were nothing like them. Seeing the war first hand Thomas and Cynthia gained a new perspective on their profession. They witnessed its ugly face in the greed and savagery of pirates and royalty alike. With the comfort of finally reaching safety soothing their beaten bodies, they dozed off with bittersweet memories flickering through their minds.

Nick Valentino's evolution of writing started with music.

Residing in Nashville, TN, his background is a curious mix of music, history and the love of all things artistic. Graduating from Belmont University with a BA in History, he played in touring bands for most of his adult life writing volumes of lyrics along the way. It was then that he discovered a love for storytelling.

Inspired by his intense intrigue with history, his travels around the world and the throngs of steampunk enthusiasts around the nation, Valentino wrote the Alternative History/Science Fiction novel, Thomas Riley.

As a pop culture fanatic, Valentino is constantly involved with the new and fresh things that life has to offer. While sometimes hard to label, readers will always find something fun and a little out of the ordinary.

Check out

www.sirthomasriley.com